He glanc[...] him, but [...] her usual intense gaze.

She seemed unsure of herself, a far cry from the capable lass with the superior air who had only to look in his direction to intimidate him. Suddenly she looked young, vulnerable and desperate. And lovely, so lovely, even in this extremity.

He hadn't quite enough courage to hold out his hand to her. "Laura, you will be safe as houses with me."

That must not have been a familiar simile in Spanish, because her expression became more quizzical than fearful.

"You will be safe," he amended. "Marry me."

He expected an immediate turn down, but she surprised him. "No one will receive me, or speak to me, *señor*," she told him. "You will be ruined, the same as me."

A Christmas in Paradise—
the first story in
Coming Home for Christmas
Harlequin® Historical #1068—December 2011

Dear Reader,

Call it curiosity, call it ego, call it whatever you want, but I've always wanted to write *all* the stories in a Christmas anthology. I enjoy writing short stories, mainly because the discipline of the shorter format is an exercise in writing, and I am always learning. A good short story is like an exquisite cupcake: short, sweet and memorable.

It's up to you to decide if I succeeded in this effort. I credit my editor, Bryony Green, with the idea to make it a series about folks trying to get home for Christmas. I think it was my idea to make them all of the same family—the Scottish Wilkies from Kircudbrightshire, a place dear to me. It was definitely my idea to make it a generational thing. The collection begins in the Regency, with our hero stranded in paradise (i.e. San Diego, Alta California) because his ship sank. The next story begins a generation later with his daughter, who is one of Florence Nightingale's nurses during the Crimean War. Our hero in the third story is the daughter's son, a post surgeon at Fort Laramie, Wyoming Territory, in 1877.

I wanted to set that final story at Fort Laramie, because a) in education and training, I am an Indian Wars scholar b) I'm writing a novel for Harlequin Historical that is set at Fort Laramie in 1876.

I hope you enjoy the journey from one continent to another, then back to the first. It's also a journey through time, as one generation yields to another. Most of all, it's a journey to that most delightful place: the holiday season.

Sincerely,

Carla Kelly

Coming Home for Christmas

CARLA KELLY

Harlequin®

TORONTO NEW YORK LONDON
AMSTERDAM PARIS SYDNEY HAMBURG
STOCKHOLM ATHENS TOKYO MILAN MADRID
PRAGUE WARSAW BUDAPEST AUCKLAND

ISBN-13: 978-0-373-29668-2

COMING HOME FOR CHRISTMAS
Copyright © 2011 by Carla Kelly

The publisher acknowledges the copyright
holder of the individual works as follows:

A CHRISTMAS IN PARADISE
Copyright © 2011 by Carla Kelly

O CHRISTMAS TREE
Copyright © 2011 by Carla Kelly

NO CRIB FOR A BED
Copyright © 2011 by Carla Kelly

Recycling programs
for this product may
not exist in your area.

To the men and women of the armed forces everywhere,
who sometimes must spend their holidays
far from home, on our behalf.

CONTENTS

A CHRISTMAS IN PARADISE

Prologue

December 25, 1809

Dear Son,
Another Christmas has come and gone. Neither your mother nor I see any sense in repining, considering how much worse off so many are. Still, we cannot help but reflect on the pleasure it would give us to see your sweet face again. I am not certain whether to blame the French or the Spanish. Ports have changed hands more often than some of my neighbours change their small-clothes—your mother says I should not have written that, but it's probably correct. She is a true Scot, though: tearing up this paper and starting over would be a waste.

Your mother and I take turns in writing to you and this month is my turn. Only this year we were made aware of your incarceration in Alta California, which seems strange, considering that Spain has been our ally for some time now. When I made a trip to London to speak to someone on the Navy Board, he informed me of your probable location. We can only assume, hope and pray that you are well and receiving a letter now and then—perhaps even this one.

If you are alive, I trust you have used your time well like a good Presbyterian, and learned Spanish. Or if you are incarcerated still, I know you have enough skills to poison the whole lot of them and hurry home to us. Your mother thinks it most likely that you are stranded on the far side of the world and have no way to get home.

Your brothers are here for Christmas, Malcolm soon to depart for Carlisle with his new wife. I know it will come as a disappointment to you to know that he married your fiancée. Cora said she sent you a letter breaking your engagement, but I do not know if you received it. If this is the first news of that event, you are probably jolted. Well, son, Cora was four years waiting for you and a woman of twenty-three is ripe and getting stale. There will be other lassies.

So, my dear son, the best of the season to you. Perhaps we will see you in 1811 or 1812. Your mother and I pray for this daily.

Your loving father,
Angus Wilkie

Chapter One

November 2, 1812

Thomas Wilkie, ship's surgeon on the long-defunct *Splendid,* folded his father's three-year-old letter and slipped it underneath the velvet covering to his capital knives. He glanced out of the window and sighed. Although the view was splendid, he wished the fort of San Diego had been built closer to the magnificent harbor. The ocean never failed to soothe him and he could use a little soothing. How many Christmases had to pass before he saw his parents again?

Years had come and gone since he had received his father's letter. Thomas wasn't surprised that Cora had decided to marry; he only wished it hadn't been to his older brother, who would probably take every opportunity to rub it in, provided Thomas ever found his way back to Dumfries.

Odd that the matter should bother him more now than when he had received the letter. Or maybe it was not so odd, considering the chain of events that had happened in short order after his Majesty's frigate *Amaryllis* had handed off supplies and a mail sack to the frigate *Splendid,* which blundered into a typhoon a week later. Dismasted and in tatters, the *Splendid* had been easy pickings for a French man o' war, cruising off the coast of Alta California.

They had been towed into the beautiful harbor of San Diego de Alcalá, then left there as a prize with the Spanish, who had been allies of France at the time. Dumped in the dungeons of the fort, the issue of staying alive had trumped any woolgathering about Cora McClean. Others had griped and complained, but Thomas had a lively mind. The food was poor, true, but the possibilities of the place had quickly made themselves obvious to him, who knew he had a skill in demand.

The *Splendid*'s captain and most of his officers— those who had survived the typhoon and the mauling by the French—preferred to maintain themselves as British to the core, making no effort to learn Spanish—it was beneath them—or engage in any way with their captors. This was war, after all, and war had rules dear to the heart of the English.

It wasn't so with Thomas. When he announced, in very poor Spanish, his medical skills, he became a man in demand. The garrison's only physician had died two years earlier. In the village, native healers practiced a level of quackery that would have made him laugh out loud—if the results of their medical practices hadn't left so many dead.

Although the medical well-being of Spaniards interested him not at all, Captain Walcott of the *Splendid* had been quick to understand his surgeon's value as a bargaining chip for better food, more bedding and such comfort as San Diego could afford his surviving crew.

Thomas was needed and he was busy, tending first to his seamen, second to the Spaniards of both fort and town, and third to the Indians in the nearby mission. Learning Spanish took his mind off any mooning about Cora McClean. He quickly discovered a facility for Spanish. It gave him some satisfaction now to dream in Spanish, as the language became second nature.

So it went. In 1810, when word came from distant Mexico City that Napoleon had invaded Spain in 1808 and they were no longer allies, the Spanish garrison had risen and killed the few French among them. This turn of events perked up the men of the *Splendid* for a brief moment, until it became obvious that nothing much had changed: they were still isolated on the far side of the world, with no rescue in sight.

So the matter had rested for several years. Captain Walcott had been kind enough to die of a fever that had defeated all of Thomas's efforts to keep him alive. Though they mourned him, the result was the unleashing of Lieutenant Ludlow, a man of ambition and innovation, unlike his late captain. Using Thomas's skill with Spanish, the lieutenant had coaxed a coasting vessel out of the fort's captain.

This would have been a foolish effort—no coasting vessel could cross the Pacific or survive a trip around Cape Horn—except for news of an American fort trading in furs that had recently been established north in Oregon country. The Americans were neutral. If a small ship could coast north, the Englishmen would eventually find a way home.

Thomas hitched himself into the window frame and

dangled his long legs over the edge, breathing deeply of the perfume of the flowers that flourished in Alta California. Now he had become a bargaining chip again. In order to acquire the coasting vessel, tools and supplies needed to make it seaworthy, Lieutenant Ludlow had bargained him away to the Spanish.

"You'll stay here, Thomas, in return for their help," Ludlow had informed him. "I give you my word we will extricate you. Some time. Do it for King George."

I am the wrong person for your appeal, Thomas had thought at the time. *I am a Scot before I am British. Georgie's your king.*

But he had a greater reason for staying behind. "Mr Ludlow, I couldn't leave anyway. Two of our crew are too sick to be put to the mercy of the ocean. The pharmacist's mate will sail with you. Duty, honor, Hippocrates and his oath compel me to remain behind."

So there, he had thought sourly. *Take your old tub and sail north.* No sense in divulging to anyone how desperately he wanted to loose the cables himself and sail north in the hope of leaning on the goodwill of Americans. He was as homesick as the next crew member.

Thomas's reverie was interrupted by a small tap on the door. He smiled, his self-pity forgotten for a moment. It must be Laura; no one else in his man's world had such a light touch.

Laura Maria Ortiz de la Garza had the run of the *presidio* because her father was San Diego's royal accountant. Laura had tried to explain his full title to Thomas once, but she had given up in disgust at his poor Spanish.

That had been three years ago. His Spanish was far

better now, but Laura Ortiz didn't seem to be a person to suffer fools gladly. More likely, she had been advised by her father, a man of minor nobility, that a mere surgeon wasn't worth her time or lineage. No matter—Laura Ortiz's black-colored hair, dark eyes and olive skin hadn't held a candle to Cora McClean's blue-eyed, red-haired Scottish buxomness.

He had known Laura for four years now, from her awkward, all-elbows phase to her most recent blossoming into a young woman of some dignity, with a face perhaps more earnest than beautiful. She had an almost disconcerting gaze that someone with a guilty conscience would find unnerving. Because Thomas had no designs on Laura Maria Ortiz beyond admiring the graceful way she had matured, his heart was pure.

"Well, *señorita,* to what do I owe this visit?" he asked in his most polite Spanish, happy to think of something besides having been abandoned on the far side of the globe.

She put her hands to her throat. *"Tumores glandulosos del cuello,"* she said. She enunciated loudly and distinctly, as though he were an idiot.

Aha, I know that one, Miss Smarty, he thought. "Mumps, eh? That's what we call them in English. And where is this victim of the mumps?"

She extended one finger and motioned to the door. "Follow me."

He did as she said, after taking up his worn remedy bag, thinking to himself that no British Isles lass would ever have used such an imperious gesture. The Spanish were different, especially those a little high in the instep. He wondered, as he had on numerous other occasions, if Father Hilario had told Laura that the navy surgeon was the son of a mere surgeon, who had begun *his* career as a barber.

It was a beautiful day in November, one of many beautiful days he had become accustomed to in Alta California. As he walked along, a few sedate paces behind Miss High and Mighty, Thomas Wilkie reminded himself that he might miss this climate, if he ever got home to Scotland.

With Laura's imperious nod and Thomas's smile to the guard, a man whose son he had saved from diphtheria, they left the *presidio* and walked down the hill to San Diego's *pueblo,* a small town of some two hundred souls. He began his usual tease with Laura, striding at her side, which was no difficulty considering his long legs. She usually tried to walk in front, as a lady would. To his surprise, she let him walk beside her.

Wonders never cease, he thought in amusement. *Maybe I am more charming than I thought.*

But no. She was slowing down because they had already reached their destination, a hovel that was home to a soldier and his ragtag family: a gaggle of children and a woman not many generations removed from Kumeyaay Indian. Thomas ducked inside the doorway, stood a moment to accustom his eyes to the smoky din and saw his little patient.

"Poor thing," he murmured in Spanish, as he knelt by the large-eyed girl; he saw tears gathering on her bottom lids while her hands grasped her throat. Gently he tugged away her hands and expertly touched her parotid glands. "Mumps, it is," he said in English.

"Mumps," Laura Maria repeated. "Mumps. *Paroditis.*"

The poor wife of a soldior, the little girl's Kumeyaay

mother hovered like all mothers. Thomas figured she must be illiterate, so he knew she would listen carefully to his simple directions involving a paste made of ginger root, which he produced from his satchel, because he knew she could not afford to buy it. Whistling softly to himself, he ground the root, added water and flour, and scraped it onto a narrow bandage, which he wrapped loosely around the girl's throat. When she whimpered, he kissed her forehead.

For no particular reason, Thomas glanced at Laura, a little surprised that she had remained in the hovel with him. The royal accountant's daughter stood with her hands clasped in front of her, her intense gaze fixed on the child, much as his had been. She seemed to be assessing what he was doing, so he explained it, much as he would have explained to a novice pharmacist's mate.

"It helps the swelling," he said, "but mostly I depend on her youth and general good health to get her through the most trying time. It isn't much of a medical arsenal, is it?"

She looked at him, startled, and her gaze softened. "But you do your best, don't you?" she asked.

"Always." He rocked back on his heels to observe her better. "Whether she be pauper or Spanish princess."

Laura nodded. When she spoke, she sounded almost deferential. "Would you have me return in the morning to renew the dressing?"

He knew she could take care of the matter competently, but he wanted to be there, too. "Let us both return." It was his turn to be deferential. "If you are interested, come a bit early to my laboratory—" such a dignified name for a closet under the stairs! "—and I will show you how to make a paste of aloe, with a little turmeric, in case the ginger doesn't work."

She nodded and gave him a rare smile. It surprised him to see how pretty her face became. Or maybe she had always been pretty and he had only just noticed. Or maybe the smoke in the room was softening his vision.

131
21
110

Chapter Two

"Tomorrow then," he said as he left the shack, not sure if the smoke was bothering his eyes more than the sudden jolt brought about by the unexpected discovery that perhaps brown eyes were as pretty as blue ones. *"Mañana."*

On the street again, Thomas felt himself succumbing to the pleasant lethargy that San Diego seemed to cultivate. Maybe it was the warm sun, even though it was November. It could have been the delightful breeze off the bay, or the aroma of flowers that never grew in any Scottish garden.

When he was much younger, he had read Homer and learned of Odysseus' dreamy days in the clutches of Circe, on her seductive island. With her direct gaze and finely honed sense of superiority, Laura was no Circe—far from it. Still, he knew he would be a liar if he did not admit to himself that San Diego was far more pleasant than life at sea in any ocean. If Laura formed any part of that realization, well, he could repent at sea

eventually. That is, provided anyone thought to send a
ship for him, once his shipmates found friendly shores
up north.

"'Why halt ye between two opinions?'"

Surprised, Thomas looked around, then laughed.
"Father, you are quoting the prophet Elijah to me?"

"Bravo, lad," the Franciscan priest said. "You
know your Old Testament in Spanish, obviously. I am
impressed."

Thomas bowed. "I *am* Presbyterian. We know our
Old Testament in any language."

The Franciscan glanced inside the hovel. "You just
appeared indecisive, a quality I seldom observe in you.
And there sits Señorita Ortiz. Did she frighten you
away?"

"Far from it," Thomas replied, willing to be frank
with this man who had become something approaching
a confidant, now that the *Splendid* crew was working
to refit the Spanish ship below in the harbor. "For a
moment, she almost treated me as an equal."

Father Hilario laughed and motioned to a bench
under a jacaranda tree, next to a woman selling chil-
lies. "First, lad, how are your own patients?"

"No better today," he said, always touched by the
Franciscan's concern for the two crew members who
were so ill, and who, by rights, Thomas should have
hated, because they were part of what tied him to San
Diego, when everyone else was preparing to sail north.
Or so he had admitted to Father Hilario recently, far
from a confessional booth, where his Presbyterian joints
would never have knelt anyway. "But it's not their fault
that I am doomed to stay in San Diego, when the crew

sails. My lieutenant promised me to your fort's captain and here I remain."

"May I sit with your patients again tonight?" Father Hilario asked.

"You know you may." Thomas shrugged. "I doubt the foretopman will know you are there, but Ralph Gooding will probably challenge you to chess."

"Perhaps I will defeat him this time," Father Hilario said with a chuckle.

"Unlikely. Consumption may be rotting his lungs, but his brain is nimble."

They sat in companionable silence. With a frown on her face, and her lips pursed in a way that Thomas had to admit could be distracting to a weak-minded man, Laura left the shack, nodding to the two men as they sat together. Idly, Thomas noticed she had an attractive way of walking that set her skirts swinging.

Thomas, you're a dolt, he thought. "Something is distracting her," he murmured, enjoying the view. *Me, too.*

"It's a touchy thing," the priest said.

Thomas waited for the man to continue. He seemed to be weighing a matter of delicacy. "If it's of the confessional," Thomas began, "I would never presume..."

"No, no, that is not it." The Franciscan sighed. "It will be out soon enough, I fear."

Thomas felt an icy hand clutch his heart, which startled him, considering that Laura had never given him any reason to think of her in too friendly a manner. "She is in trouble?"

Father Hilario shook his head. "It is her father, the accountant." He shrugged. "Which, I suppose, puts her in trouble." He turned to look at Thomas and lowered his voice, even though the market square was bustling and noisy. "He has been caught, so to speak, with his hand in the till." He peered closer. "Do you understand that idiom?"

Thomas nodded. "It translates well into English, Father." *There are scoundrels everywhere,* he thought, feeling suddenly sorry for Laura. "What happened?"

The priest shrugged. "Who knows? Maybe it takes a man of strong character to resist greed." He gave Thomas a knowing look. "Those of us with no fortune and few prospects are never tempted, are we?" He looked around and leaned closer. "Some say he is a gambler."

"Ouch," Thomas said. "What will happen?"

"If this is true, Señor Ortiz will be trundled off to Mexico City for trial."

"Laura?"

The priest shrugged again. "She has no family here. I suppose his fate will be hers, as well."

Thomas thought about the misfortunes of others as he returned to the garrison. Even though it had been a long time since the crew of the *Splendid* had been liberated from the fort's noisome cellar, he had seldom walked past the *presidio*'s open gate without a feeling of relief. And now the royal accountant was cooling his heels in that miserable hole. Too bad for him.

He decided not to worry overmuch about Laura; she must have friends in San Diego to look out for her. At least she wasn't thousands of miles away from people who spoke her language or practiced her religion. As his own father had told him on occasion, a little humility never did a body any harm.

* * *

He mentioned the matter to Ralph Gooding, the carpenter who lay in bed with fever-bright red spots in his cheeks, as classic a presentation of consumption as Thomas had ever seen. Poor man. Gooding had come to Thomas's attention several years ago when the *Splendid* had rounded Cape Horn in a monstrous storm and entered the Pacific.

Thomas had finessed Gooding through good moments and bad, but the disease was finally taking its inevitable course, no matter how balmy the air in San Diego, or how plentiful the seafood and other choice victuals, now that they were no longer imprisoned.

Ralph had been cajoling Thomas to take ship with the coastal lug when it was finished. "Davey there and I are finished, sir, and you know it," had been Gooding's most recent argument. There was no denying Thomas was tempted. Davey Ewing, the foretopman, traveled in and out of consciousness and the carpenter was right about his own prognosis.

"You know I cannot leave you," Thomas had said, hoping his resolution sounded firm and reassuring.

Bless him, Gooding tried again, this fourth day of November, as the purple hues of late afternoon began to spread across his coverlet. "Davey Ewing is a no-hoper and Father Hilario can close my eyes as well as you can, Surgeon," was Gooding's latest attempt. "Why should you remain?"

Thomas propped his stockinged feet on the carpenter's bed. "Ralph, you're a trial and a blasphemer, but the answer is still no!"

Gooding smiled and Thomas knew he understood.

"Did some learned professor feed you a cock-and-bull story while you were in medical school?"

"Indeed he did! Happens I believed it and still do," Thomas concluded gently. He ran his hand down the carpenter's skinny arm. "And there is this—in order to get a ship and permission to leave, Mr. Ludlow promised the fort's captain that I would remain here to treat his own sick." Thomas smiled. "See there, Ralph—it isn't just about you!"

Gooding laughed appreciatively, as Thomas had hoped he would, but the laugh turned into a racking cough that ended with a handkerchief to his lips.

Thomas calmly wiped away the blood. "I know my duty," he said simply.

Gooding nodded. When he spoke, it was just a whisper. "Then you'll hear no more about it from me." His good humor had not deserted him, though. "I suspect you prefer the fleshpots of San Diego to any of his Majesty's frigates."

"You've found me out," Thomas teased back, slapping his forehead dramatically. "Seriously, it is San Diego's beaches I would miss."

Now that was a lie. Thomas sat with his patient until the man drifted to sleep, trying to think of the last time he had visited the harbor for any purpose other than to wish himself aboard the coastal vessel the *Splendid* crew was reinforcing for the trip north. Finally, it had become too painful, so now he stayed away.

When Gooding slept, Thomas strolled outside the fort's adobe walls to admire Alta California's bewitching twilight. He would have enjoyed it more if Laura Ortiz hadn't stumbled into him as she came into the *presidio,* her limpid eyes too full of tears to see him.

He had tried to sidestep her, but ended up grasping her shoulders to keep her from running right into him. When she looked up, he couldn't help sucking in his breath at all the misery in her eyes; it easily had his own misery trumped in spades. He was a man of some experience—life in the Royal Navy made that imperative—but he was not prepared for such raw sorrow.

So much so that he lightened his grip, but did not release her, blurting out, "Señorita Ortiz, is there something I can do for you?"

Him? Him? A former prisoner, a Protestant, a man who soiled his hands with actual work? If she had hauled herself back and slapped him, Thomas would not have been surprised.

She did seem to rear back in disbelief at his impertinent invasion of her privacy. She opened her mouth to speak, then closed it into a firm line. Resigned, he waited for the cutting reply he fully expected, but it never came. Instead, she shook her head slowly and passed him.

He was almost too embarrassed to look at her, except he did. For one tiny moment, she looked like a woman who desperately needed a friend. The moment was as ephemeral as the smoke starting to rise from little shacks outside the fort on the way to the *pueblo*.

Thomas Wilkie stored it up for the moment. He knew he had a good instinct for other people's troubles. That was another lesson he seemed to have learned in medical school.

Chapter Three

Less than a week later, three incidents happened in cruel succession: the *Almost Splendid*—as the crew had christened her—sailed with the tide for Fort Astoria in Oregon country; Davey Ewing died, nearly at the moment the *Almost Splendid* disappeared over the horizon; Laura Ortiz was turned out of her house, a victim of her father's circumstances. Thomas was hard put to think which incident bothered him more, particularly since he was deep in a pool of self-pity that rendered him less than useful.

Against his inclination, he had gone to the harbor for the ship's embarkation. It was a typically misty morning in San Diego, with fog here and there, but destined to burn off by four bells or so in the forenoon watch. He had two express purposes in attending the coasting vessel's send-off. The first was to give his pharmacist's mate all the useful advice he could think of. True to his nature, the mate paid attention for a few minutes, then his focus began to wander. *God protect the men of the*

Almost Splendid, *for I know I cannot once they sail,* Thomas thought.

The second matter of business involved getting Lieutenant Ludlow, captain of the vessel now, to put his signature to a document attesting to Surgeon Thomas E. Wilkie's reasons for remaining in San Diego—to tend to crew members too sick to embark on the *Almost Splendid* and as a bargaining chip in return for the Spaniards' help in outfitting the vessel.

Father Hilario had suggested such a document over supper the night before, after the soup and before the fish and tortillas. "Tomás, suppose an English vessel should appear in our harbor, and wonder why *you* are here, instead of aboard a ship? Could this get you into trouble?"

"Ay de mi," Thomas had said, startled at the possible implications and startled that he had thought automatically in Spanish. "I could end up swinging from a yardarm, if a British captain thinks I held back because I was a cowardly malingerer."

Thomas had drawn up a document to cover himself, in the event an English ship actually did arrive. Father Hilario had taken it to the *presidio*'s captain, who added his additional reasons. The capitan's secretary was far more skilled than the overworked purser on the *Almost Splendid.* With baroque swirls and furbelows, he had written in Spanish that Tomás Wilkie, surgeon, Royal Navy, had been expressly required to remain behind to provide medical care to England's illustrious allies, the Spanish, who were without a physician of their own. The captain's seal was far more impressive than Lieutenant Ludlow's mere signature.

Lieutenant Ludlow and his now-former surgeon

had shaken hands on that matter as the crew unfurled
the sails. "The Americans at Fort Astoria will help us.
Between the two of us nations, we'll get you home,
Thomas," Ludlow had said, with one eye on the sails.
"And now, I have work to do."

"That's all I ask, sir," Thomas said to the captain's
back. With a sigh, and one last look around, Thomas
left the small lugger. He stood on the dock, hands in
his pockets, head down, as the ship tacked out of the
harbor.

Now he felt well and truly alone, discounting his
helpless patients in the *presidio*'s hospital. As he
climbed back to San Diego, he turned a few times to
look down at the harbor again. "I am so far from home,
Father," he murmured. "I do not know if I will ever see
another Christmas with you and Mum."

He swallowed a few times, declared himself too old
to cry, but let the tears fall anyway.

The second incident happened immediately upon his
return to the *presidio*. At some point between Thomas's
morning ward-walk and his entry through the *presidio*'s
always-open gates, the foretopman had died.

Well, damn me, Thomas thought, as he closed Davey
Ewing's eyes. He glanced at the carpenter, who was
observing him thoughtfully.

"I hope you don't hate me, Thomas," the man said.

"For being alive?" he asked. "You're troubling the
wrong man about that. I'm your surgeon. I'd like to keep
you on this side of the soil."

It was true; he meant it. He also felt himself succumbing to the worst case of self-pity he had ever
indulged in. *But for you, and the Spanish captain, I*

would be sailing north, he couldn't help thinking, even though he knew it must be a sin to feel that way.

He could tell Ralph Gooding didn't believe his *bon-homie;* he scarcely believed it himself. He made himself look Gooding in the eye, except the carpenter had already sighed and turned his face to the wall.

Thomas assuaged his guilt by taking extra care over the body of Davey Ewing, dead so far from home. His innate curiosity made him want to perform an autopsy, but he resisted. He doubted anyone in the *presidio* would think kindly of him after such a procedure and he did have to get along with the Spanish.

Still, he couldn't help but be touched by the way Father Hilario gently helped him with a soft cloth and stood silently by the dead man, his hands clasped together. When he had finished praying, he put a crucifix between the profane and adulterous foretopman's tight grip.

"He wasn't a very good man, Father," Thomas said.

"Who among us is?"

The words were softly spoken, but Thomas felt the rebuke settle around him like mortar. "Forgive me, Father," he whispered, and left the room.

Perhaps if his father had been a cruel man, and his mother an indifferent woman, Thomas would not have yearned for home with quite the longing that attacked him now. If he were honest, he could recall many a moment in the far northern latitudes when he would have gladly committed all seven deadly sins for the privilege of rotting in so blissful a prison as San Diego. In fact, he knew there would be many a San Diegan who, suddenly transported to Dumfries, would have been shocked at being exiled to such a spartan environment.

But home was home and he was far from his; the matter was as simple as that. Thomas knew himself well enough to know that he would probably mope about for a few days and then resign himself to the current affair. Still, it was hard, and he knew he had to tough it out on his own.

The third cruel incident was not specifically his problem, but made him feel considerably less sorry for himself. After a night of tossing and turning in his tidy quarters off the ward, Thomas had wakened to a disgustingly lovely morning. Even though it was November, the shutters were open and the fragrance of various tropical flowers wafted inwards, daring him to think ill of Alta California. Sourly, he could and did, until he glanced out of the window off the surgery to see the royal accountant being led toward the inner courtyard in chains.

"Good Heavens!" he exclaimed, setting down the bowl of warm water he had poured with which to wash Ralph Gooding. The water sloshed onto the bedside table and Ralph looked at him with amused eyes.

"Is it Napoleon?" the carpenter joked.

"Not quite. It looks as though Father Hilario was right. Laura's father is being led away in chains. I guess the Spaniards suffer fools no more gladly than the Navy Board would."

The carpenter frowned. "Is he the man accused of pilfering money from the *presidio* treasury?"

"The very one. Father Hilario has kept me abreast of the audits and investigating committees," Thomas replied. "I swear the Spanish are even more diligent bean counters than our own *fiscales.*" He stopped and smiled at his use of Spanish where English was expected. "Accountants, I mean."

"What happens now?"

Thomas shook his head. "I have no idea, but it can't be pleasant."

It wasn't. Father Hilario gave him a full report that afternoon while Ralph dozed. According to the Franciscan, all of the Ortizes' possessions were to be auctioned off that very evening. "Yes, there were gambling debts. Not only did he siphon off money from the *presidio*'s coffers, but he also cheated a number of local residents." He shook his head. "He cried and carried on and vowed to pay it all back, but there was no sympathy in that room! Talk is that he will be on the king's highway in chains tomorrow, heading for a trial in Mexico City."

"So soon?"

The priest shrugged. "If he stays one moment longer, I fear the San Diegans will garrote him." He made a twisting gesture with his hands and Thomas winced.

The priest bustled off; mid-afternoon prayers were approaching. Thomas assumed his favorite position in the broad window. It was a good time to resume the pity he had been showering on himself since the *Almost Splendid* had sailed, except that he had a more nagging thought: What would happen to her High and Mighty Doña Laura Maria Ortiz de la Garza?

He knew it wasn't his business. Either she would go with her father to Mexico City or perhaps stay with friends in San Diego.

* * *

His mind on Laura, Thomas sat with Ralph Gooding while his patient ate his gruel and soft-boiled eggs
a few hours later. Apparently the carpenter had similar
thoughts, because he folded his arms across his stomach
and looked the surgeon in the eye.

"Sir, what will happen to that pretty lass?"

"I have no idea."

There was a long pause. Thomas glanced at Ralph,
wondering what it was the man wanted to say, but
appeared uncertain how to say it. "Look, Ralph," he
said finally, "call me Thomas, please. We're both a long
way from home and I'm not inclined to continue any
protocol. What's on your mind?"

"Laura is," Ralph said promptly. "You need to find
out what will happen to her."

"Why?"

Even to Thomas's own ears, it sounded so bald,
almost as though he was still sulking about being left
behind. He felt his face go red with the shame of his
own meanness.

Bless him, Ralph was too kind a man and too chari-
table to think ill of his doctor. There was no reproach in
his reply, only a certain reasonable quality that forced
Thomas to admit he was in the presence of a better man
than himself.

"Because she's pretty and you like her a little, I think.
Unlike you, I doubt she has any friends at all in San
Diego right now."

"Surely you are wrong," Thomas replied.

"I wish I were, sir…Thomas. Speaking as one who
has a lived a bit more on the edge than you have, people
don't look kindly on anyone—the perpetrator *or* his

relatives—who cheats them. I think the milk of human kindness in San Diego is turning sour right now."

You could be right, Thomas thought later as he made his way to the *pueblo* outside the *presidio,* wondering if there really was going to be an auction of all the Ortizes' possessions. There was. For people who enjoyed a lengthy siesta each afternoon and considerable lassitude, they seem to have made an exception today.

Spread out in the plaza were what looked like everything the disgraced accountant and his daughter must have owned. *This isn't right,* Thomas thought to himself, looking around for Laura. She was nowhere in sight, which didn't surprise him. He felt his face grow red from such humiliation visited on someone who, as far as he knew, barely tolerated him.

The women of the *presidio* pawed through a mound of intimate clothing. They held up Laura's delicate chemises to their own ample fronts, laughing among themselves. Thomas turned away, embarrassed. And there was Father Hilario, watching from the portico in the late afternoon's shadows. Thomas walked to him, shaking his head.

"This is shameful, Father," he said, speaking low.

The priest nodded. "True, but this is a crowd of upset people. I almost cannot blame them."

Thomas remained where he was by the priest as the auction began. He astounded his Presbyterian soul by bidding on and winning the family's surprisingly simple prie-dieu, and a triptych of Father, Son and Holy Ghost that caught his eye with its primitive style. Thanks to doctoring among the San Diegans, Thomas had money enough to buy more and he did. For some reason he could not explain to himself, he bid on housewares, a table and chairs, a blue-painted cabinet and what was probably Laura's bed.

He didn't question why he was doing this, except that he knew what it felt like to be alone and left with little, beyond his medicines and capital knives. Maybe whoever took in Laura would take more kindly to the imposition if her possessions came, too.

Thomas said as much to Father Hilario, who shook his head. "Tomás, I fear you are awarding these San Diegans more virtue than they deserve," he cautioned.

"What do you mean?" he asked, his eyes on the auctioneer, who was now holding up a calfskin trunk of clothing.

"No one will take her in."

"You're quizzing me, Father!" He hadn't meant to speak so loudly. People turned to look. "Seriously?" he asked in a whisper.

"After what her father did, she has no friends."

Thomas threw up both hands in surprise and suddenly found himself the owner of a trunk of female finery. The women around him tittered as he blushed, then turned back as the auction continued.

"Someone should do something," he said, glaring at the women's backs.

"My thought precisely," Father Hilario said in his most matter-of-fact voice, the one he probably reserved for the confessional. "Marry her, lad."

Chapter Four 6

Thomas couldn't have heard Father Hilario correctly. What the man had said must be an idiom he had never encountered before.

"I beg your pardon?" he asked, his voice really low now.

"Marry her. She has nowhere to live. For unknown reasons, you have just purchased some of her clothing and much of her furniture. She will thank you for the prie-dieu—we call it a *reclinatorio.* Your own quarters are rather sparse and could use some nice furniture, if I may say."

"You may not," Thomas snapped. He felt light-headed, but he was damned if he'd take his own pulse in front of the Franciscan. "That is the craziest thing I have ever heard. She doesn't even *like* me."

"Ah! So you have thought of it!" the priest chortled, pouncing.

"I have not!" Thomas whispered back furiously. "Well, only a little."

"I could ask why you purchased so many of her possessions, but I know how easy it is to get caught up in the spirit of a bargain," the priest said generously, with only a hint of a smile.

"Um, yes."

"You English," the priest said, his voice kind.

"Scot. Scot," Thomas said weakly.

The auction was over. His mind traveling in all directions at once, Thomas went to the auctioneer and paid what he owed.

"Shall we deliver this tonight to your quarters?" the man asked.

"Of course not! Find Doña Laura Ortiz and give it back to her," Thomas declared.

The auctioneer pressed his lips together in a thin line, disapproval etched deep. "That child of a cheat and a gambler has no home now. I do not know where she is." He waved his hand at Thomas's new possessions. "This is now yours and it is going to your quarters. And that is that." He turned on his heel in the way only a Spaniard could—or would—and left the surgeon standing there.

"Do it, then, man, damn your eyes," Thomas muttered in English. He turned to the priest, his voice low. "Marry her? That is out of the question."

Father Hilario only nodded. "Find her and see what she says."

"I know what she will say!"

"Are you so certain?" Father Hilario murmured. "Good night, lad. Go with God. Find her."

"A fat lot of help you are," Thomas had muttered to himself as he returned to the fort. In another moment he was seated beside Ralph Gooding. The carpenter's constant fever always burned brighter in the evening, so he wiped the man's face and neck.

Ralph didn't open his eyes. "Did you go to the auction?"

"Aye, more fool me," Thomas replied. "Out of the goodness of my heart I bought some of Laura's things. Just to return them to her, mind you. Father Hilario thinks I should marry her!"

Even at the worst of times, Ralph Gooding had a sense of humor. Thomas expected him to laugh, but he was disappointed. The carpenter opened his eyes and his expression was thoughtful.

"Oh, no, not you, too," the surgeon said, holding up his hands to ward off this odd contagion that had spread from the Franciscan to the English patient.

"It's an excellent idea. She's so pretty, and who knows how long you will be stuck here in paradise? I don't intend to live forever, you know. She'll make you happier than I will."

Thomas smiled in spite of himself. "Ralph, you are an antidote, but this is no joking matter."

"I never thought it was." Ralph's eyes were closing. "I'm tired. Would you snuff that wick and let me sleep? Go find that pretty lady." He sighed and tugged at his blanket. "Father Hilario is so clever. He can probably find a million ways to marry a Roman Catholic to a Presbyterian in Alta California." He smiled. "Some of them might even be legal. G'night."

"I don't know where she is," Thomas protested, as he tucked Ralph's blanket higher.

"Don't you?" was Ralph's drowsy reply.

"Why would I?" Thomas said. Even as he said it, he

did know where she was—at any rate, where he would be, in similar circumstances.

Obtaining permission to visit the cells was easily granted by the turnkey in charge, whose twins he had recently delivered. There she was, sitting on the floor by the iron bars, her hand looped through and resting on her father's shoulder. Thomas squatted beside her, saying nothing because there was nothing to say. He glanced at Laura, admiring her creamy complexion. He had been close to her before, but maybe the way the light from a single torch glinted off her hair brought out the auburn highlights. The dungeon stank as usual, but she smelled sweetly of lavender.

She was moving her deliciously lovely lips just slightly and he thought she might be praying. Then she sighed and sat back, looking at him with the intense gaze he was familiar with, but with something more besides. He wouldn't have thought it possible earlier, but he saw shame and humiliation in her expression.

"I did not think that you, of all people, would come to gloat."

Startled, he frowned. "Laura, you know I would never do that."

He had spoken just as quietly. Her eyes filled with tears. "I'm sorry. I should never have said that. This is hard."

Thomas understood hard. He nodded and looked at her father, who, in his shame, looked away. Tentatively, the surgeon reached his hand through the bars and grasped the accountant's shoulder. The man began to weep.

Thomas decided it was a good thing that he was

there, and not someone unfamiliar with tears. He kept his hand on the man's shoulder, thinking of the times his instructors had told their students that often a kind touch was the sum total of their medical arsenal, when all else was gone.

"She wants to go with me to Mexico City," Señor Ortiz said finally. "It is nearly a six-month journey, so hard, and through Apachería. I fear the trip alone would be a death sentence." He raised his eyes to Thomas's then. "But I have shamed us both and no one here will take her in."

"I will," Thomas heard himself saying. When Laura gasped, he hadn't the courage to look at her. "I will," he said again. "Señor, may I have your permission to marry her? She'll be safe. No one will harm her, because I am valuable to this garrison."

"She comes with no dowry," the Spaniard said, the mortification of a proud man almost palpable.

"Not precisely," Thomas said, still not brave enough to look at the woman seated beside him on the floor. "I…uh…I purchased quite a few of her possessions at the auction. That would count for something in Scotland."

Whether that was true or not, he didn't care. Here he was, sitting by a man who did not think he—or his daughter, if she accompanied him—would survive the trip to Mexico City. He glanced at Laura, who was looking at him, but without her usual intense gaze. She seemed unsure of herself, a far cry from the capable lass with the superior air who had only to look in his direction to intimidate him. Suddenly she looked young, vulnerable and desperate. And lovely, so lovely, even in this extremity.

He hadn't quite enough courage to hold out his hand to her. "Laura, you will be safe as houses with me."

That must not have been a familiar simile in Spanish, because her expression became more quizzical than fearful.

"You will be safe," he amended. "Marry me."

He expected an immediate refusal, but she surprised him. "No one will receive me, or speak to me, *señor,*" she told him. "You will be ruined, the same as me."

At least she was considering his impulsive offer. "No, I will not," he contradicted. "This *presidio* needs me. The people will not dare to ruin me, because I am probably the only surgeon between Los Angeles and Tucson." He chuckled, aware of his own pride. "At least, the only good one."

"I know what you mean," she told him, then leaned close to her father. "Papa?"

Thomas got to his feet and stood in the doorway of the dungeon, allowing them a moment of privacy. Father and daughter whispered together, both cried, and then Laura stood up. She looked at him, then glanced away, her lovely face pale.

There wasn't time to think about what he had done; no time to consider how foolish it probably was; no time to reflect on how it might actually affect his life here, or in the future; no time to do anything except square his shoulders and take whatever came. Whether that was the refusal he expected or acceptance, which would complicate his life in Alta California, at the very least.

The turnkey was standing by him in the doorway. "Did…did I hear you right, *señor*?" he whispered.

"You probably did, Emilio," Thomas whispered back.

"She's awfully superior," the turnkey warned.

"Not now," Thomas said, and his heart went out to the young woman seated on the floor of the filthy prison, in tears. "Not now."

He held his breath as Laura looked at him. The tears slid down her face. She glanced at her father for reassurance, then gracefully stood up, smoothed down her dress and squared her shoulders. To his everlasting pity, she glided across the floor in that magical way he had observed before and knelt at his feet.

"No, no," he said, reaching for her.

She raised her hands to his and he helped her up.

She could barely lift her eyes to meet his gaze. "I will marry you," she said, her voice soft. "Only, please treat me well."

Thomas knew he could promise that. If there was one lesson he had learned in life, at sea and in school, it was to do precisely that. But a wife? Thirty minutes ago, he had been a little foolish at an auction. Now he was about to become a husband.

"Of course I will treat you well. I could never do anything else, Laura," he told her.

She nodded. "I will find Father Hilario," she whispered and left him standing there, wondering what he had just got himself into.

Chapter Five

Ralph Gooding was right: Father Hilario was perfectly capable of finding a way for a Presbyterian to marry a Roman Catholic in the royal *presidio* of San Diego. The matter was accomplished the next day, with nary a cried bann in sight. A bit dazed by the whole and the speed of the proceedings, Thomas signed a document in Latin, the gist of which revolved mainly around his agreement to raise any children as Catholic.

He blushed and signed, even as Laura did the same. He didn't dare meet her eyes; a quick glance assured him that she no longer wore a superior air. To his dismay, she looked worn down and weary beyond her years, which made him wonder whether she had slept at all last night.

He knew he hadn't. True to his word, the auctioneer had delivered Laura's possessions to his modest quarters, located just off the small hospital's ward. He had nothing more than a bed and a chest of drawers in one room, and a few chairs and a table in the other.

Since there was less furniture in his sleeping chamber, Thomas had directed the men to put Laura's bed in with his. *She won't like this,* he thought, as he tossed and turned all night. Still, better here than in the other room, where patients from the town sometimes came for consultations.

Her prie-dieu, table and chairs and cabinet went in his consulting/sitting room. The bright blue table and chairs made him smile, which was a good thing, because nothing else did. He who was known fleet-wide as a careful man, one who weighed all options, was about to plunge into marriage. While cooling his heels in the small antechamber at the garrison chapel, he consoled himself by acknowledging that no one in the entire Royal Navy knew what he was about to do.

His next thought was one of shame at his callous nature. He might have been uncharacteristically impulsive, but it didn't follow that he would abandon Laura Ortiz de la Garza, soon-to-be Wilkie, as soon as the first Royal Navy vessel hove into view. No. He was to be married, and married he would stay. One didn't rescue a damsel in distress, only to show a clean pair of heels when times were better. He was in for the long haul. Whether Laura knew that or not was the unknown quantity.

They were married before noon, but after the disgraced accountant was chained into an oxcart and driven with an armed escort from the *presidio*. A few whispered words with the *presidio*'s captain left Thomas feeling less than sanguine about Señor Ortiz's future. The plan was to avoid Apachería after all. The military caravan would travel south to Baja California, gathering felons along the way who were deemed important enough to bind over for trial in Mexico City. A short crossing of the Sea of Cortez would land them in Puerto Vallarta, and then across to Durango, and down to Mexico City, where a long prison sentence awaited.

"If he lives that long," the captain said. "It's a long trip, and much can happen."

And probably would, was the implication. Thomas had no inkling that the captain would be much disturbed if justice along the king's road was a bit rough on his former royal accountant. Perhaps he had lost money to Señor Ortiz's gambling. At least he did not try to discourage Thomas from marrying the man's daughter.

Thomas did not know where Laura had spent the night, but from the look of her rumpled dress, it was probably on the floor by her father's cell. No matter— she could sleep well in her own bed tonight, under his protection.

He watched her as the melancholy oxcart procession left the *presidio,* skirted the town square at the foot of the hill and disappeared down the king's road. She stood alone on the porch of the garrison church, her eyes downcast, her hands clasped together in that way of Spanish gentlewomen. He thought she was crying and wanted to go to her, which made him different from most of his sex, who tended to run from a woman's tears. The difference was his profession; he knew he could comfort.

But he hesitated. Depending on how long these matters took, he would be married to her in less than an hour. He knew it wasn't the moment to be shy, but he wanted to give her room to grieve. Whether she was mourning the loss of her father, or the upcoming loss of her freedom, he couldn't have said.

She couldn't see him as he stood in the shadows by his quarters off the hospital, so he watched her, touched by her air of calm, when he suspected she was feeling anything but. After a moment, she raised her eyes from their contemplation of the tile and dabbed at them with a lace handkerchief that looked like one of the items he had bought back for her at yesterday's auction.

Her quiet beauty took his breath away, as he wondered just when, in the past years of knowing her, she had turned into such a lovely lady. While it was true she was much slimmer than Cora McClean, his faithless fiancée, she had a figure that was beginning to make him warm under his shirt.

She stood alone, without a friend in sight. He watched as she looked heavenward, as though seeking aid. Seeing none, she sighed—he couldn't hear her, but her breast rose and fell eloquently. Then she squared her shoulders and straightened her back, as if preparing herself for another ordeal: the ordeal of marriage to a stranded surgeon in the Royal Navy, because not one of her own would take her in.

"I won't be so bad," Thomas whispered. "I promise you, lass."

If Ralph Gooding hadn't insisted on being carried across the courtyard on a stretcher, there would have been no guests at their wedding. The effort made Gooding's fevered cheeks even brighter. When Thomas rose and took a step toward him, the carpenter shook his head.

"As you were, laddie," he managed to say, with a

touch of his humor that even consumption couldn't steal away.

Thomas nodded and resumed his place at the altar on his knees beside his bride. He had brushed his uniform into submission, but he had lost weight and now it hung on him. Lately, he had been going about in Spanish trousers and linen shirts, and the worn blue wool felt almost alien. Laura had changed into another dress, one not so wrinkled and smelling of the dungeon, but plain and dark green with a crocheted collar. She had coiled her pretty hair around her head like a coronet. He wondered how long it actually was and grew a little warm, thinking that he might actually find out in a few hours. Her black-lace mantilla hid her hair, but not her face, and certainly not her frightened eyes.

He had a ring, a little silver bauble given in payment several years ago by a fisherman after he extracted a hook from the man's lip. Thomas was too cynical to believe the man's tale of treasure from a Spanish galleon of the Philippines trade, but it was a pretty ring so he had kept it, rather than bartering it for something else.

This was the ring he slid on Laura's finger, surprising them both because it fit. For the only time in the ceremony, she looked him in the eye and smiled slightly, before dropping her gaze to the tile floor again.

The service was in Latin, of course, and Thomas had no idea what Father Hilario was saying. He supposed it was something about loving, honoring and obeying. He imagined his ancestors looking down on the two of them with Presbyterian disapproval, but it bothered him less than he would have thought. They were dead and he was not, and they had probably known as much as he did about the general uncertainty of life.

He knew, by marrying Laura Ortiz, that he was doing a kind thing. Whether it was a wise thing remained to be seen. Still, the whole matter had quite wiped away his disgruntlement at the sailing of the *Almost Splendid* without him. He had more pressing concerns now.

Ralph Gooding had taxed himself sore by attending the wedding, and then signing the wedding book as one of two witnesses—the other was the sexton. With a smile at his new bride and a nod to Father Hilario, Thomas had seen to his patient's return to his bed, and then sat with him for part of the afternoon as the man coughed and hemorrhaged. Ralph slept finally, exhausted, and Thomas had nowhere to go except his quarters, located off the ward. He hoped Laura would be there.

She was, just sitting in that still way of hers, hands clasped on her table this time. He looked around appreciatively. Laura had removed a colorful tablecloth from her trunk of possessions that he had purchased at the auction and spread it on the table. He had made a settee of sorts out of a discarded packing case. She had found two embroidered pillows and placed them on his make-shift sofa. A saint now looked at him benevolently from a small alcove, which had probably been waiting for such an occupant a few years, rather than the tin cup and grog bottle he usually kept there.

"Who's she?" he asked his new wife.

"St Cecilia," Laura replied. The sudden bloom in her cheeks gave him ample proof that she was just as frightened and shy as he was. "She is the patron saint of music." She swallowed, and he knew what an effort she was making. "My mother's name was Cecilia."

She looked at him then, and, with a pang, he wondered where the confident, imperious Laura had gone. "I thought I had lost her, but you bought so many of my things. Thank you."

"You're welcome," he replied, touched. "May...may I sit down?"

There was just the hint of her former spark. "Of course you may! This is your house."

He sat down opposite her, feeling suddenly large and clumsy and red-faced, so unlike the people she was used to. He wanted to assure her that he was a kind man who would never hurt or frighten her, but a sudden pounding on the door took him out of his quarters. A garrison bull had gored one of the soldiers and he was needed at once.

A goring, what a relief, he thought.

Without a word, he picked up his remedy bag and slung it over his shoulder. Laura was standing by the table now, her eyes full of concern. "Is there anything I can do?" she asked.

"You're a dear to ask," he said in English. "Yes, there is," he said in Spanish. "I don't know how long I will be. The garrison cook always delivers dinner to my quarters and food for Señor Gooding. Will you see that he is fed?"

She nodded, her expressive eyes filled with purpose now. "Will he eat much?"

"I doubt it. He had a bad spell this afternoon. If he does not want to eat, just sit with him, will you?"

Laura nodded again. He couldn't help himself. He reached out and touched her arm. "Don't be afraid if he starts to hemorrhage. Just raise up his head and keep his mouth clear. Will you do that? I am asking a lot."

"No, you are not," she replied. She hesitated. "And may I eat, too? It has been a long day."

"Laura, everything I have is yours now," he said simply. "Even the beans and tortillas."

He smiled to show it was a joke, but she was looking at him in that serious way he was more familiar with. "Of course you may eat. Just save me something and put it in that cupboard."

She nodded. Her cheeks blossomed with pink again. "Should I wait up for you?"

"No. Just go to bed, Laura. I'll be quiet when I come in."

She took a deep breath. "In which bed?"

"Yours, of course. We need to talk…first."

The tears in her eyes surprised him. He didn't have time to think about it, not with something as interesting as a goring waiting for him in the stable, a problem he might actually be able to solve. Wives were probably different, especially a wife on such short notice. Did she think he didn't want her? Was she relieved? Nervous?

Thomas Wilkie prided himself on being a man of science. Too bad he had no idea what to do next.

Chapter Six

Thomas knew the goring should have fascinated him, considering that it was something he could never have hoped to treat at sea, but all he wanted to do was return to his quarters. He rendered the best care he was capable of, all the time thinking about the length of Laura's hair and how lovely it must look spread on a pillow.

Calm down, Wilkie, he warned himself. *You just told her you weren't going to bother her and you're not.*

He wavered for a moment between leaving the unconscious but stable soldier where he was, or taking him to the little ward off his quarters, where he could observe him more closely throughout the night. His training won out.

It was a small ward and, thankfully, a healthy garrison; the only other patient right now was Ralph Gooding, who slept. Working quickly and quietly, Thomas settled his new patient into a bed and stood over him for a long moment, taking the time—he always did it—to second-guess himself, play devil's advocate and assure himself that he had done all he could for the moment. When he was satisfied, he let himself out of the room quietly and went a few steps to his own quarters, which could be entered from the ward as well as from the outside door leading to the fort's plaza.

He smiled to see a candle burning on Laura's table, thinking she had lit it for him. He remembered the many times his mother had done just that for his father, out late on a call. Maeve Wilkie had generally left a small snack by the candle. He looked closer, touched to see that Laura had left him a tortilla. She must have found some butter somewhere, because she had spread it on the tortilla and then sprinkled a little cinnamon and sugar on it.

He sat down quietly and ate, pleased at her concern and a little surprised by it. Maybe wives of surgeons had a sixth sense about what to do. He would have to ask his mother some day, if he ever saw her again.

Thomas looked toward the door to his bedroom, a little amazed that he was already thinking of Laura Ortiz—Wilkie now—as his wife. He shook his head, still wondering why he had bought so many of her personal effects at that auction. *I must be the softest touch in all of Alta California,* he thought.

Taking off his shoes, he tiptoed to the closed door and opened it, hesitant to go in. He reminded himself that it was his bedroom and moved with more assurance. He left the door open; from the little lamplight from the other room, he saw Laura asleep in her bed. She had gathered herself into a ball; perhaps she was chilly.

He looked closer at her, saddened to see the tears that had dried on her cheek. *What a day for you,* he told himself, in complete sympathy. *You bid* adiós *to your father, not knowing if you will see him again, and find yourself in a strange new situation, one not of your own choosing.* "Believe me, I can understand," he said under his breath, thinking of his four years in San Diego, a lovely sun-kissed paradise for seamen that he would happily trade for one glimpse of chilly, foggy Dumfries.

He was only going to find his Mexican sandals, one of the numerous pleasant side effects of life in California, and return to the ward. He found the sandals, but stood for another long moment looking at Laura, admiring the length of her eyelashes and still surprised by her beauty, which he had never really noticed before the last few days. He was oddly touched by the way that, in sleep, her thumb rested under her curved fingers, rather like a baby at rest.

I don't even know you and you are my wife, he thought. He decided that stranger things than this had probably happened in the whole history of the world. Before he left the room, he took his extra blanket from his bed and draped it gently over her. Laura stirred in her sleep and murmured something, then returned to slumber, if she had ever left it. He closed the door quietly behind him.

As nights went, it didn't seem so long. Thomas had spent many such nights at bedsides and by hammocks, on all seven seas. He made himself comfortable on the sling-back canvas chair he had rescued from the old *Splendid,* before it was broken up for firewood. He positioned his slat-sided lamp just so and shook out the fort's sporadically published broadside, pleased that he could read in Spanish as easily as in English now.

* * *

The soldier—his name was Juan—woke up halfway through the night, just when Thomas was starting to doze. He groaned, and Thomas was awake in an instant, checking the drain he had put into the young man's groin, then feeling his forehead for a fever that might signal infection. Blessedly, he was still cool. Thomas sprinkled a frugal amount of opium in a glass and raised the man slightly to drink it. In moments he was asleep again.

Thomas settled in his chair again. He heard Ralph stirring and turned his chair around. "Have you been awake long?" he whispered.

His other patient shook his head. Thomas put his hand on Ralph's forehead, sighing to feel the heat there and knowing there was little he could do to change the matter. After the past year, he had to wonder what the carpenter was using for lungs now. Not even the beguiling climate could trump the ravages of consumption.

"What say you, Surgeon Wilkie?" Ralph whispered. "Will I make Christmas this year? Be honest now."

"I don't know," Thomas replied.

He knew his patient well. Ralph only smiled and settled himself more comfortably, not a man to complain. "Well, at least I saw you married to a lovely lady," he whispered. "Maybe San Diego will turn into the best thing that ever happened to you."

"Hardly," Thomas replied. "I can't imagine what I was thinking."

Ralph chuckled. "Oh, you can't? Sir—"

"Just Thomas," the surgeon reminded him.

"Thomas, you know as well as I do that she's pretty enough to raise the dead."

Thomas was silent. He felt his face going red in the gloom of the ward. "Go to sleep, you rascal," he said finally and turned his chair around again.

"All it takes is time," Ralph told him, "something you have a lot of."

Thomas sighed again, but more quietly. *And something* you *have so little of,* he thought.

The ward was silent then. Thomas relaxed when he heard Ralph's steady breathing, even though it was more labored with each passing day. *Will you make Christmas, my friend?* he asked himself. *I sincerely doubt it.*

The rest of the night passed more slowly. The soldier woke again, in pain and trying to tug loose the drain. Thomas stayed his arm and then stroked it, speaking quietly to him, until he returned to restless slumber. When the man finally relaxed just before dawn and slept, Thomas slept too, his bare feet propped up on his patient's cot.

He woke hours later. The room was light now and he heard birds singing in the jacaranda tree in the courtyard. The *presidio* was rousing itself for another beautiful day. Thomas glanced at the soldier, who still slept, then looked down in surprise.

At some point in the early morning hours, Laura must have covered him with the extra blanket he had spread over her. *What a sweet lassie you are,* he thought, as he carefully pulled back the blanket and got out of his chair, stretching. Laura must have extinguished the bedside lantern, too, which made him smile and think of his own frugal Scots mother.

Walking to the door that opened onto the courtyard,

he stood a long moment in thought, watching the soldiers assemble—most of them lived with their women in the nearby *pueblo*. In the past year he had doctored many of their families. They generally paid him in tortillas and tamales, and the occasional hen past her laying prime. The families of the officials were more generous because they had more, which meant the occasional blanket—or even a pearl from Panama, paid after he had successfully bored into the skull of a small boy with swelling on the brain after a fall from his father's horse.

He looked at the door to his own quarters, still shut, wondering if Laura would have the courage to face her own kind again, since they had turned so relentlessly against her father and her. He knew there was a way to make it happen, but it would certainly test her mettle.

The first test was coming; he could see it walking across the courtyard right now, heavily laden with breakfast. He stepped aside, nodding his usual greeting to the kitchen hand who brought his morning meal of tortillas and mush.

"*Hola,* Pablo," he said, raising his hand in a friendly greeting. "*Como estás?*"

The man smiled his own greeting. Thomas gestured to the table beside the closed door and he set down the tray of food, hot and fragrant from the *presidio*'s mess hall. He gestured again to the stool and the kitchen hand sat.

"Pablo, I have a problem that only you can help me with," the surgeon said, after the pleasantries that his Scottish upbringing had learned to offer to these people who seemed to naturally have more free time than his own kind.

"Anything for you, *señor*," Pablo replied. He touched his own arm. "After all, think of what you did when I burned my arm."

"Ah, yes, I did help you, didn't I?" Thomas smiled. "That is what I am trained to do."

"Of course, *señor,* but not even our own garrison doctor—" he crossed himself "—rest his memory, could be bothered with kitchen workers."

"Perhaps he was too busy," Thomas replied diplomatically. "I know how that can happen."

"Perhaps," the man agreed, but he sounded doubtful. "*Señor,* your food will get cold."

Thomas nodded. He leaned forward, so Pablo leaned forward, too. "Pablo, yesterday morning I married Doña Laura Ortiz de la Garza."

Pablo nodded, his eyes troubled. "She is the daughter of a very bad man. Begging your pardon, but you should not have done that."

"*She* is not a bad person, Pablo. Far from it. I find her most pleasing and charming." *Well, I do,* he thought to himself, *even if she thinks I am a low-class barbarian.* "She feels sad because no one will speak to her now."

"Why should we?" Pablo said with a shrug.

"Because she is my wife, Pablo," Thomas said gently, feeling a pang in his heart for the woman he had so precipitately married. "I have been a friend to you and many others in this garrison. It would pain me to see her treated unkindly. Especially after I have been so kind to you," he added, with a sorrowful shake of his head. "It's just a thought, Pablo. Here, let me open the door for you."

Thomas swung the door wide. Laura stood there, her hands tight together. He didn't think she had heard any of their conversation through the heavy door, but there was no overlooking the dread in her eyes when she came face-to-face with a member—albeit a lowly one—of the garrison her father had cheated.

There they stood. Thomas gestured to the table. "Thank you, Pablo, for the breakfast. And this is Señora Wilkie."

It could have gone either way; Thomas knew that. All Pablo had to do was nod to him and turn on his heel. He did not. To the surgeon's relief, the kitchen hand—lowest of the low in the garrison and destined always to remain such—beamed at them both.

He turned specifically to Laura and Thomas held his breath. He shouldn't have worried.

"Señora Wilkie, if there is anything more you wish from the kitchen, only tell me."

Letting out the breath that Thomas knew she was holding, Laura smiled her thanks. "I will let you know, Pablo," she said, her voice scarcely above a whisper.

The man bobbed a bow to Thomas and left the *sala*. Laura sat down, as though her feet could no longer hold her. There was nothing in her face of condescension and Thomas almost found himself missing her dignified, superior air. Almost.

She did not speak for a long moment, swallowing a few times. Then, in a voice no louder than before, "I did not expect him to be kind, *señor*," she said.

"I did. And please, call me Thomas, not *señor*."

She blushed. "I do not think I can." She swallowed. "Yet."

Not yet? he asked himself, as he took the cover from the tray of food. Actually, that was more than he had hoped for. Maybe the little plan—such a wee plan—he

had forged in the early hours before he slept had some
hope of success.

He set out two bowls and Laura went to the cabinet where he kept his utensils. He smiled to see that,
womanlike, she had already acquainted herself with
everything in his tiny household.

He bowed his head while she murmured her prayer
and crossed herself. Like a practiced wife, she dished
out the mush and set it before him before serving herself.

They ate in shy silence. Since she could barely bring
herself to look at him, Thomas couldn't help but admire
the length of his wife's eyelashes again and the delicate
way she held a spoon. She was grace personified.

And now he would put her to dirty work; it was all
part of the plan.

"Laura, my pharmacist's mate sailed with the ship
a few days ago."

She looked at him then, curious, perhaps not understanding the way he had translated pharmacist's mate
into Spanish.

"The man who assists me when I perform surgeries
or help patients in the ward," he explained. "I have no
help."

She nodded. In the brief moment she looked at him,
he saw the interest in her intelligent eyes.

"I already know how you have helped me and Father
Hilario with the poor folk in the *pueblo,*" he continued,
after a few more bites. He nodded his thanks when she
handed him the little plate of tortillas.

He rested his elbows on the table then, and could
have laughed out loud to see the way she frowned at

his bad manners: almost the old Laura again, but not quite.

"You are going to be my pharmacist's mate," he continued, swabbing the inside of the bowl with the tortilla. "You will accompany me on my rounds of the garrison and into the *pueblo,* and we will tend the sick together."

She turned pale at that, looking at him with stricken eyes. "I cannot," she whispered. "They would never allow it. I am…" She paused as the tears rose into her deep brown eyes. "Oh, *señor,* I should have left with my father! They hate me now!"

He took the corner of his napkin and gently wiped her eyes, even as he writhed inside over her anguish. "Don't be so sure of that, Laura."

She stood up, unable to remain seated, humiliated by the misdemeanors, even though she had not authored them. "You don't understand, *señor!* I know these people!" She sobbed out loud. "They will hate you, too!"

Touched, he took hold of her hand before she could retreat to the bedroom, pulling her closer, but not forcing her beyond what she was willing to do. "I know them, too, Laura," he told her. "They're going to discover that we are a matched pair."

He knew he had not translated that well by the sudden mystification in her eyes. "Two horses pulling one cart, my dear," he said, trying again in Spanish. "Bacon and eggs," he said in English. "Tea and toast."

Laura just shook her head, but she was no longer tugging against his hand. Thomas released his grip and she stood there. He knew she could bolt to the other room and refuse to leave it, or she could hear him out. He was counting more on her curiosity than her affection, of which he had no gauge.

"Listen to what I say, *señora,*" he said, as formal as she. "Let me make you indispensable to San Diego."

134
62

68

Chapter Seven

10

Laura might have been uneasy, but she didn't falter when Thomas took her by the hand and led her into the wardroom. Her grip got a little tighter when she saw the wounded soldier, but she didn't hang back.

Thomas glanced at Ralph, who still slept, and whispered in Laura's ear, "When Ralph wakes up, I want you to help him eat."

She nodded, her eyes still on the gored soldier. Gently she freed herself from Thomas's grasp and, to his relief, sat down in the canvas sling chair. She glanced at Thomas for permission; when he nodded, she smoothed the young man's hair. "There now," she murmured.

Thomas knelt by the bed and raised the light blanket that covered Juan's wound, moving the bedclothes to protect the man's modesty. "He was gored in the thigh. I cleaned the wound and put in a drain, which needs to be irrigated every few hours. Let me show you how."

He taught her as he had taught any number of pharmacist's mates through the years: one eye on the wound, and the other eye on the student. If she fainted, she wouldn't be the first, but she didn't. Her normally full lips came together in a tight line and she swallowed several times, but she watched with that intense gaze already familiar to him. When he finished his demonstration, he handed the tube to her and directed her hand as she inserted the drain into the ugly wound.

Juan regained consciousness as she finished her task. Thomas moved closer. "Well, soldier, you've survived the night. I have high hopes."

The man's eyes were on Laura. "This is my wife, Laura Ortiz Wilkie," Thomas said. "She will be helping me care for you."

The man's eyes narrowed for a moment and Laura looked anxiously at Thomas. Hoping she would not mind, he put his hand on her shoulder. He thought she leaned towards him a little, but he could have been mistaken.

"Señora Wilkie," Juan said, and this time he managed a slight smile. "I would like something to eat."

Thomas felt his wife's slender shoulders raise and lower in a silent sigh of relief. "The mush?" she asked over her shoulder.

"That would be fine. Pablo brought enough for these men, too. He always brings enough. Add a little of the cream to it, then feed your patient."

"Aye, aye," she said, which made him laugh. It touched him a little, too. She continued in Spanish. "Actually, I am Laura Ortiz *de* Wilkie, to be proper." She smiled, and looked more her usual self. "I intend to correct your Spanish, if needed."

Thomas bowed. "I thought you might," he said in

what he knew was poor Spanish. This elicited an overly dramatic eye roll from his new bride, which suggested she might be regaining her equilibrium.

He watched her hurry from the room, intent on her errand. Thomas glanced at Ralph, who was awake now. "When she finishes feeding the soldier, it will be your turn," he told the carpenter.

Ralph put his hands behind his head. "You plan to work yourself out of a job?" he teased.

"I do, indeed," Thomas replied. "I want everyone in the *presidio* to need Laura Wilkie as much as they need me."

And maybe the moment will come when my wife needs me, he thought, as she came into the room again—such a graceful walk—and sat beside the soldier. He looked at the clock, marveling that he had been married twenty-four hours and wondering just at what moment he had decided he already loved her. Maybe it had happened during the night when he sat up with his patient, thinking of ways to resurrect Laura's good name in the eyes of—oh, let us be honest—this hypocritical group of busybodies. Maybe it was when he woke up warm, because she had covered him with the blanket. Possibly it had happened months before, when he had started admiring her, back when she'd had all the class and style and he'd had none. Perhaps it was when she had given him that anxious look, as if he could make it all better. Well, he could and he would, because she was his wife.

He watched his patient for another hour, leaning in the doorway, his eyes drooping, until to his delight, Laura took him by the hand and led him to his own bed. "There now, *señor,* you have showed me what to do and Juan is sleeping. You sleep now."

He didn't argue, especially when she knelt to remove his sandals, as though she was his servant. He protested, but she merely told him to hush as she slipped them off and displayed one of those peremptory gestures that reminded him of the old Laura.

"Very well, madam," he told her, happy enough to lie down and close his eyes.

He didn't open them until much later in the day, comfortable in his bed, even though the day was uncharacteristically cool for San Diego. On opening his eyes he discovered, to his delight, that someone had wrapped a warm stone and placed it under the cover at the foot of the bed. *This could be a better bargain than I reckoned,* he thought drowsily and drifted back to sleep.

He woke up later as shadows were beginning to slant across his bed, prodded awake by gentle pummeling, which grew more insistent. He took her hand. "Laura, what on earth…?" he said.

A look at his wife's anxious face had him up and scuffing for his sandals. "Is it Juan?" he asked.

"No, no, he is sleeping," Laura said, her hand still on his arm, tugging him. "It is Señor Gooding. Please hurry!"

As his head cleared, Thomas noticed the smears of blood on her apron and fingers.

Still she clutched him. "I didn't know what to do!" she cried.

He paused long enough to touch her face, then tug gently on her auburn hair peeking out from under her matron's cap—where had she found such a thing so fast?—because she looked so terrified. "Don't worry, Laura. I've been expecting this."

She had hold of his hand now, and she didn't release it as they went quickly into the ward, where Juan still slumbered and Ralph bled.

Thomas went right to work, propping up the terrified carpenter, then applying styptic and gentle pressure to the open lesion on his neck. All the while, Laura knelt beside him, holding Ralph's hand, as the bleeding slowed and then stopped. Calm returned to his patient's face, even though his pallor was more pronounced than before.

And now it begins, Thomas thought. *How much longer can he survive?* He glanced at Laura, who was on her feet now and pouring warm water in a basin to cleanse away the blood. She was pale, too, her fine eyes betraying all the worry he knew she was too shy to express.

He went to her and gave her shoulders a gentle squeeze. "Would you rather I tended Señor Gooding alone, or do you want to learn?"

"Let me think about that," she whispered as she returned to the bed with the warm water and a soft cloth. She helped Thomas remove their patient's nightshirt and replace it with a clean one, then delicately dabbed at his face and ruined neck. Through it all, Ralph Gooding's eyes remained closed, his feelings a mystery.

When she had finished, Ralph opened his eyes and smiled at her, which only brought more tears to her eyes.

"You're a pretty one," the patient said to her, then looked at Thomas, the anguish in his eyes unmistakable. "Pretty or not, too bad I didn't reach this point a month ago, eh? You could have sailed with the *Almost Splendid* and still been free to marry your sweetheart." He closed his eyes again, then fell into exhausted clumber.

Maybe out of pride, Thomas had never said anything to the other navy men about his father's letter, which broke the news of his fiancée's marriage to his older brother.

"What did Señor Gooding say?" Laura asked.

Thomas translated automatically, not thinking until the words were out of his mouth. *Lord, I am a chowderhead,* he thought in dismay, as Laura gasped.

"Oh, no, wait," he said, as she got to her feet, looking everywhere but at him. "I could never have left my patients. Laura, wait! My fiancée married my older brother years ago. There's no one back home for me! Oh, this is a jumble."

He was speaking to an empty space. She was out of the door, pouring the contents of the bloody basin into the dirt of the courtyard. She stood there a moment, wavering. Heartsick, Thomas went to the door and watched her, knowing how badly she wanted to run and also aware of how frightened she was now of her own people, who had rejected her along with her father.

When he just stood there, Laura looked at him, tears on her cheeks. She swallowed. "There is no one back home for me, either. Or here."

With a small curtsy, avoiding his eyes again, Laura went into their bedchamber and closed the door quietly behind her.

It was a long afternoon spent, repentant, in the ward. Juan woke up hungry and Thomas fed him, happy for any distraction. He cleaned the drain and replaced it, then sat beside the sleeping carpenter, flogging himself for his own stupidity. The door to his bedroom—oh, God, their bedroom now—remained closed.

His misery must have showed. When Ralph woke up he raised an enquiring eyebrow and Thomas told him what had happened. "I have just proved to myself that I am the biggest fool in the Western Hemisphere, at least," he concluded. He threw up his hands. "Ralph, I barely understand women—I mean, how often do we even *see* them?—and certainly don't understand wives." He moved closer to the bed. "I'm embarrassed that I don't even know this about you—are you married?"

"I am, indeed," the carpenter said. His voice was weak. "She's a bonny lass from Portsmouth and we have two sons."

Thomas leaned forward in the canvas chair, his eyes on his patient. "Well, Lord smite me when I whine," he said. He took Ralph's hand, distressed how light it was, how frail the man. "Make sure I have their direction in Portsmouth. I'll deliver a message when…"

"…when you eventually get home," his patient concluded. "I'd like that." He regarded Thomas and Thomas noticed the shrewd light returning to his tired eyes. "Want advice? Apologize for being an idiot. Then do something nice." His voice turned wistful. "Buy her one of those pretty veils the ladies here wear." His eyes were closing. "You're married now. Watch your mouth and you'll be a happy man."

Thomas chuckled. "I suppose humble pie in Alta California tastes the same as humble pie in Dumfries."

In fact, I'm certain of it, he told himself, as the carpenter returned to sleep, worn out with conversation. "Carpenter Gooding, believe me when I say I would never abandon you." He smiled at the sleeping man. "What would Hippocrates think?"

Trusting both of his patients to slumber for a while, Thomas stood up, took a deep breath and girded his loins. He stood a long moment outside the door to his room, and knocked. He listened. Nothing. He listened a moment longer. She didn't throw anything at the door, so he went in.

Funny, that. They had been sharing his room for barely more than a day and a night, and it already smelled better. Of course, when they had sat close together at Juan's bed that morning, Thomas had appreciated the pleasant fragrance of her hair. Maybe it was lavender, something he had noticed growing here and there in the *presidio,* almost like a weed.

She was lying on her back staring at the ceiling, her naturally downturned lips making her look sadder. She didn't turn away and face the wall to his relief. He sat down beside her, figuring the stool was safer than actually sitting on her bed.

He cleared his throat, wondering what was sticking there. He decided it was pride and swallowed it. "Laura, when I was a wee lad and I said bad things, my mother would make me take a bite of soap and chew it."

Startled, she looked at him. "I will never do that to our children," she blurted out, then blushed when she realized just what she had said.

It was as though she had forgiven every thoughtless word he had ever uttered. The power of that little sentence nearly made him giddy. *All right, ninnie,* he ordered himself. *Say the right thing.*

"I know you would not," he said. "Will not," he corrected himself. "Laura, Ralph was wrong. I could never leave him, even though he chastises himself. He knows he is dying and wonders what difference two or three weeks would make. He's probably right; my staying here or leaving him to the local healers would probably make no difference."

She shifted herself to face him and raised up on one elbow. "You would never do that, even though I know you would rather be with your crew."

"I would," he agreed, knowing that for all her youth and vulnerability, she was a plain-spoken woman; it seemed to be the Spanish way. "But only if I had not met you and decided that your need was greater than Ralph's, even. You're not dying, but you needed my help and I gave it. Forgive me?"

She nodded, and wiped the corner of her eye. A smile played around her lips. "You said that rather well, *señor.*"

"Call me Tomás," he asked. "I don't think I got all the subjunctives right. That's a lot of speculative reasoning."

She repeated "If I had not met you" correctly. "That is how you should say it. See how close you were?"

"I want to be closer," he said in English.

"Qué?"

He shook his head. "Not important." He regarded her for a long moment, which didn't seem to make her uncomfortable. "Laura, with my pharmacist's mate gone with the ship, I miss his help."

Now that *was* a lie. He had discovered years ago and early in their ill-fated voyage that his pharmacist's mate was the laziest help ever inflicted on a hard-working surgeon. Laura didn't need to know how worthless the man was.

"It's this way—you can tell that Juan and Ralph are happy for your help. I want you to come with me when I am asked to make calls in the *pueblo*."

"I dare not!" she exclaimed, her eyes filled with fear. "You…you saw how they looked at me."

He had truly frightened her. *Trust me, wife,* he thought, *even if I lacerate your confidence.* "All you need to do is help me once or twice. When they see how much they need me *and* you, you'll have friends again."

The look she gave him was doubtful and he didn't press the matter. He wanted more than anything to lie down with her, gather her close and take her fears away. There was one fear he knew he could end now. He went to his battered sea chest and pulled out that last, well-creased letter from his father. He pointed to the passage he had memorized.

"My brother married my fiancée in 1809," Thomas said, smiling a little at Laura's sudden intake of breath, as though she could not imagine such disloyalty. "Listen— 'Well, son, Cora was four years waiting for you and a woman of twenty-three is ripe and getting stale.'"

He stopped there, not reading the rest of it: "There will be other lassies." He felt suddenly too shy to say more.

No fears, apparently, from his wife. She sat up, taking the letter and looking at English words she could not read. "Twenty-three? Tomás, she is an antique and that was almost three years ago!"

Her woman's logic amused him, if that's what it was. "Aye, lass. An antique. I suppose you will tell me you are a mere twenty!"

Her eyes were still big, but her voice was proud. "Eighteen, *señor,* and that is old enough in my country."

He thought he would try his luck then. "I am tired, wife. Move over."

She could have pointed to his own bed, but she did not. She did as he asked and he lay down next to her. Since his luck was holding, he held out his arm. Laura curled close to him and he knew by that simple gesture how distressed she was. She pillowed her head on his shoulder, as though seeking warmth.

"You'll come about again with the people of San Diego," he murmured, his eyes closing.

He could feel her shaking her head. "I am certain I will not. They have long memories."

"We'll see, Laura."

131
14
———
57

Chapter Eight

As November turned into December, Thomas didn't mention again her helping him in the little village outside the *presidio*. Laura seemed relieved to work beside him in the ward. After a week, Juan had returned to the barrack, but there were other soldiers needing the surgeon's help. It was the season of catarrh with coughs and runny noses, which seemed to constitute a major portion of his work on land or sea—so much for the glamour of medicine.

Thomas had taught her how to care for Ralph Gooding and the carpenter seemed to respond to her tender ministrations. More than once or twice he had observed the two of them engaged in what he knew must be curious conversation. Her English was rudimentary at best, and Ralph's Spanish was limited. But they seemed to find some common ground and Thomas was content.

The only ruffling of calm waters came on the night he was called out to a difficult delivery and tried to convince her to come along. She burst into tears and he had no defense against that. "It's all right, Laura," he soothed, even as the mayor waited—none too patient, and who could blame him?—for Thomas to hurry to his pregnant wife's bedside.

"Don't make me!" she whispered, clutching his nightshirt.

"I won't," he promised. He touched her forehead with his. "But the moment might come, Laura, when you have to be brave enough to prove your value to everyone here besides just me."

He already knew her value and so did his usual customers. She tended his soldiers and fishermen and the Kumeyaay Indians from the mission a few miles away with care equal to his own. Laura Ortiz de Wilkie was a quick study and even brighter than he had thought. "Have a care," Ralph told him one day. "Maybe I'll ask *her* to close my eyes, after I die."

The carpenter's gallows humor would have upset Laura, so Thomas did not translate any of that for her, even though she stood close by, alert, should the carpenter need her. Her loyalty touched him, but her proprietary air—so Spanish—made him chuckle inwardly.

He was no closer to her bed and Thomas knew better than to press the matter. True to his nature, he analyzed his feelings. Did he just want a female, or did he want this particular female? Did she touch his heart, that seat of more exalted emotions, and not just his baser desires? He could have taken her many times over and she would have had no choice but to submit, but that much cruelty was foreign to him. He could wait; he was good at waiting.

On those occasional nights when no one needed his medical skills, Thomas fell into a pleasant bedtime routine with his new wife. He had always enjoyed reading in bed and he continued the practice, retiring to his bed with a good book and a sturdy candle. He kept the door to their shared chamber open. Out of the corner of his eye, he watched Laura kneel at her prie-dieu and begin that comforting click of her rosary beads. He even fancied that she prayed for him, but never had the nerve to ask.

When she finished, she invariably went into the ward for a last look around, even though he knew everyone in there was buttoned up for the night. She might spend a few minutes with Ralph Gooding. Once in a while Thomas heard them laugh, and he had to wonder what mutual language they could possibly communicate in. As December replaced November he even heard them humming a time or two. The tune was familiar, but he couldn't quite place it.

The sibilant splash of water in the washbasin signaled her ablutions next. There was no room for her clothes press in their bedchamber, not with the extra bed, so he listened then for the rustle of her clothing as she disrobed, put on her nightgown and draped an all-encompassing shawl around herself. The shawl stayed around her until she was safely in her own bed, then she draped it across the end of her bed and generally sat up, cross-legged, to brush her hair.

Once he almost got out of bed and took the brush from her, to handle that office himself. Her hair was such a beautiful deep black and snapped and crackled as she brushed it. Her expression was often dreamy then, as though the homely exercise soothed her. It soothed him, too, when it wasn't exciting him. The fun began when he blew out his candle and the room was dark.

Then, and only then, did Laura Maria Ortiz de Wilkie seem to feel confident enough to talk to him about her childhood in Spain, their removal to the viceroy's court in Mexico City, and her mother and baby brother, both of them long dead in a cholera epidemic.

"Could *you* have saved them?" she had asked one night.

He thought it over and had to tell her that he probably could not. By the light of the moon shining through the eucalyptus leaves outside their window, he saw her raise up on her elbow to give him that intense stare of hers.

"But you would have tried everything, would you not?" she asked.

"You know I would."

"Even if it meant you came down with cholera?"

"Even then."

Silence. And then, "Do you ever wish you could save everyone?"

No one had ever asked him that before. He had to try not to show his emotions when he replied, "All the time."

He must not have been convincing, because the next thing he heard was her covers pulled back and her bare feet on the floor. She did nothing more than pull his covers higher over his chest and then kiss his forehead before returning to her own bed, but it was enough to melt his heart entirely.

In his turn Thomas told her about Dumfries, where it rained all the time and the wind blew, and his parents' house—stone and substantial—was never warm enough. One night he probably woke up Ralph with his laughter, when Laura looked at him and mused in all innocence, "Only an idiot would yearn for a place like that."

"It's home," he had replied, when he stopped laughing.

He could tell she was not convinced. She was even less impressed with Christmas celebrations in Scotland, which amounted to very little.

"The cook will fix a slightly better-than-usual dinner and we will go to church."

"You can't be serious," she had said, in her now-familiar voice, the tone reserved for the truly misbegotten.

"I never lie, Laura," he lied. "What do you do here that is better?"

"Most nearly everything," she said succinctly, which made him smile in the dark. "We have special food, singing and dancing." He could hear her sitting up in her bed. "We have *fun.*"

"Fun is against the law in Scotland," he told her and was rewarded, to his amusement, with a huge snort of disgust from the other bed. "No. Seriously. England outlawed fun."

"Then I cannot comment on such stupidity," she said, pulling her dignity about her like a shawl, which never failed to make him smile. "We have a *posada* and that is the best of all."

Thomas listened appreciatively as Laura told him of the nine nights of processions of the Holy Family from door to door, seeking in song a place to spend the night. With growing enthusiasm she described their tender plea for succor, and the innkeepers' disdain, also sung. "And on the last night, the eve of Christmas, Maria and José go to the final house and the innkeepers let them in," she concluded in triumph, obviously aware that her Christmas far trumped his. "We pray and we eat." She laughed softly. "A lot of both."

He knew what she spoke of, thinking of his years in San Diego and discounting the one year where the English and Spanish had still been officially at war and which he had spent mainly in prison. Even when the English and Spanish were friends, no one from the *pueblo* or *presidio* had included them in the festivities. "I remember the singing and the music," he told her, his hands behind his head, as he lay there in the dark. "Can we have Maria and José visit us here in the infirmary?"

She was silent a long time and he thought she had drifted to sleep. When she spoke, he heard the tears in her voice. "No one will have me, *señor*," she said. "Just as there are innkeepers who would not have the Christ Child."

"Damn them all, then," he said softly in English.

Thomas didn't hesitate. It was his turn to throw back the bedclothes, cross the room to her bed, tug up her blanket and plant a gentle kiss on her forehead. Before he returned to his own bed, she took his hand and kissed it, which made him swallow, then kept him awake much of the night as he contemplated the depths of her shame at her father's scandal, and his own emotions.

I wish you would trust me enough to understand that if we help your people with medical attention, you'd be astounded how many friends you will have, he thought. He wanted to tell her that, but her even breathing told him that she slept.

"Call me cynical, but it is true," he whispered in Spanish, before his eyes closed. "Something needs to happen, because I cannot bear to see you so sad."

* * *

From his lips to God's ears. Thomas wasn't sure what woke him so early on that morning of December 8th. He lay there listening; Laura was breathing gently on the other side of the little room. When he had got up around midnight to check on Ralph and the other patients, as he always did, he had left the door between the ward and their sitting room ajar. Now he listened, frowning. Nothing. Ralph's breathing was labored, but that was to be expected, with advanced consumption.

He listened harder and then it came to him that the animals taken into the courtyard were stirring restlessly, the cattle lowing and the horses whinnying, as though a wolf were among them. He got out of bed quietly and went to the door in the sitting room that opened onto the courtyard. He opened it a crack and watched the animals moving about; he could see no predators to disturb them.

Thomas had just crawled back into bed and stretched out with a sigh, when the ground began to shake. The whole room seemed to sway. It was only seconds, but enough to nauseate him.

He leaped from bed, his legs far apart as though he stood on the quarterdeck, because the movement continued. He heard tiles falling from the roof and glasses breaking in the next room. He knew he should rush to the ward, but that wasn't his first instinct now. In a few seconds, he had scooped Laura from her warm bed to the floor, lying on top of her on the heaving tiles, cradling her head in his hands. He slid them both under her bed. She was suddenly wide awake and as terrified as he was, clinging to him, wrapping her legs around his body in a strange caricature of lovemaking and fear at the same time. He pulled her close.

The room continued to move; the heavy bed even started to shift, so he moved them farther under it. Laura groaned when her cupboard with all its dishes crashed to the floor in the other room. "It's all right," he murmured, kissing her somewhere in the vicinity of her ear. "It's just dishes."

She didn't say anything, but tried to burrow as close to him as she could, her breath coming in little gasps. He put his cheek next to hers—she was so soft—and said in a commanding voice, one usually reserved for the orlop deck, when patients were piling up at the foot of the gangway during battle, "Breathe slowly. In and out. Do it."

She did. In a moment, he felt her heart slow down, beating more in rhythm with his now. He could feel her body relax under his, even though her legs were still firmly anchored over his back. This was not the time to do what he wanted to do, but Thomas Wilkie, practical surgeon and Scot in the Royal Navy, had to admit he was beguiled by the idea.

"Can you breathe?" he asked, his voice more normal now.

Laura nodded, but clung tighter when he tried to move off her.

"Honey, I have to go in the other room." It was the first endearment he had attempted. She made no objection. After more precious seconds, while the earth still trembled, she released her hold on him just enough for him to slide out from under her bed, and tug her after him.

He wasn't sure he had ever seen another human being's eyes as wide open as his wife's were just then.

"I can never get accustomed to these," she said as she trembled.

He kept his arms around her a few more moments, then duty called; in fact, it clamored from the ward where Ralph was coughing. He released her and hurried into the other room, after lighting his lantern.

The ward was filled with plaster dust. His own eyes wide, Ralph coughed, his hand to the tubercular lesion on his throat, which began to ooze.

"We have to get him out of here," Thomas muttered to Laura, who had thrown her shawl around her nightgown. He grabbed a stretcher and Laura helped him move the carpenter onto it. Ralph was light enough now—too light—and she had no trouble taking one end of the stretcher and helping him move his patient into the courtyard. Ralph stopped coughing and Thomas stood over him a moment before following Laura back into the ward. Together they helped out a broken leg and a bad cold.

When his patients were comfortable enough, now that the frightened livestock had been herded outside the *presidio*'s courtyard, he motioned to Laura. "We'd better get dressed," he told her.

They hurried inside. Laura wasted not a moment on propriety and threw off her nightgown, standing naked before reaching for her chemise and then her dress. For several weeks now it had been his duty to button her up the back. He couldn't help it that his fingers shook. Whether it was the shock of the earthquake or the sight of his wife's substantial and beautiful breasts, he had to remind himself to breathe.

Oddly he felt shy about disrobing in front of her, as she looked about for her apron and shoes at the same time. *When in Rome,* he thought, stripping. He found his trousers before his smallclothes, which was a time-saver. A shirt and his surgeon's bibbed apron completed his *haute couture,* plus sandals. His medical bag was always in the same place. He slung it around his shoulder and reached for the cloth bag full of bandages.

"You're my pharmacist's mate," he told his wife, handing the bag to her. "Just follow me. We'll check the garrison first."

She nodded, clutching for his arm when the floor started to sway again with an aftershock. *"Dios mio,"* she muttered, holding tight to his arm. "Why do people live in San Diego?"

"Must be the beaches," he said, trying to make a joke, as the floor heaved and then stopped. "This never happens in Dumfries."

It pleased him that Laura could still tease in turn. "From what you have told me, nothing else ever happens there, either, including Christmas," she whispered in his ear. "We may have to do something drastic about Dumfries."

Chapter Nine

Impulsively Thomas kissed her cheek, then started for the small barrack on the opposite side of the courtyard. Few soldiers lived there permanently. The captain had explained to them several years back that *soldados* in Spanish forts generally lived outside the walls with their families, or even in bachelor houses.

He held out his hand for Laura and she took it, hanging back for a small moment. He turned around and noticed the tears in her eyes.

"I'm afraid," she whispered.

"I am, too," he told her honestly, "but I know what to do, and you know far more than you think you do."

She must have believed him because she nodded and squeezed his hand. His reassurance grew when she corrected his Spanish.

They found the captain nursing nothing worse than a bump on his head, caused when the bookcase with government regulations had collapsed against his desk, spilling out more than a century of parchment docu-

ments bound with red ties. While Thomas felt his forehead the captain remained serene, contemplating the
piles of regulations. "I doubt any of us paid much attention to them anyway," was his philosophical comment.
"Spain is so far away."

Their visit to the mess hall took longer. The cook and
his minions still crouched under tables, one Kumeyaay
boy clutching his foot, cut when he'd run across broken
china to slide to safety with the others. After Thomas
coaxed them out, Laura bound the lad's foot and gave
him a handful of sweets from a box that had burst open.
The cook glared at her for wasting delicacies on a mission Indian, but Laura just glared back, winning that
staring contest handily. Thomas could have told the man
to save his glares; his wife never suffered fools gladly
and was not inclined to start now.

They finished up quickly in the *presidio,* hurried
along by soldiers from outside the walls, begging for
help with their families. Laura hung back for only a
moment, looking to Thomas for reassurance. She had
not left the comparative safety of the fort since her
father had been led in chains from the *presidio.*

"I need you, Laura," was all he said. He gave her
hand a tug and she followed.

The *presidio* was well built, courtesy of Spanish
engineers decades ago; the *pueblo* itself was another
matter. Thomas saw the injuries he expected he would
see: broken limbs caused by falling beams, lacerations
and burns from overturned cooking pots. These were
the worst, but Laura waded right in with him, her eyes
fierce in their concentration. Only once did she throw
up. As he wiped her mouth, Thomas assured her there
wouldn't be anything worse than burns.

"How do you do this?" she asked, from the safe nest she had made of his shoulder's hollow, as he held her tight.

"How? I know how," he said simply. "So do you, my dear."

With a quick squeeze of her shoulder and a pat on her hip—he had taken that liberty without a qualm—he sent her back to applying salve to the less-horrific burns as he did what he could for the others. As they worked, Father Hilario, his eyes serious and his lips set tight, followed them with prayers and, in two extreme cases, final rites.

By the end of a day filled with frightening after-shocks, Father Hilario needed to remind no one that San Diego could have fared far worse. Although the tower in the partly constructed *presidio* chapel listed at a precari-ous angle, almost no crockery had survived anywhere and few windows with glass in them remained, San Diego itself still stood.

Laura had changed. It was a simple transformation; Thomas doubted she was even aware of it. When the mayor's wife had been found in her plaster dust-covered bed with her foot trapped under a beam, Laura had not hesitated, going quickly to the new mother's screaming child—the one he had delivered barely two weeks ear-lier—and covering the infant with her own body in case the roof chose to cave in just then. The child's helpless mother had watched, her eyes huge with fear. Crouching in the middle of destruction, Laura had crooned to the baby until he slept.

When the baby slept, Thomas gestured Laura closer. Soldiers had moved the beam from the new mother's foot and stabilized the leaning roof with their backs. Unmindful of her injury, the mayor's wife held out her arms for her child and Laura made them comfortable with a pillow and a blanket.

"You fit the space better, so you set her ankle," Thomas said and she did, working more efficiently than he could in the small space to splint and bind up the woman's ankle. Thomas smiled to watch the injured woman's face when she first realized that her help was coming from the hated daughter of the man who had swindled her husband and other people of quality in the *pueblo*.

The woman's eyes softened as she watched Laura. When Laura finished and sat back, looking to him for approval, the new mother touched Laura's cheek lightly, then closed her eyes in relief. "Bless you, Señora Wilkie," she whispered.

"Back out with the baby and we'll move her now," Thomas said, nodding to the soldiers propping up the precarious walls.

With no coaxing, the mother handed her baby to Laura, who crawled out on her knees, the child held tight in her arms. After Thomas gently lifted the mother from the ruin, the men lowered the beams and leaped out of the way as the walls collapsed inwards.

The mayor stood there now, tears streaking his dirty face as he thanked them for saving his darlings. "The thanks go to my wife," Thomas said. "I couldn't fit in that small space."

Without a word, the grateful hidalgo kissed Laura's hand and burst into tears when she gently placed his son in his arms.

"That wasn't such a small space," Laura whispered

as she picked up the bandage duffel again and followed him down the street littered with adobe shards and roof tiles. "You could have squeezed in there."

Thomas only smiled. "I get sweaty in tight places."

She laughed out loud, then covered her mouth with her hand. He took her hand away. "You have a wonderful laugh, Señora Wilkie," he said.

"I'll save it for a day when we do not have a catastrophe on our hands," she said, looking around, obviously hoping no one had heard her.

They had spent the rest of that long day in the *pueblo* patching wounds, and then later in the mission, where there had been less damage. He had returned to the *presidio*'s courtyard a few times to check on his bona fide patients. The bad cold had fled the scene and the broken leg snored peacefully. Ralph Gooding lay there with his eyes open and troubled. Thomas had sighed to see more blood on his nightshirt. He had applied styptic until the slow ooze stopped and had no hesitation in giving the man a dose of laudanum from his precious stores.

He had still been squatting on his haunches by Ralph's stretcher when Laura returned to the *presidio,* looking as tired as he felt. She had patted his shoulder, which made him smile, then gone into the small hospital. In another moment he had heard her sweeping the glass and plaster.

In companionable silence, they had cleaned up the ward, pausing only to stand in the doorway with each aftershock. Invariably she had leaned against him; just as predictably, his arm had gone around her shoulder. He had found himself looking forward to the after-shocks. By the time darkness had fallen, the broken leg was back in a newly made bed, and Ralph was comfortable again, propped up against a grain sack because his pillows were bloody and needed washing.

Dinner had been nothing more than *posole* with more parched corn than pork, but delicious because they had eaten nothing all day. Summoned by more emergencies beyond the *pueblo,* he had left Laura spooning the stew down the carpenter's ravaged throat and gently wiping his neck.

When he returned hours later, all was peaceful in the ward. Laura had admitted three new patients in his absence, two soldiers and one mission Indian he had sent to her, escorted by Father Hilario. Everyone was clean, fed and sleeping. *Goodness, she will work me out of a job,* Thomas thought with satisfaction as he checked his patients.

When his exhausted mind realized there was nothing more he needed to do, Thomas opened the door to his sitting room and peered inside. All was orderly now—Laura's blue-wooden cabinet had even been righted, although its glass and china contents must have been relegated to the midden. The prie-dieu had a crack in it, but he thought he could fix it. Her heavier wardrobe still lay on its side, but there were plenty of men in the *presidio* who could help him tomorrow.

Leaving his sandals in the sitting room, he tiptoed into the bedroom where Laura had left his ward lamp burning. For safety's sake, she had set it in his battered metal basin, the one that had followed him from Portsmouth and around the world a time or two.

He glanced at his wife, who had drawn herself into

a ball, probably more from residual fear than cold, because the night was still mild. Quietly, he looked for his nightshirt, tossed somewhere that morning, hours ago. When he couldn't find it he sighed, stripped and climbed between his sheets, weary right down to his Achilles' tendons.

He was almost asleep when he vaguely heard Laura pull back her bedclothes and pad across the space between their beds. He wanted to be more alert, but all he could do was yawn as she tugged back his blankets and crawled in beside him. He put his arm around her and pulled her close.

"I can't stop shivering and it's not even cold," she whispered.

"You're shocky," he murmured, not sure of an approximate Spanish word.

"Chalky?" she repeated.

"Shocky," he said again in English, then reverted to her language. "It's what happens when hard-working wives are ignored during a major crisis."

"Is there a cure?" she asked, still shaking, but drowsy now.

Both of his arms went around her and she clung to him, gulping down her tears and keeping them quiet against his bare chest.

"Honey, you were magnificent," he whispered. "You'll warm up in a few minutes, I promise."

Then—churl or exhausted surgeon, she could decide which—he slept.

He woke up once in the night, more from habit than anything else. He found his nightshirt and put it on, then took the lamp into the ward for a look around. All was orderly. He opened the door into the silent courtyard, piled high with ruined bits and pieces of people's lives and destined to be carted away tomorrow. He stood there a moment, wondering what the next day would bring besides more work. He leaned against the door-jamb, overwhelmed by the longing to be home. Even if Dumfries was misty and gray and probably as unprepossessing as his wife suspected, he yearned for a place where the ground did not move.

Here it was, December 9th, and he was no nearer home than he had been years ago, when he had received that Christmas letter from his father. In his mind's eye, he saw his father making his own surgical rounds in dreary winter weather, while his mother probably knitted by the fire. He thought of his own wife, working so hard beside him all day, stopping for nothing, and then reduced to shivers and tears. Thomas Wilkie wasn't sure he deserved someone as brave in the face of catastrophe as she was. And the funny thing was, she would never think of herself that way.

"Thomas, you could be a dumb cluck and moon about what you don't have, or appreciate your current lot in life," he said out loud, as he looked through the *sala* and into his bedroom. "Go to bed, you idiot, and keep Laura warm."

Thank goodness he wasn't so stupid as to need to talk himself into going back to bed. He set the lamp back in the basin and returned to bed with a sigh. Laura huddled close to him again. He smiled in the dark, thinking of the improbability of spending another Christmas in San Diego with a beautiful wife. *If my friends could see me now,* he thought. He kissed the top of her head.

She was warm now and heavy against his side. He

liked the feel of her, especially the fragrance of her hair, even if she did smell of plaster dust, too. She woke up when he placed a tentative hand on her hip, but only long enough to murmur something, then sink into sleep again. It seemed like such a good idea that he followed suit, his hand still on her hip.

Chapter Ten

Dawn was breaking when Thomas woke. Startled, he wondered for a millisecond why Laura was sleeping in his bed, then remembered her fears of the night before. Obviously, she hadn't taken the trouble to follow her usual bedtime routine, because her dark hair was spread across his chest, instead of confined in its usual chaste braid.

He fingered the ends of her hair, admiring the way it curled. He knew he should get up, but he stayed where he was, unwilling to wake his sleeping wife. Still, duty called. Carefully, he slid out of his bed, dressed quickly and opened the door to the ward in time to see the mission Indian, head bandaged, leap out of the back window.

"I'm surprised you stayed this long," Thomas murmured in English to the retreating figure. "Look out for infection and take out those sutures in a hygienic place." He smiled and shook his head.

"*I* won't take French leave," Ralph said.

Thomas hoped he kept his expression neutral. The earthquake had taken its toll on his oldest patient. "You had better not, or I'll put you on report."

"Ooh, I'm all a-twitter."

Ralph could barely speak, but Thomas chose to overlook that fact. He swabbed gently around the tubercular lesion on his neck, wishing for cures where there were none. He knew he should be concentrating on Ralph, but he thought of his father and mother instead. He had been doing this increasingly since his sudden marriage, wondering how his mother would treat Laura Ortiz de Wilkie. Probably very well, he decided, as he quietly tidied his patient. Mama had not thought he would ever survive so many years at sea, much less find a wife. *They don't even know if I am alive,* he thought. *Or I, them, I suppose.*

"I wish we were home," he said to Ralph.

"Laddie, I think you already are," Ralph said, after a long pause to either assemble his thoughts or merely find the energy to talk.

Thomas looked toward the closed door to his bedroom. "A ship will come eventually."

"What then?"

It was a fair question and he had no answer. "I know I can secure passage for her to England, but will she want to leave Alta California?" he asked out loud, even though he did not expect an answer. "What do you think?"

Ralph's eyes were closed, as though the effort to keep them open was too much. "Just ask," he said finally. Eyes still closed, he gestured. "Don't be so afraid."

"Is that what I am?" Thomas asked, surprised.

"Mebbe."

He tried to think of a worthy retort, but he had none, because it was probably true. And only a moment later, there were far bigger fish to fry than his own romantic life.

With no preamble, Father Hilario and the captain came through the outside door one after the other, both with eyes so serious that Thomas was on his feet and looking around for his surgeon's bag before either man spoke. When the captain did speak, Thomas felt that familiar plunk in his stomach, where the worst news seemed to land.

"Who needs me?" he asked the officer.

Father Hilario answered, not bothered by protocol. "The entire mission of San Juan Capistrano," he said.

"Heavens above," Thomas said, feeling the blood drain from his face. He had been to the lovely mission last spring, two days' distance by horse, just for the pleasure of watching the swallows return. "What has happened?"

"As you know—" Thomas didn't "—yesterday was the Feast Day of the Immaculate Conception of the Blessed Virgin..." Father Hilario began. Emotion choked him and he could not continue, so the captain spoke.

"When the earthquake struck, the chapel was full of worshippers, mostly mission Indians. The doors jammed and the roof fell in. There are at least forty dead, and Father Barona and Father Boscana are doing their best..." The officer's voice trailed away.

"We will go at once."

Startled, Thomas looked around to see his wife standing in the doorway to their sitting room, her hair still wild about her head, but her shawl and her bear-

ing giving her considerable dignity. He looked into her
eyes and saw nothing but calm there. How was it that
she could even make herself look *tall?* What a mystery
women were.

"Anything you can do there will be a blessing,"
Father Hilario said.

"Very well." Thomas looked at Ralph, then, and the
broken leg in the other bed. He didn't try to hide his
doubt. "Laura should stay here to…"

"No, Laura will *not.* Father Hilario will tend these
men," Laura said.

There was nothing in her voice but steel and Thomas
thought it wise not to argue. *I'm learning already,* he
thought. "This is true; he can." He looked at the captain.
"How did the news travel here?"

"By a coasting vessel. It was quicker than horseback."

"We will go that way, too," Thomas said. "Laura,
get the bandage box together. Maybe some food, too."

She obeyed him without a word, gathering up more
bandages that she must have had the foresight to roll last
night, when he was out tending last-minute victims and
thought she was asleep. While Thomas gave instructions to Father Hilario for the care of his few patients,
and the more difficult cases he might encounter in the
pueblo, Laura finished her work and went back into
their room to dress. When she came out she was tidy,
dignified and neat as a pin, which made him smile.
*Laura Ortiz de Wilkie, you are a lady right down to
the soles of your feet,* he thought with admiration. He
knew he had never met anyone like her in his life.

The captain left to secure a cart to hurry them down
to the harbor. Thomas sat beside Ralph for a moment.

He took his hand and just held it. "I should leave Laura here," he said, "but this is such a crisis. We will have to trust Father Hilario."

Ralph was too weak to move his head, but his eyes followed Laura as she gathered the bandages and set them outside the door. "I don't think she would have stayed," he managed to croak. "She is a determined woman, laddie."

When did you start calling me "laddie"? Thomas thought, his eyes on the patient who had, in some way, become his dear friend. *Was it that moment when you realized I couldn't do anything more for you? At least you know I have tried.*

He patted Ralph's shoulder, dismayed to feel bone, sinew and little else. Tuberculosis was a bitch of a disease; he doubted there would ever be a cure. For a moment Thomas rested the back of his hand against Ralph's always-warm forehead. *"Vaya con dios,"* he said.

They made the trip to the harbor in record time, Thomas clinging to his surgeon's satchel with one hand, and to Laura with the other. The wheeled cart was noisy on the dirt path, so Laura put her lips close to his ear, which made him shiver with pleasure.

"I do not do very well in a boat, *señor,*" she told him.

"I do even worse on horseback," he said, speaking in her ear, in turn. "I would have embarrassed you."

"I fear I will embarrass *you,*" she replied.

Perhaps she would have, if he hadn't loved her so much. The usually placid water of San Diego Bay was choppy—perhaps because of the continuing after-shocks—and the small vessel tossed them about. He held his wife steady over the gunwale as she threw up. Her normally perfect complexion turned sallow. At one point on the voyage, he thought he heard her ask him to throw her overboard and let her die, but his Spanish wasn't perfect, he knew.

He found no fault with the sailors, fishermen who had been pressed into service in Mission San Juan and who knew the coast like their wives' bodies. When Laura had seemingly thrown up everything she had eaten for the last six months, he held her tight against his side with his boat cloak around them both, their only defense against the salt spray. He listened with deepening alarm to the sailors' stories of massive waves even farther north, near Mission Santa Barbara, and a ship that had foundered there.

His mind was on the mission though, and the sailors told him what they knew of the nave collapsing on early-morning worshippers. Some had survived and others in the mission houses had been terribly burned by cooking fires, as in San Diego, but worse. The earthquake must have originated under the unstable soil at San Juan.

Laura listened, too, her face as grave as his. He barely noticed when she took his hand and held it. He did notice when she raised his hand and pressed it to her lips.

"What is that for?" he asked, surprised, and gratified.

"I wanted to," she said simply.

If he hadn't needed her help so badly, it would have bothered him to take a barely trained woman into such a place of distress as Mission San Juan. Father José Barona and Father Gerónimo Boscana were the walking dead themselves, after toiling for two days and nights

among the injured and dying. Without a murmur, they
did what they could. Father Barona even smiled faintly
and apologized when he sat down. "It's been hours,"
was his only comment.

Her lips tight together, Laura followed Thomas to the
priests' refectory, which had become the hospital. She
assisted as he set bones, amputated and cleaned burns.
When he gave her supplies from his dwindling medical
bag, she set off on her own with no word of complaint.
It tugged at his heart when she walked away from him
and stopped to square her slim shoulders on which he
had placed such an awful burden.

It must have been well past midnight when the worst
cases were either dead or tended to. His face gray with
fatigue, Father Boscana had fallen asleep leaning
against a wall. Laura sat beside a small child, crooning to it. Stupefied with weariness, Thomas watched
the little one relax and finally sleep. He came closer
and rested his hand lightly on his wife's shoulder.

She looked around, then gestured to the child's
mother. "I fear she is dead," Laura whispered.

She was. Thomas sighed, covered her face and
nodded to Father Barona, who knelt and began to pray.
When the priest finished, he just sat there, too tired to
move.

"We can take turns sleeping," Thomas told him. "I
will watch first."

He thought the Franciscan would argue with him,
but Father Barona lay down next to the dead woman
and closed his eyes without a word.

Laura protested as Thomas took her arm and helped
her to her feet. "Mind me, Laura," was all he said and

she did, letting him lead her to a pallet that Father Boscana had pointed out earlier, close to the door. She lay down, but patted the grain sack. He lay down beside her. "Just for a moment," he told her, putting out his arm and pulling her close so her head rested on his chest. She didn't seem to mind his leather surgeon's apron, stiff with blood from yesterday in San Diego and now today in San Juan.

"How do you do this?" she asked. She was shivering. That troubled him, because he wasn't certain if it was from shock or cold.

How did he do it? His mind was too tired to form words in Spanish or English, but he thought she deserved an answer. "It is my choice," he said finally, but she was asleep.

He walked among the rows of wounded Indians, doing what he could, until Father Boscana woke up from his bench and took over. Thomas returned to Laura's side. She didn't wake up, but she must have known he was there, because she moved closer, shivering still.

They stayed two more days in San Juan Capistrano: ample time for the critically wounded to die and the less injured to begin to heal. The last night, they were both able to sleep together in a small room off the refectory, provided by Father Barona. There was even a pillow this time and a surprisingly soft wool blanket, probably woven by mission Indians. He wondered briefly if the weaver was still alive.

Laura seemed inclined to talk, as she did back in San Diego, once the lights were off. Her voice low, she told him again about Christmas in San Diego—the parties, the *posada,* the singing.

"I played Maria once in Mexico City," she told him, putting her hand over the one of his that was gently exploring her hair, running his fingers through the strands. He felt her chuckle. "I was young. When the innkeepers told us that we could not stay because there was no room, I cried."

He kissed her head. "I think that is a natural reaction. You have a soft heart, wife."

She raised up on one elbow to look him in the face. "That was kindly said," she murmured, then astounded him by kissing his lips. "You are the first man I have ever kissed," she said when she finished. "I doubt I am very good."

"I think that was fine," he said, pulling her closer and kissing her. "Let's do that again," he told her, his hand on her breast now.

With a sigh of contentment, she moved his hand and began to unbutton her dress. He helped, pulling the blanket higher to shield them from the open doorway. His hand was inside her bodice and caressing her bare skin when he heard footsteps and stopped.

Father Boscana tapped on the door frame. "I have a duty for you," he began, sounding apologetic.

It can't be better than what I was about to enjoy, Thomas thought, as he withdrew his hand from his wife's breast. "Certainly, Father. I am coming."

"It is a childbirth," the priest said. "Our midwife is dead and I have no skills along those lines."

"We're good at childbirth," Thomas said. "Lead on, Father. My wife will follow." *After she buttons her shirt-front again,* he thought, amused now, because he had been summoned and had no choice in the matter.

*   *   *

The birth took them down to San Juan's dock where a fisherman's wife was laboring over twins. It was a simple matter of organizing arms and legs, which Laura and her small hand managed with considerable proficiency, once Thomas had told her what to do. The twins came out quickly, crying and protesting such an abrupt disturbance of their crowded universe, which made Laura grin at him.

Dawn came as they left the fisherman's hovel, both of them smiling as they heard the babies crying—such a pleasant sound after the terror of the past few days and nights.

"Life just keeps going on," he said to his wife. He sat with her on the end of the dock, both of them dangling their legs off the pier. "Maybe she will name them Tomás and Laura."

Laura giggled and put her arm around him. "You have a high opinion of yourself!" she scolded, but he knew her well enough to know she was teasing.

"I am also an amazing lover," he joked back. "Probably the best in the Royal Navy."

She swatted his arm. "And how often are you on land?"

"You have me there," he said, ruffling her hair.

Thomas looked at the peaceful water. His back was to the mission, the smoke that still rose from smoldering buildings around the mission, the rubble everywhere and the incessant keening of Indians in despair. He could hardly imagine a more unromantic setting, but there was no overlooking the contentment filling him just sitting beside his bride of a few weeks.

"We can go back today," he told her. "And look over there—isn't that the pinnace we came on?"

Laura shuddered. "Could we not take horses? We would be two days, three at the most."

"The pinnace is faster and I have patients in San Diego, too," he reminded her. "This is the life of a surgeon, Laura."

She snorted, but was otherwise silent as he hailed the *pescador,* who was folding his nets into the boat, perhaps getting ready for a fishing run now that as much order had been restored to San Juan as anyone would see for a while. Life went on and the fish waited.

Hand in hand, they walked down to the beach. "Would you take us to San Diego?" Thomas asked.

The fisherman nodded, his face troubled. "Better south than north," he said.

"It's worse there?" Thomas asked.

"That man over there told us more than one ship foundered off Mission Santa Barbara."

"It's a tragedy," Thomas agreed. "We can be ready any—"

The fisherman wasn't finished. "One of the vessels was a strange sight. Apparently, members of your navy had jury-rigged a coastal vessel."

"Oh, Lord," Thomas breathed, as the blood drained from his face. "But…Santa Barbara? It can't be the vessel I know. The *Almost Splendid* left San Diego weeks ago."

The *pescador* shrugged. "Hard to say. I do know the British men had put into Santa Barbara two weeks ago, because they were taking on water." He sighed. "Everyone drowned in a rogue wave. How sad."

His legs wouldn't hold him. Thomas sank to the sand and bowed his head.

Chapter Eleven

H e stayed that way a long, long while, hearing a great roaring in his ears and feeling an enormous urge to cry his heart out. These were men he had sailed with, cured of ailments, heard their complaints and shared the evils of war. And now they were dead, fish food off the California coast, far from home.

He couldn't cry though, not when people depended on him. He tried to rise, but found he could not, until Laura helped him. Unable to speak, he nodded his thanks, then glanced at her.

What he saw in her eyes took away his breath. He had never seen such devastation on another human's face. Jolted from his own sorrow, he grabbed her shoulders. "Laura! What is the matter?"

She sobbed and threw her arms around him, trying to grab him everywhere, as if he were smoke and would disappear if she did not try. She clung to him, her face muffled against the bib of his surgeon's apron, wailing as though her heart would break. It was foolish to expect her to speak rationally; Scottish women did not behave like this. He held her just as tightly as she held him, knowing by now that her apparently fragile construction was an illusion. She was as strong as steel, every bit his equal.

He had no idea how long they clung together. When he opened his eyes, the fisherman was back coiling his nets, ignoring them as would any man who was "born to trouble as the sparks fly upward." So it was with Job; so it was with these citizens living in paradise on the Alta California coast, where the earth moved without warning.

His wife's wails ceased finally. She sagged against him and Thomas realized they were holding each other up.

"Dear heart, what is it? You didn't even know those men."

She raised her tearstained face to his, cupping it with her shaking hands. "Tomás, *you* could have been on that ship!"

Dumbfounded, he stared at her. She was right; he hadn't even thought of that, so horrified was he by the death of friends and the agony that the Americans at Fort Astoria would never even know how badly their assistance was needed by the Royal Navy, farther down the coast. He was stranded in California for the foreseeable future.

Selfish man. He had only thought of himself and not of his lovely, sudden wife. His father would have been ashamed.

Laura sat down in the sand then, and he slumped beside her. He put his arm around her, swarmed by more emotions at once than he was capable of processing through his tired brain. Death on land and sea surrounded them both and here was this precious gift: Laura Ortiz, descendant of grandees and Spanish nobility, who loved him. She loved him so much that even the mere thought of his death rendered her inconsolable. He didn't deserve such devotion.

She was saying something else, but there was that roaring in his ears. He breathed deeply and slowly until the noise went away. The sound of water lapping against the fishing boats, a sound he was familiar with, restored his equanimity. He was able to listen to what his wife was saying.

"I don't know when it happened," she was saying, her voice soft. She rubbed his chest. Her voice changed, and he could hear the shyness now. "Maybe it was even when you…when you did not take me at once, as was your right, once I was your wife."

"I would never have done that, Laura," he said.

She nodded. "I know. You were kind and you never had to be."

He pulled her on to his lap because beside him wasn't close enough. "Probably the populations of large countries would not say I have been kind to drag you into… into this hell that is San Juan Capistrano."

"Probably not," she agreed and her Spanish practicality made him smile. "If you will recall, *señor,* I did not ask. I told you I was coming."

"So you did, my love."

He kissed her then, mindful of nothing except her. There was nothing tentative in his urge and nothing shy in her response. He kissed her lips, her neck and the warm space between her breasts, where her heart pounded. By God, he would have taken her right there on the beach, if it hadn't been broad daylight. The fisherman was ignoring them—wise man—and Laura was breathing as heavily as he was. He owed what little restraint remained to him to his Presbyterian upbringing.

He held himself off from her. "I don't even pretend to understand any of this," he told Laura, when he could sling foreign words together.

Was she always going to be better than he, in fraught situations? "Let us get on the boat and go back to your bed in San Diego," she whispered in his ear. "Earthquakes can wait."

So they could. While she waited on the fishing vessel, Thomas gathered together what remained of their medical stores, leaving most of them with the two Franciscans along with more instructions. He took one last ward walk through the refectory, assessing his Indians. Two were still no-hopers, but he felt sanguine about the rest.

Touched to his very soul, Thomas knelt, as Father Boscana directed, and let the priest pray his thanks to God and make the sign of the cross on his forehead with his thumb.

"I'll return in a few weeks," he said, when he was on his feet again, blessed for his work and amply paid.

"Bring your wife, too," the priest said.

As if he would ever travel anywhere without her again. Laura kissed him when he was seated beside her in the vessel's gunwales and whispered in his ear. "I love you. You know I am going to be seasick soon."

He smiled and nodded. She was.

The fishing vessel only took them halfway down the coast to Mission San Luis Rey, a mission Thomas was familiar with from a measles epidemic last year. "The fish are running and I cannot waste my time with you," the *pescador* said. He was apologetic, but he was adamant.

He was even thoughtful. As he helped Thomas over the rail and handed him his medical bag, he gestured him closer, his eyes lively with good humor.

"*Señor,* this mission appears to be standing. The fathers at the mission will provide you and your wife with a fine room for the night. The walls are quite thick."

Thomas blushed and looked away, then shook the fisherman's hand. "*Gracias,*" he said simply.

It was a fine little room with thick walls. The bed was narrow, and Father Peyri apologized to them both. "If you wish, your wife can sleep in an adjoining cell," he said. He patted Thomas's arm. "And we will be honored to furnish you with horses for your return to San Diego tomorrow." The priest looked at Laura. "We can do no less. Your husband aided us monumentally last year, when so many suffered from measles."

"He is good that way," she replied. "And, no, we do not need an extra room. Is there a bath? We worked so hard at San Juan Capistrano."

There was a bath house and Laura used it first, coming back to their room with her hair damp, but in its usual braid, her shawl over her nightgown, her feet bare. By the time he had finished, she was already in bed, the nightgown spread across the foot of it. He hadn't been aware that she had freckles on her breasts.

Neither of them wasted a moment worrying about the narrowness of the bed, probably intended for priestly travelers from one mission to another. She had a few practical questions, which he answered while he was caressing her breasts and then her trim waist, then lower. He had made a clinical observation a few years ago that Spanish women were nicely rounded—far more so than Scottish women. Laura was no exception, despite that air of fragility she had discarded forever the night that neither of them had slept.

He was gentle, but he knew she was ready. And practical, anchoring her legs around him so he couldn't fall off the narrow bed, no matter how strenuous their exertions, once she got into the rhythm and hang of lovemaking. Her breath was rapid and tender in his ear as she told him of her love again and showed him, with no qualms, no restraint, no fears about the future.

She protested when he left her body, tucking herself close out of more than necessity. Father Peyri had kindly left them a pile of blankets. When reason triumphed again, Thomas spread out those blankets and she unmade the little bed and added them to create a larger bed on the floor.

"Much, much better," she said, when they were still tight together, but without the fear of falling.

The room was dark and he was post-coitally drowsy, but he enjoyed her usual conversation in the dark, particularly as it was punctuated this time with a low moan when he decided to familiarize himself with her soft mechanism that hardened and made her shift about restlessly, until she sighed and put her hand on him in turn.

Toward morning, he woke to her tentative exploration, which turned into a symphony that left them both sated and exhausted.

"Maybe you *are* the best lover in the Royal Navy," she told him, her voice drowsy this time.

"Told you."

She punched his arm at that, but she followed her brutality with a thorough massage of his body that ended only when Father Peyri tapped on the door and invited them to Mass and then breakfast.

In his four years in San Diego, he had been to many a Mass, but never one when he was so alive to the serenity around him, which seemed to begin and end in his beloved wife. When her expressive face grew solemn and sober, and she glanced at him and slid closer, he knew without words that she was thinking of his now-dead comrades, and what would have been his fate, had he left his two dying patients and sailed with the *Almost Splendid.*

Ralph Gooding was on his mind in the late afternoon as they rode into the *presidio.* Laura was the far better rider, leading his horse for the last few miles as he abandoned all pretence of dignity and clung to the tall pommel and suffered. She helped him dismount and took his arm as they entered the *presidio*'s small hospital.

Thomas sighed with relief to see Ralph lying there, his eyes bright with fever, to be sure, but alive still. He took a step back, jolted out of his pain, when his eyes registered in the late-afternoon shadows and he saw the man scated beside his patient.

He was dressed much as Thomas had dressed four years earlier, in a plain navy blue uniform, with only the chains and knots on the collar to proclaim him a surgeon in the Royal Navy. The uniform was much worn, proclaiming a long cruise. The young surgeon stood up and held out his hand.

"Ah, you are Surgeon Wilkie." He laughed. "I guess you did not look in the harbor, did you?"

Dumbstruck, Thomas shook his head. He groped for Laura's hand.

"His Majesty's frigate, the *Glenmore,* lies at anchor. Don't look so amazed! We've come to take you home."

131
113
18

Chapter Twelve

The *Glenmore* well and truly rode at anchor in the harbor. A glance at Laura's pale face told him worlds about her feelings. She probably had no idea what Surgeon Fletcher was saying, but her suddenly frightened eyes remained fixed on the man's uniform and what it meant to her world. The only reassurance Thomas could offer her at that moment was her hand firmly held in his. He hoped it was enough.

Fletcher had certainly noticed it. "Gone native, have we?" the surgeon said to Thomas in English, which brought a pithy oath from Ralph Gooding.

"Remember yourself, carpenter," the new surgeon said.

"She is my wife," Thomas said, suddenly hating Tobias Fletcher.

"This complicates matters," Fletcher replied.

Thomas took a good look at the man: young, his uniform still fairly new, even after what must have been a long voyage from the other side of the world. "Ever been cast ashore, Surgeon?" he asked.

A head shake.

"In a Spanish dungeon? Away from England more than a year or two? On your own?"

More head shakes.

"Then don't tell me about complications," Thomas said.

The *Glenmore*'s surgeon at least was wise enough to know when to stop talking. "And now, sir, I had better see to my patient," Thomas said, moving the other surgeon aside. He took Ralph's hand, hot and dry and even thinner than before.

"Any more bleeding?" Thomas asked.

"Aye, once or twice." Ralph tried to smile and failed. "Father Hilario took good care of me, but he is more prone to prayer than styptic."

"A little of both probably didn't hurt." He spent a long moment looking at the carpenter's widening tubercular lesion. With a chill, he noticed another one forming on Ralph's chest. "Can I get you anything?" he asked, almost wincing with the inanity of his question.

"A new body—barring that, no," Ralph said. He tugged weakly on the surgeon's hand. "Just do this: let your pretty wife sit with me this evening." He glanced at the other surgeon without moving his head. "I believe you are to have dinner aboard the *Glenmore*." He sighed then. "Time to make plans for the voyage…home." He closed his eyes.

"I still won't leave you here," Thomas said, wishing he sounded more positive.

"You may not have a choice, laddie," Ralph replied.

Tobias Fletcher's plans were precisely what the carpenter suggested. "You'll have dinner aboard the Glenmore now," he said; it was no suggestion.

"I suppose I will," Thomas murmured. He looked around for Laura and saw her in their sitting room. "Just a moment, please." He went into their quarters and closed the door quietly behind him.

"He will take you away," she said, trying to hold her lips in a firm line so they would not tremble.

"Not without you," he assured her, holding open his arms.

She hesitated for a small moment, then reached for him in that all-encompassing way he already cherished, holding as much of him as she could, and he was not a small man.

"Not without you," he said again, then made a monumental mistake. He held her off for a moment, to see her better. "Not unless that is your choice."

He knew he would never forget the look she gave him. It was as though he had struck her. Her eyes grew wide as she carefully extracted herself from his embrace. Her face turned pale and then solemn.

"How could you even think that?" she asked, then added quietly, "Unless, of course, you *are* thinking that."

"Oh, no, never," he replied quickly, but the damage was done.

Fearful now, he watched her face as she calmly regained her Spanish dignity. She smiled, but there was no joy in her eyes, the joy he had seen in the last few days and nights, when they had worked as equals in San Juan and made love as husband and wife.

He didn't know what to say. He wanted to take her in his arms again, but he was afraid. "We'll…we'll discuss this when I return from the ship," he said, afraid to meet her gaze and magnifying his wrongs by his cowardice. "Would you…would you sit with Ralph?"

"You didn't need to ask that," she said quickly, stung, because he was trampling on her pride.

"I'll be back soon, Laura. We'll talk then."

Silence. She had shouldered past him and opened the door into the ward. He watched her a moment as she sat beside the carpenter, her hand in his.

"Well, then," Tobias Fletcher began. He clapped his hands together, which made Laura jump. "To the ship, Thomas. I am certain you outrank me in years of service, but we are brothers in arms, after all. May I call you Thomas?"

No, Thomas thought sourly. *You may call me a fool, you mushroom.* "Certainly." In utter misery, he bared his teeth in a grin.

Thomas couldn't deny that his heart lifted to step aboard a frigate of his Majesty's Royal Navy again. The *Glenmore* looked hard used, as most frigates did this far from Portsmouth or Plymouth. He sniffed the air—foul, indeed, after the fragrant blossoms and pine-scented cooking fires of San Diego.

Captain Livermore introduced himself and invited Thomas to the wardroom, where the other officers were already at their dinner. He gestured toward the empty chair and the other officers began passing him their kegged beef and ship's biscuit. Funny. According to Tobias, they had been riding at anchor for two days and were still eating kegged beef. He took a little on his plate.

"Captain, you really should try some of the tuna and

ceviche, while you are here in port," Thomas said, by way of small talk. "In fact, I can—"

Livermore waved his hand, as though dismissing a bad smell. "One of the local fishermen tried to cheat us with something he called tuna. 'Pon my word, it was brighter than a baboon's ass and he claimed it was cooked!"

"Oh, it was, Captain," Thomas said. "Nothing tastes better than—"

"And what did he have the nerve to do next but try to sell me a bucket of raw fish, by God, octopus and squid marinated in goo! With limes yet! I sent him packing. Does he think we are idiots?"

I do, Thomas thought. "That was ceviche, and it's delicious. I can arrange—"

"You've been here too long," the captain said, over-riding him again. "Good thing we arrived."

"Aye, isn't it?" Thomas replied. He pushed away the spoiled beef in front of him. "I think I'll eat later, sir."

"Just as well," Livermore replied. "Tell me your story. That fat Franciscan in the ward spoke a little English, but what he said sounded too fantastic."

"It wasn't, sir," Thomas replied. He pushed back his chair and made himself comfortable.

For the next hour, he described the *Splendid*'s encounter with a much-larger French frigate that mauled them and sent them limping finally into the harbor where the *Glenmore* was now moored. He described the year in the dungeons, and their change of fortune when Spain's alliance with France dissolved. He had to stop now and then to remember the English words.

"This autumn the first mate jury-rigged a coasting

vessel in hopes of seeking help from the Americans
north of us at Fort Astoria."

The Glenmore's officers looked at each other and
chuckled.

"Thomas, we are at war with the United States now,"
Captain Livermore said. "They're probably in irons in
Fort Astoria!"

Thomas shook his head and continued his story of the
Almost Splendid, foundering from a rogue wave after
last week's earthquake. "They're all gone, sir, except for
me," he said, unable to keep the catch from his voice.
"I'm only alive because I stayed behind with my two
patients." He looked at Surgeon Fletcher. "A foretopman
died just a day after the ship sailed. And the carpenter
remains as you see him. He's still too ill to travel."

"I don't give him more than a week, at most,"
Fletcher said. "You can leave him with that Franciscan,
or your wife."

Thomas couldn't help the dismay on his face at the
surgeon's callous words. He looked around the table and
saw no sympathy anywhere. "I cannot do that, Tobias,"
he said quietly. "Could you?"

The other surgeon flushed and drew his lips into a
taut line.

"Even if it is a direct order?" the captain asked, his
voice genial, as though he spoke to an idiot.

Lord, I have landed among Philistines, Thomas
thought in disgust. "I, uh, have taken a higher oath,
sir," he said. "And I *am* married. I cannot just discard
my wife."

The silence that settled was unpleasant in the
extreme. Thomas looked around again at stolid faces,
British faces. He had sailed with men like these for

fifteen years, since he was lad of fourteen. It was as though he had never seen them before. "I know we are at war, but it is no hardship to take along my wife, especially since she is the best pharmacist's mate I ever had."

To his embarrassment, everyone laughed. "She is," he insisted, but quietly, because no one was listening to him. *Think, Thomas, think,* he ordered himself. *Be devious, you plainspoken sawbones. Remember that you are dealing with the English now, more your natural enemies than the Spanish ever could be.*

He wasn't much of a liar, but he knew he could bend a truth well enough. He willed himself to calm and looked at the captain for a long moment. "Sir, she is no ordinary female, but the daughter of the *presidio*'s *subdelegado,* a powerful man, indeed."

He had to admit that *subdelegado* sounded massively more impressive in Spanish than mere royal accountant did in English. No need to tell them that his last view of the *subdelegado* was of a humbled man in chains, sitting in a squeaking oxcart, bound for either Mexico City or death at the hand of Apaches on the way.

"Indeed," was all Captain Livermore said, but at least he had stopped laughing. "Where is this man?"

"He is on his way to Mexico City right now," Thomas said without a blink. "He has been summoned and is under orders to appear before the captain-general at the first opportunity." He glanced around; the officers seemed to be buying that, and why not? It was true. Here came the bend. "Ah, sir, it would be a breech of protocol for you to anger our allies, the Spanish, if you forced me to abandon the daughter of grandees and hidalgos." Well, his lovely Laura looked as though she was descended from Spain's elite; probably, she was. He was no genealogist.

The captain was silent, mulling that around. He poured himself more rum. "We entered the harbor here because of rumors of a frigate lost these past four years. And you are all that remains, eh?"

"And the carpenter. I cannot abandon him, either, sir. I have a duty to perform," Thomas said simply.

"How much longer will he live?"

Thomas knew it was not a callous question, not from the captain of a warship far from England and sailing in questionable waters.

"A few days. My wife and I can probably sail by Christmas."

"And if he is not dead by then?"

Thomas didn't answer, but gave the captain the calmest look he could muster, the one that set him apart as a surgeon and made him different. *I will not look away first,* he told himself.

Captain Livermore sighed and looked away. "And what are we to do in the meantime, Surgeon?" he asked. There was no overlooking his testy demeanor.

Learn to love ceviche and rare tuna, you dolt, Thomas thought. "There is something. A week ago, this area had a terrible earthquake. I would like your permission for Surgeon Fletcher to accompany me and one of the priests into the back areas. I'd like to take whatever you think the *Glenmore* can spare from her medical supplies. There are people suffering." No need for the captain to know that most of them were mere Kumeyaay Indians.

"I suppose we must," the captain said, sounding amazingly put upon. "They are our allies."

And people in need, Thomas thought. "I also recommend that you put your carpenter in charge of repairs around the *pueblo*." He smiled around the table at the wary faces. "Yes, these people are Popish, but they are kind. I've noticed through the years that seamen can turn a hand at nearly anything. Your help would do a great deal to foster relations with our allies, even on this side of the world."

He knew he had the upper hand, invoking allies and diplomacy, even if no one in the world was destined ever to know about it.

"I suppose we must," the captain said at last.

Thank you for your enthusiasm, Thomas thought. "We must, sir," he said firmly. "And my wife comes with me, when we sail."

Captain Livermore smiled at that, but it wasn't a congenial smile. "If you can convince her to leave her own kind, sail into danger for a year, and, if my ears don't lie, settle in the land of chilblains, oatmeal and haggis, provided we survive."

Put that way, Thomas had his doubts. Damn the man.

Chapter Thirteen

T he longboat took Thomas back to the dock and he stood a long time, watching the water and the *Glenmore*. What he wished for so fervently had finally happened—he had been rescued by the Royal Navy. Too bad he did not want to leave San Diego now. He ordered himself not to think of the captain's words, which were making him doubt. Heavens, a Doubting Thomas! But what if Laura really didn't want to leave?

He could have asked anyone in the *pueblo* to give him a donkey ride back up to the *presidio,* but he preferred to punish himself with a long walk. It was a slow journey, because besides feeling sorry for himself, he knew he was duty-bound to look in on his San Diego patients.

He made the mistake of stopping at the mayor's house to check on the man's wife and child and was met with hand kissing and exclamations of joy. Through eyes that threatened to tear up, he saw the San Diegue-ños as they were: kind people, for the most part, who had treated him well because he rendered service and learned their language. In their hour of need, he had been there and they would not forget it.

After he had looked at *la señora*'s leg—the mayor watched him closely—and checked out the baby, whose only mishap had been a small cut on his forehead, Thomas let the maid bring him a bowl of bean soup. He listened with growing peace and satisfaction as the woman of the house chattered on about the *posada*.

"You do not think the earthquake will stop the celebrations?" he asked, a smile on his face. *La señora* had given him her baby to hold.

She laughed and waggled her finger at him. "*Señor!* Have you not lived here long enough to know that we do not postpone parties?"

He had, but he wanted to let her have the last word. "Let's see: Maria and José will go from house to house and then an innkeeper will finally let them enter?" he asked. "I forget."

She was generous with his stupidity and waggled that finger again. "You are a tease, *señor!* You have seen our *posadas.* I wonder that Laura Ortiz tolerates you."

So do I, he thought, reminded of his troubles.

Saying her name had reminded the mayor's wife, as well. She was silent a long moment, looking down at her leg that Laura had bandaged so expertly. "*Señor,* we may have been wrong about Laura Ortiz."

He could have cried with relief. Thank God the *pueblo* had seen his wife's worth, as she had labored at his side without a murmur, all that terrible day of the earthquake, helping the very people who had wanted nothing to do with her.

"She is a kind lady," he said simply. "Whatever her father's faults, they are not hers."

La Señora nodded, the color high in her handsome face. "We were hasty. I am sorry." She leaned closer. "In fact, after you went to the ship, I visited Señora Ortiz. I apologized, on behalf of all San Diego."

"That is kind of you, *señora*," Thomas said. "I am certain it meant a lot to her."

She nodded and took the baby from him. "I also told her that when the ship sails, she is welcome to stay with us."

If the mayor's wife had suddenly brained him with a stick of firewood, Thomas couldn't have felt worse. "Oh, but—" he began.

It was his night to be overridden in every conversation, apparently. The mayor's wife looked at him kindly. "*Señor*, what kind of a life would she have, so far from her own kind? I assured her it was for the best." She laid a hand on his sleeve. "You can sail without worrying about your wife. Never fear; we will take care of her here, where she belongs."

He mumbled something then about seeing his other patients and left the house, blinded by tears. Had Laura agreed to stay? He had to know.

The night was cool in that pleasant way of San Diego that he knew could never be duplicated in Dumfries. With a feeling close to pain, he realized how much he would miss this fair land, this paradise that could turn treacherous when the earth shook. There was no question of remaining behind, because he was a warrant officer in the Royal Navy who had been rescued by HMS *Glenmore*. His country was still at war with France, and now with the upstart United States—

heavens, would it never end? All he wanted to do now was survive the war with Laura, the woman he adored, resign his warrant and practice surgery with his father in Dumfries. The dear man had probably been writing him a Christmas letter for years now; if God was good, he was still alive.

Thomas walked faster. He wanted to teach Laura how to grow roses in Dumfries, deliver their children and grow old with her, his Spanish darling. Was he asking so much? Was there a point at which war paled in the face of love? He doubted it supremely, but he hoped.

He thought she might be asleep, but she was still sitting in the canvas chair beside Ralph Gooding's bed. He stood silently in the open doorway, listening to the dying man's labored, irregular breathing. He hated it when patients died, but as he stood there, leaning against the doorframe now, he heard the quiet click of Laura's rosary. He closed his eyes as the sound soothed him.

After a moment, he opened his eyes, startled to see Laura's level gaze appraising him. She had been crying, but her gaze was calm. In another moment he was on his knees, his head in her lap. She smoothed his hair, murmuring something that might not have even been words.

"Laura, I know the mayor's wife visited you and made you an offer," he said into her lap.

"She did," Laura whispered. "I told her I would think about it." Her fingers were gentle in his hair. "I don't have to think about it, though."

"I love you."

Her hand stopped. "Is that the wisest thing you ever did?" she asked, after a long pause.

Heartbroken, he knew then he had lost. He opened his mouth to say something, anything. He was overridden again, this time by Ralph Gooding.

"Laddie."

Thomas raised his head from Laura's lap. Still on his knees, he rested his elbows on Ralph's bed. "Right here," he said distinctly, in command of himself again because he was a surgeon first, even as his own life crumbled like the nave in San Juan Capistrano.

"I tried to teach her. Not enough time."

Puzzled, Thomas shook his head. "I'm sorry, Ralph."

The carpenter smiled. He closed his eyes. "You worry too much."

Thomas shook his head again. The man was making no sense at all. All things considered, this was hardly surprising. Death had come knocking and never liked to be ignored for long.

He sat back on his heels, loving this patient of his, this carpenter in the Royal Navy who had sailed on many a ship through many an ocean. He had never complained or mourned his lot, even as he suffered and faded. And here he was, thousands of miles from his home. Or was he? Thomas turned his head and looked out through the open door. The earthquake had crumbled a portion of the wall. Even though it was dark, and he couldn't see it, San Diego Bay was down there; the *Glenmore* rode at anchor, and the sea was home to the likes of Ralph Gooding.

Thomas turned back to his patient, forgetful that his wife was even in the room. He raised up on his knees and kissed Ralph Gooding's cheek. "Do you want to be buried at sea? I can easily arrange it."

He thought for a moment that he was too late, until the labored breathing began again. "No, laddie. Find me a pretty place here. Shouldn't be hard."

Thomas nodded. "I wish I could have cured you," he whispered.

"Ah, well. I've had a good time."

Thomas sat on the bed, taking Ralph's hand in his. The carpenter's breath started and stopped several times, then he opened his eyes and looked at Laura, who had pulled the canvas chair closer.

"Laddie, tell her in Spanish…"

"Tell her what?" Thomas asked gently, when the breathing resumed.

"To sing the song. You wanted to hear an English carol and I taught her." A bubbling sound came from his ruined throat. "No time."

Thomas looked at his wife and repeated Ralph's request in Spanish. Her eyes turned into deep pools of sorrow.

"I didn't learn it all, *señor*. The earthquake got in the way."

"Sing what you know," Thomas said, still mystified. "He doesn't have long."

"He taught me for you," Laura said. "He knew you were homesick and wanted to be away from here. He wanted me to sing it on Christmas Day."

"You need to sing it now," he said softly. "For Ralph."

She rose gracefully to her feet. She went into their sitting room. He heard her rummaging around in the blue cupboard he had bought on a whim, almost as

impulsive as their marriage. In a moment he heard the
snap of castanets.

"I've never heard a Christmas carol with castanets,"
he murmured to Ralph.

"Hush. Enjoy the moment," his patient said. "Raise
me up."

Thomas did as he was asked. He looked at his patient,
seven-eighths dead, and went to the cabinet where he
kept the rum. He poured a small glass for Ralph, even
though he doubted the man could swallow. He couldn't,
but Ralph opened his eyes and licked the rum off his lips.

"We did this for you, laddie," Ralph said. He waved
his index finger to a beat only he could hear.

Laura nodded. She cleared her throat and looked
down modestly, then up at Thomas. She hummed a note,
clicked her castanets, then sang. Her voice was sweet,
her English fractured.

He knew the tune at once, thinking of a midnight on
deck in the Arctic when he had sung that very carol to a
thoroughly bored tern that had happened to land nearby,
forced down by freezing rain. It had been Christmas
then, too, one of many he had spent at sea.

He wanted to laugh out loud, but he knew his wife
well enough to know that would be the wrong thing,
especially since her expression was so earnest.

> "I sore tree cheeps come siling een, own Crees-
> mus Dye, own Creesmus Dye,
>   I sore tree cheeps come siling een, ta dum, ta
> dum ta ta dum dum."

As Ralph watched, a half-smile on his face, she sang
it again with more assurance—but no better English—

employing a syncopated chatter with the castanets that would have astounded any British choirmaster. She added a solemn little dance that looked more Spanish than Mexican to Thomas, but which made him smile.

"I don't know any more, Tomás," she told him.

"Well, accompany *me* then, my lady," Thomas said, and began to sing. "'And what was in those ships all three, on Christmas Day, on Christmas Day? And what was in those ships all three, on Christmas Day in the morning.'"

Laura twinkled her eyes at him then, and he felt his spirits rise. "'The Virgin Mary and Christ were there,'" he sang and nodded at her.

"'Own Creesmus Dye, own Creesmus Dye,'" she sang.

They went through the whole carol that way, to the syncopated click of Laura's castanets, ending up in each other's arms, laughing.

"My love, say you won't stay here, when the *Glenmore* sails," he asked, his lips in her hair.

His love gave an unladylike snort, not something one expected of a hidalgo's daughter. "Did that old prune tell you I was staying?" she asked. "As if I would let you sail without me!" She dropped the castanets, put both hands on his face and kissed him soundly. When her lips were barely separated from his, she asked, "Will I like Scotland?"

He gathered her close. "I rather think you will."

They both stopped then and looked at Ralph. Laura sighed and turned her face into his chest. Thomas kissed her hair and tightened his grip on her. "Well, Ralph, we sang you out," he murmured. "'Own Creesmus Dye ta ta dum dum.'"

With tears they laid the carpenter out, washing his wasted body and dressing him in a clean nightshirt. Thomas shrouded him and wrapped him tight, then summoned two of the kitchen help to carry Ralph Gooding to the deadhouse. In the morning, he would make arrangements with Father Hilario and the *presidio*'s captain to find a good place for a man who had sailed the seven seas and died far from home.

He sat a moment with Ralph in the deadhouse. He had fulfilled his final obligation to the HMS *Splendid* and to Hippocrates himself, in this distant land. It was time to go home, after he had dragged the *Glenmore*'s young surgeon through some cleansing surgery in the back country, tending Kumeyaay. He stood in the doorway a moment more, looking at the shrouded man. He gave a small salute.

He hoped Laura would not think it strange if he reached for her even before he had blown out the candle, later that night. She must not have minded, because she was raising her nightgown over her head even before he closed the door to the *sala*. They made wordless love, assuaging their sorrow, celebrating their marriage, and planning for a future. Warm and drowsy, she cuddled close to him, her leg thrown over his thigh, running her foot down his shin.

"Laura, after Ralph's funeral, Surgeon Fletcher and I will be going into the back country to check on the more remote *pueblos*."

"He is a foolish man," she said with that former superior air of hers that he had been missing.

"True. In a few days, I will bring him back here much wiser." Thomas kissed her sweaty hair. "Perhaps you can arrange with the mayor's wife for us to be the innkeepers for that final posada on the 24th."

"We can welcome in Maria and José?" she asked, kissing his chest. "You and I, who have no home?"

"Who better than us?" He patted her hip. "And then we will have to sail on Creesmus Dye."

"You're making fun of me," she said, softening her accusation by running her tongue inside his ear.

"Aye, lassie," he replied in English, pillowing his head on her breast. "I have six or seven months to teach you English," he continued in Spanish.

Sleepy and satisfied, she was soon asleep. Thomas yawned and held her close, breathing in her fragrance. He hoped she wouldn't be too seasick once they hit the Pacific rollers. But that was marriage, taking the bitter with the sweet.

He thought about his father's Christmas letter and smiled in the dark. He'd have to make a special trip to Carlisle to thank his brother for marrying Cora.

* * * * *

O CHRISTMAS TREE

199
735
64

Prologue

Dumfries, Scotland—October 10, 1855

Dearest Daughter,
Like you, now that the Russians have surrendered
Sebastopol, we wish the British High Command would
hurry up and bring the boys home, so you could come
home, too. And if you could actually be home in time
for Christmas, even better, my dear—I have to chuckle
here, remembering how many years my own dear father
had to wait for me to come home for Christmas! I trust
you will fare better, but I do understand delays. Still,
weren't we all assured that this nasty little war would
end in six weeks?

You are continually in our prayers. Your dear mother
has burned enough candles in St James to ignite Dumfries—or at least they would, if there were more Cath-
olics. I continue with my less-colorful Presbyterian
prayers. Between the two of us, I believe we have the
Lord Almighty surrounded. Let me assure you that your

sweet Will keeps you in his prayers, too, even when he says grace over his porridge. He's mature for an almost ten-year-old, but he misses you.

If you have a moment, tell us more about Major Wharton, your unusual hospital administrator, since he is an American. I am less surprised than you, perhaps, that the US Army sent observers to the Crimea; such a thing is commonplace in military circles. If he is as effective an administrator as you seem to think, then we must applaud Miss Nightingale's split-second wisdom in sending him to Soulari Barracks Hospital to straighten out the mess caused by others. I imagine she had to tug a few strings for that to happen, but I hear she is resourceful.

We love you, we miss you. Will is my right-hand man. He accompanies me on my visits about Dumfries and likes to ward walk, when I let him. I think you have a budding surgeon in your son. Are you surprised?

Best of Christmases to you, Lillian, even in that awful place. Your *mamacita* wants you to find someone there to kiss under the mistletoe, although I doubt there is mistletoe on the north shore of the Black Sea.

Love,

Papá

P.S. My dearest, this is a broad hint, but I managed to find a husband in the middle of a war. At Christmas, too. *Adiós.*

Mama

Chapter One

Lillian Wilkie Nicholls ached everywhere. As she tossed the scrub brush into the bucket and rocked back on her heels, she looked with some satisfaction down the barrack room. It had been dubbed a ward last year by Miss Florence Nightingale on a brief visit to this satellite hospital in Anatolia. *One down, two miles to go,* she thought, with a slight smile. *Too bad I look washed out in gray.*

"And that shows how shallow I am," she said out loud to no one, because the nearest nurse was at the other end, making beds. She looked down at the ugliest gray dress ever conceived by the mind of woman, then at her chipped nails. "Papa always told me never to volunteer for anything."

Lily knew he hadn't meant any such thing. Still, even he had been taken aback when she'd arrived home in Dumfries more than two years ago, her hand tight in Will's, and declared her intention of traveling to Constantinople with others ladies determined to Do Good.

"I have it on good advice—Lord Aberdeen himself—that the war will not last above another six weeks," she had told her parents. "If you can watch Will for me, I can do some good in that limited time." That was two years ago—so much for politicians.

By the end of the week, she'd been on her way back to London to plead her case with Miss Nightingale's London liaison. There had been some objection to her general good looks. It had faded as soon as Lillian had said she could pay her own way, plus the way for four other nurses. Although she had known no more than most cultured ladies about nursing, her chief reference had come from Lord Aberdeen, prime minister and her late husband's cousin—end of argument. How kind of her dead husband to continue to be useful.

Will hadn't minded being left with his grandparents; since his papa had died two years before, he had worn mourning clothes at the request of his London grandparents and walked slowly when he would have preferred to run. Even before the illness that had led to his death, Randolph Nicholls had been a distant figure: the perfect London gentleman, with time for clubs and horses, but not one scholarly little boy.

True, Will had clung to Lily a long time at the Dumfries train station, until Grandpapa Wilkie, after whom he'd been named, had knelt beside him and gently pried him away. Grandpapa had promised to let him come along on doctor visits to the neighbors, Will's idea of fun—end of another argument. Lillian had been at liberty to leave England and Do Some Good in the Crimea. After all, it would only be for six weeks.

Lily sighed and looked into the filthy wash water, wishing herself home with her son. Trouble was, she had proved too efficient to release and had had no choice but to stay. Even now, almost three months after the Russians had surrendered Sebastopol, it seemed neither side could believe the long siege was over. British and French patients still languished in hospitals throughout northern Anatolia and across the Black Sea in Crimea. Soldiers still made their way to her hospital in Soulari. They should have been going home to England, but nothing about this nasty little war had been well organized, not even victory.

With a groan, Lily stood up. She sniffed the air, happy to smell dinner cooking in the detached kitchen behind the barracks. A year and a half of scrubbing and carbolic had gotten rid of truly noxious odors. She smiled at the nurse at the other end of the corridor, one of the silent, efficient Sisters of Mercy from France who had arrived six months ago and spoke no English.

"It *is* my hospital," Lily murmured. "You can have it back, oh mighty Ottoman Empire. I am through."

Somehow, she had managed to avoid typhus and even cholera. Between death and transfers and feminine tantrums, she truly was the last remaining Englishwoman who had come to serve in Soulari; therefore, it must be her hospital.

Any time now, orderlies would trundle in the dinner cart and she would spend the next few hours assisting those patients who needed help. For a few minutes, she could walk the corridor in peace, checking on her men, for so they were. The wounded were silent, something Miss Nightingale herself had once remarked on. Wounds and illness seemed to create their own torpor, as men rested and gathered their strength. Thank goodness at least they could do it in a warm hospital, with clean linen under them and good food coming. Lily remembered the battles of Inkermann and Balaclava, when the wounded had lain in their own blood and gore for weeks, because nothing had been ready. Those days were over.

She walked through the wards, observing her patients and noting, with a sinking heart, their air of resignation. Victory wasn't supposed to look like this and it bothered her.

Of course, who wouldn't be affected by it? Only this morning, the chief surgeon—Captain Pompous himself—had gone from ward to ward, reading aloud a letter from General Simpson, Lord Raglan's successor, crowing about victory, but advising the men there would not be any transport home until after Christmas. So much for England remembering her heroes on far-off battlefields. Damn Captain Pompous anyway.

She walked silently, smiling at the few patients who made eye contact. A former patient, long furloughed home, had remarked to her in a late-night, candid moment that most of his bunkies agreed that the hospital's most comforting sound, even more than the food wagon, was the swish of women's skirts through the halls, signaling that they had not been forgotten. After that comment, Lily had begged a noisy taffeta petticoat from Mama, who had promptly sent two.

Lily observed as she walked. The wards were airy and comfortable, the beds properly spaced to receive all the good oxygen required to maintain standards, as interpreted by Miss Nightingale in one of her many dispatches to the hospitals within her jurisdiction.

In the third ward, Lillian Nicholls realized what was missing. At first, the notion was absurd; the nursing staff would laugh her out of the building, if she mentioned such a trivial matter. Of course, none of the Sisters of Mercy spoke much English, so it didn't matter.

The more she thought about it, the more her resolve grew. There was time before dinner rounds to discuss the matter with the one man who might understand. A purposeful walk down a flight of scrubbed stone steps took her to his office. She knocked right away, not giving her doubts time to gather strength. A good idea in a ward was just as good in front of the hospital administrator's door, or so Lillian reasoned.

Major Trey Wharton, USA, opened the door himself, making her wonder—not for the first time—if he knew the very sound of her knock.

"Mrs Nicholls, I wondered if you would stop by today to give me a pithy comment on the nitwittery of Captain Penrose. Who in God's name would read aloud a letter like *that*?"

If Lillian had been holding her breath, she let it out in a little sigh; trust Major Wharton to understand, even if he was an American. Or perhaps *because* he was an American.

A handsome one, too. She admired his posture, and the fine cut of his blue uniform, with its gold buttons, epaulets and collar trim denoting an engineer. His uniforms looked tailor-made and expensive, and he always appeared perfectly proper. That aside, her first encounter with the complexity that was Major Wharton had happened in surgery, his well-tailored coat tossed across the room, and the major watching with great interest the surgeon at work. With no hesitation, he had held a retractor when the surgeon required it, then had grinned at her. "Mrs Nicholls, is it? Are you ever amazed how some people meet?" And then he had blushed like a schoolgirl.

Shyness was another of Major Wharton's endearing qualities. She had decided early on how much she liked him. Lily was used to men appreciating her company—she had a stillness about her and was ornamental in the way that men of her class seemed to prefer. Once Major Wharton had recovered from a monumental case of tongue-tied-itis, as he had jokingly dubbed it late one weary night, he had become her friend, but nothing more. She chose to be philosophical about the matter. After all, she was here in the Crimea to nurse, not flirt.

With a smile now, she sat in the chair drawn up before his ornate desk, a gift of Sultan Abdul Ahmed Wasiri. The two men regularly played poker, a game that the sultan always claimed had originated in Persia. The desk had formed part of Major Wharton's considerable winnings.

The major sat down in the chair next to her, not bothering to retreat to the other side of the desk to look intimidating, as Captain Penrose would have. He smiled back and Lillian felt her own heart lifting, even as she reminded herself that Major Wharton seemed to want no more than friendship from her.

It was the smile. Until he smiled, he was handsome in that understated way of capable men. His brown hair was turning gray here and there, and his eyes were dark blue. He had a deep dimple in one cheek and carved lines around his mouth that gave his face character. The smile changed everything because he had a gap between his two front teeth, making what should have been an intimidatingly perfect man quite human. When he smiled, Trey Wharton looked just slightly off-kilter. She knew her mother would find him amusing.

"Major, you'll just have to endure Excelsior Penrose," she reminded him, not for the first time.

He never failed to laugh when she used the physician's full name. It was a laugh as comfortable as he was, even in dismal surroundings.

She looked at an ornate rug he must have recently hung on the wall. It blocked out a portion of the window, which leaked heat notoriously. "More winnings from your disreputable game?" she asked, indicating the *objet d'art*.

He nodded. "Our friend the sultan would be worthy pickings for any riverboat gambler I can think of," he said. "If the British High Command lengthens out the evacuation of patients, I believe I will own Abdul Wasiri's palace and chattels. Probably the harem, too." He blushed furiously. "Has he made *you* any more offers recently?"

"Not one!" She laughed, remembering one straitlaced London lady who had reported the major to Miss Nightingale for his vulgarity. That bit of self-righteousness had earned her a prompt transfer to another hospital. Flippant the major might be, but he could run a hospital. What's more, Miss Nightingale knew it.

"No more offers from the sultan," she said. "If I am honest, perhaps I did not entirely understand what he was proposing. I will give him the benefit of the doubt."

"Wise," Major Wharton said. And then he was all business: her great friend, but first and foremost a hospital administrator. "I'll wager you've come here to tell me that our patients are a bit morose."

Our patients? Lily asked herself. She nodded, pleased that he had included them both. "They are, indeed."

"I observed that, too, Mrs Nicholls." He looked her in the eye, something he was generally too shy to do. "I'll wager you have a solution. I've never known you to complain without a remedy."

Her doubts returned. It was such a small thing. "Nothing grandiose, mind," she said, ready to explain it away.

"Say on, Mrs Nicholls. I value your opinion."

He did, too, and so he had told her on several occasions. Major Wharton was a far remove from the condescension she was accustomed to from British surgeons. Of course, he made no claims to being a surgeon. "I'm just an observer," he had said, on more than one occasion. "Miss Nightingale must have had a momentary lapse of judgment to request my heretofore-unknown administrative services."

Lily knew better. For six weeks before her transfer to Soulari, she had watched the genius of Florence Nightingale organize order from chaos and recognize such skills in others, even those among US Army war observers. Miss Nightingale was never deterred by red tape. Lily smiled to herself.

"I want a Christmas tree for the main corridor." There, it was out in the open and it did sound silly.

He didn't laugh, but continued his observation of her. Never was his gaze anything but thoughtful, which reassured her.

"I've never seen any around here, but I hear there are pine trees in the Taurus Mountains. I think it might do wonders for the men's morale," she added, then thought to herself, *And mine, too.* "Would it be so hard to transport a tree here?"

"Probably not in times of less disorder." He reached for a neat stack of forms on his desk. "I'll fill out a requisition right now. One tree, comma, Christmas?"

She couldn't help laughing. "Major, you seem to labor under the misapprehension that someone in the commissary department—or should it be the quartermaster's?—has a sense of humor."

He shrugged. "Let's start with proper channels first. What can it hurt?"

What, indeed? she asked herself, as she left Major Wharton's office after a few pleasantries. *I know I will miss you, Major, when I am given leave to bid Anatolia farewell and return to my darling boy.*

Chapter Two

The requisition went on its way that afternoon. It was returned, rejected, in the mail pouch early the next week. Major Wharton brought it to her after she had finished feeding those men too weak to care for themselves and was tidying her small diet kitchen off the main hall.

Still impeccable, still dignified, he sat at the table and absently folded a pile of laundered dishcloths.

"Really, Major, I can do that," she protested, but not too vehemently, in case he should think she actually meant it. With only French-speaking nuns around, she was coming to relish her encounters with the American, even if his English had a distinctly foreign sound to her ears. He was the first American she had ever met.

"Mrs Nicholls, I can no more sit idle than you," he said, working his way quickly through the pile of dishcloths as she scrubbed the sink. "Is there anything else to fold? Tablecloths? Deck of cards? A tent, and silently steal away?"

She laughed, always appreciative of his droll wit, especially when compared with Captain Pompous, who wouldn't know a joke if it barked in his face. Indeed, the physician had wasted a quarter-hour of her time only that morning complaining about Major Wharton's levity in a place of contagion and disease.

You are a nitwit, she had thought, while fixing Captain Pompous with her blandest face. *I appreciate a man who can make an entire ward roar with laughter and forget, for even fifteen minutes, that some of them are dying.*

"Nothing else?" Major Wharton asked. He rested his hands on the table. "How about this? If I am not a dreadful nuisance or an opportunist of the grossest sort, would you object to a glass of champagne?"

She stared at him, wondering where his shyness had gone. Before she could say anything, he continued, his familiar blush back. This reassured her in an odd way, because it meant all was right in the major's world again.

"I know it should be served in a flute, but I have only two drinking glasses, army issue."

"Where did you…?"

"Acquire champagne?" He caught the tablecloth she tossed his way to fold. "It came in the same delivery that brought that prissy note from the commissary officer regarding our Christmas tree."

"A consolation prize?" she teased in turn, catching the end of the tablecloth and folding her share.

He finished folding the cloth and handed it back to her. "I probably shouldn't tell you this, considering that Captain Pompous already thinks I am a vulgarian."

"That has never stopped you before," she said,

amused. Her casual treatment of Major Wharton reminded Lily of her relationship with her own easy-going brothers.

He peered at the label. "A bottle of Perrier-Jouët came from General Albert Pasquier. He seemed to think I had something to do with getting most of his wounded troops transferred home to Paris ahead of schedule."

"You know you did—what a nice effort that was, considering that his son was among the wounded," she said gently.

He sighed. "I only wish we could have moved him sooner, so his *papa* could have had more time with him. It's nice of the general to remember me." He looked at her again, his gaze direct, with no blush this time. Lily had noticed that he never seemed shy when talking hospital policy. "If I ran this war, there would be a change in the transport of wounded. As it is, thank goodness for your Miss Nightingale. She does all she can."

"The champagne is payment for your impressive sleight of hand with a bunch of wounded Frenchmen?" she asked, smiling in spite of herself.

"Absolutely. Care for some bubbly?"

She did, actually, and told him so. While she waited in the kitchen, Major Wharton returned to his office and came back with a dusty bottle and two glass receptacles used for blood cupping.

"Can't find my glasses," he muttered. "I think one of the nuns has decided to organize my desk. Stand back, madam. No telling how far this Perrier-Jouët will fire. I'd hate to lose you after the war is over."

He popped the cork expertly and the bubbles fizzed out demurely. "Ah, it is a dignified wine," the major said. He poured a respectable amount into the cup and handed it to her. "What shall we toast? The war is over and we're still languishing in this most trying backwater."

"To Christmas and the tree I still want," Lily said.

He nodded and clinked her cupping glass. "Fine. To next Christmas at home?"

"I would have preferred this one, but, aye, I'll drink to that," she said.

The major propped his slippered feet on the table as he leaned back in his chair. She watched him over the rim of the cupping glass, remembering their first encounter a year ago, when he had arrived unannounced, with the astounding directive from Miss Nightingale herself to install him, a US Army observer and an engineer, as administrator of the overstretched satellite hospital.

Such an assignment was unheard of, but both surgeons on staff had been forced to swallow their objection to the directive, because it was also signed by FitzRoy Somerset, Lord Raglan. Within a fortnight, Major Wharton had organized the hospital until it ran like a top. Modestly, he gave all credit to a month of observing Miss Nightingale's genius for organization, which mollified the British Army physicians.

It had been Lily's turn to provide the libation late one night, when only the two of them had been still awake and ward walking. The drink had been rum instead of the cupping glass of champagne she held now.

"Major, I believe we used cupping glasses with that rum I stole from the densest surgeon in the British army."

"I believe we did," he said. He tipped his chair down and poured more champagne. He amazed her by leaning forward and touching her hand lightly. "I have never thanked you for being my champion with those twits with cotton wadding for brains." He raised his cupping glass. "Let's toast the late Lord Raglan, may he rest in peace— Thank you, sir, for recalling both twits home and sending better surgeons in their stead!"

She drank to that, enjoying the way the bubbles worked on her brain. The major tipped his chair back again and he sipped slowly. She watched him, remembering that earlier evening of rum. Maybe the alcohol had loosened his tongue. He had told her about himself, unabashedly describing his wealthy Philadelphia family—part of the Main Line, he called them—and the general uses of wealth and influence. His parents had had no objection to West Point—America's premier, and only, engineering school—but they had expected him to resign his commission after a dignified time and join the Wharton's banking firm. He had told her this over rum last year, after a long and exhausting day of disease and death.

Since then, there had been little time for such leisurely chat. She sipped her champagne and remembered that earlier conversation, when they had become better acquainted.

"My parents rejoiced when I was selected to accompany Captain McClellen, and Majors Cooke, Delafield and Mordecai to the Crimea as observers," he had said. She remembered that his voice had turned a little bleak then. "Observation of others' fighting methods is a time-honored military tradition." He had shrugged. "I have always been more interested in how things *run*. Hospitals interested me more. I intend to write a whacking fine report to vindicate my choice. In fact, I promised Miss Nightingale I would."

"What does your family think of you now?" she asked, recalled to the present, even as the champagne infiltrated her brain. "I remember our rum-filled conversation quite well."

He glanced at her and laughed. "They want me home for Christmas, probably the same as your family does." He put his hand to his chest in a gesture worthy of Edmund Kean. "'All is forgiven, Trey! Return, resign your commission and join the banking firm.'"

"Oh, dear, you are the black sheep," she teased, then sighed. "I went with my parents' blessing, but I miss my son. He will be ten right after Christmas."

She held out her class for more champagne, and Major Wharton obliged. "With a young child, why did you do it?" he asked, then held up his hand. "Stop me if I am being intrusively rude, but I have been wondering."

"Not at all, Major. My husband, God rest his soul, died of consumption and I decided not to be buried with him." She took a deep breath.

It sounded so blatant that she stopped, her hand to her mouth. Again the major put down his chair and touched her hand, as though giving her permission to continue.

"Two years of the blackest mourning, for Will and me both." She looked at him, uncertain if she should say more, but he nodded. "My late husband's family is as rich as you Whartons, I suppose. Major, I couldn't be an expensive ornament for one more minute, so Will and I escaped to Dumfries, where people eat oats for breakfast and make their own beds. I wanted to prove something to myself."

"Did you?" he asked. "No, I can answer that for you— Yes, you did. Mrs Nicholls, you are a useful woman."

She smiled at his courage in delivering so much sensible praise with only a slight blush. "What I am is naive and foolish to actually think the war would end in six weeks." She had to smile at her own stupidity, to keep the tears from welling up. "I miss my son."

Lily had to give Major Wharton credit then, despite his shyness. With his little finger, he brushed gently at the tears in her eyes and changed the subject to spare her. "Dumfries, eh? I wondered where that delightful brogue came from," he said. "And your marvelous red hair?"

It was her turn to blush. No one had ever described her hair as marvelous. "You should see my father!"

"There's more to you than red hair, a brogue and *naïveté,*" he said. "Now remember, Mrs Nicholls, I am an official observer. I have a document from the U.S. Army saying precisely that, if you are skeptical. Your mother's not from Scotland, is she?"

Why did we never have this conversation sooner? Lily asked herself, charmed by this casual side of Major Wharton, now that the worst press of war was over and they had the time to linger over champagne, even if it was served from cupping glasses. "She was born in Spain and raised in Mexico City. My father met her in San Diego, Alta California. I believe it is one of your states now. He was a prisoner of war."

"You're more interesting than the Whartons!" The major shook his head, his eyes full of something that looked like admiration. "Your father is a surgeon still?"

"A very good one. So are two of my brothers. The

third brother is the family black sheep. He went to Cambridge and became a successful banker. He met my husband there and brought him home once during the Long Vac."

They laughed together, conspirators, in the ways of families. She felt a pleasant glow edge down her body. She felt as though she sat close to a glowing brazier, not a handsome man with a gap-toothed smile. Lily sat back, surprised at herself, and wanting a moment to consider what she was feeling.

That was a split second before she heard labored footsteps up the narrow flight of stairs to the administrator's office, and a moment later saw the red face of Sister Marie Xavier. She was breathing heavily from her exertions, but not too fatigued to scream "Fire!" in French.

199
154
———
45

(45)

Chapter Three   4

That's what Lily assumed she said, considering the aroma of smoke that began to drift over the barracks hospital. Equally startling to Lily was the way Major Wharton grabbed her hand and hurried her toward the stairs.

He didn't let go of her until they stood a safe distance away from the detached kitchen, where the roof threatened to collapse. Shocked, Lilly counted to twelve, relieved that all the nuns—in various stages of undress, to be sure—were out of their quarters behind the ovens and standing in the walkway between the kitchen and the hospital. And then the major only let go of her to clap his arm around her shoulders as she contemplated the loss of every possession she had brought to Anatolia, except for the clothes she stood in, hairpins currently employed and a pair of scissors in her apron pocket.

She turned her face into his chest, stunned at the loss of the kitchen more than her possessions. "How on earth can we feed all those men?" she muttered into his uniform.

"Dear Lily, you have just lost all your possessions and what worries you is porridge for invalids?" he asked gently. Able-bodied men from the hospital were already pouring water on the flames. "Bless your heart."

She looked at him, startled. "Of course it is. All we have now is that little diet kitchen off the main hall." Lily looked at the nuns, who seemed to have dragged out their few possessions. "If someone can spare a habit, I'll be Sister Lillian until I get my marching papers," she told him.

To her further surprise—where *was* his courage coming from?—the major touched his forehead to hers. "I have another idea, Sister Lily."

He did, to the consternation of the French nuns and Lily's own amusement. Before midnight, they were comfortably settled in Sultan Abdul Ahmed Wasiri's seraglio, with his harem and his wives. "Look at it this way, Mrs Nicholls," the major said, as he escorted her to the harem's elaborately curved doorway, where a eunuch stood watch. Wharton eyed the tall man, who was obviously not used to suffering fools gladly, especially infidel fools. "You'll have a wonderful story to tell your grandchildren some day."

The Sisters of Mercy had taken longer to bring themselves to enter the harem, requiring all of Major Wharton's rudimentary West Point French. With considerable chatter, and even more flailing about of hands, they had finally succumbed with the air of potential martyrs.

Captain Penrose had been beside himself, turning an alarming shade of purple at this affront to British

womanhood and French ecclesiastics. His acceptance
of the idea came with great reluctance, and only after
the major reminded his subordinate that he, Major
Wharton, U.S. Army, had been put in charge of the
barracks hospital a year ago by Lord Raglan himself.
"The hospital is full and there isn't anywhere else in this
Godforsaken town that is safe," he had said, speaking
slowly, as though he addressed an idiot. "Could they
be any safer than in a harem?"

"Just humor me, Captain Pot Roast," the major had
muttered under his breath as the other surgeon returned
to his pony cart, looking less than dignified in a Paisley
dressing gown and red nightcap with a tassel. "Mrs
Nicholls, I am certain he will waste not a minute firing
off a vitriolic protest to his own high command and perhaps to Captain McClellan, who thinks he is in charge
of me in the Ottoman Empire."

"Is he?" Lily asked, pleased that the hospital administrator could be so lighthearted about possible career
disaster.

"Little Georgie? Mercy, no!" He leaned closer. "The
rest of us outrank him, although you'd never know it to
listen to him crow. My dear Mrs Nicholls, small men
fight like terriers over small stakes." He gave an undignified snort. "Lord help us if Georgie McClellan is *ever*
put in charge of an entire army! I can't see it."

He told her good-night at the seraglio door, assuring
her that carriages would be available in the morning to
take them the short distance back to the barracks hospital. "I'm afraid your little diet kitchen will be taxed to
the limit, Mrs Nicholls. Hopefully we can make rapid
repairs on the other one." He sighed. "Wouldn't it be

nice of the British High Command to move out the men now?"

He touched her shoulder, which made the eunuch move forward and brandish his curved sword. Major Wharton backed away, smiling his most charming gap-toothed smile, which made Lily turn away to hide her own mirth.

She stood beside the eunuch, who towered over her. "Major Wharton," she said to his retreating figure, "I still want a Christmas tree." She laughed. "My, but I sound petulant."

Maybe there was something wistful in her voice, because the major turned back to look at her, his gaze soft. "It's all a bit much, isn't it?"

He moved toward her again, but the eunuch elaborately ran his thumb and forefinger down the flat of his scimitar. Major Wharton chose discretion over valor and quit the field.

"I mean it," Lily said softly. A few minutes later, one of the sultan's pretty wives took charge, chattering in melodious Turkish as she led Lily down the hall. In a few minutes more, Lily looked at the sumptuous chamber the wife had assigned her. After the door closed, she removed her clothes, stained with a day's typical work and smelling of smoke now. She took off everything, standing naked and wondering what she would wear to bed. She always wore *something* to bed.

She yawned, wondering why the loss of all her possessions meant so little, then wondering how long she would stand there, bare. She laughed a little, imagining the shocked look she would have got from her late husband, who was the most proper man she had ever met. An imp seemed to take possession of her mind then, as she considered what Major Wharton would do, if he could see her now. Her cheeks reddened as she thought a most improper thought. And then she laughed to think how embarrassed *he* would be.

"All right, Lillian, what *do* you wear to bed?" she asked out loud. "You're getting tiresome."

Nothing, obviously. She got into bed, enjoying the unexpected heat of a cloth-covered warming pan, remembering how nice it used to be to put her cold feet on her husband's legs. To her chagrin, that imp returned. She wondered whether Trey Wharton would object to her bare feet on *his* legs.

She lay on her back in strange surroundings, looking up at a gauzy canopy. The bed was amazingly soft. Her eyes closed, just as she was wondering what on earth she would wear tomorrow.

199
159
40

Chapter Four

When she woke the next morning, Lily wasn't sure if she was glad or sad that her ugly gray uniform was gone. Clutching the sheet around her, she raised up on one elbow, looking for the pitiful thing, before deciding it must have crawled away in shame.

I am in a harem, she thought, and couldn't help the laughter that bubbled inside her, despite the gravity of the situation that had caused it. She folded her hands properly across her stomach, aware that for the first time in ages, she hadn't braided her long hair into tight pigtails before sleep claimed her. Her hair lay all curly and abundant on the pillow. All she wanted to do was lie there and enjoy the feeling of silk sheets on bare skin.

I could maybe like a seraglio, she thought. *I wonder if someone would bring my meals, scrub my back in a scandalous bathing pool and brush my hair? A massage would be nice, too. So would shaved ice brought by runners from the Caucasus Mountains.* She turned

her head and giggled into the pillow, curious to know
if the sultan—bless his elderly, overstuffed hide—liked
to dally with his numerous bits of fluff in beds like this
one, and probably in broad daylight. Goodness, what
wicked thoughts for a straitlaced widow!

That thought was enough to make her draw the sheet
tighter around her and look more seriously for her clothing, as pathetic as it was. All she saw was a robe as
diaphanous as the canopy overhead, in a lovely shade of
pale yellow that she knew would look perfect with her
hair and coloring. Of course, every curve and outline
of her body would be visible to all, but this was, after
all, a harem.

"When in Rome," Lily murmured as she reached
for the robe. She sighed with the softness of it, thinking how much her Mexican mother would enjoy such
luxury, living as she did now in Dumfries, home of oatmeal and woolies. She admired herself in the full-length
mirror, thinking to herself, *I will be queen this morning,
or at least until someone returns my ugly dress, and I'm
Cinder Ella among the ashes again.*

Shy now, Queen Lillian opened the door to her chamber a crack and was immediately pounced upon by a
trio of servants, all speaking at once. Seeing this as an
adventure, rather than a trial, Lily let them lead her to
another room. It turned out to house a marble-lined
bathtub big enough for a discreet dog paddle.

There was no point in hanging back, especially since
one woman, laughing, untied the sash to her robe and
helped her out of it, while the other two led her to the
tub and helped her in. The water was warm and divine
and Lily surrendered without a protest. *If they could
see me in Dumfries,* she thought, as she offered no

objection to the slathering of soft soap everywhere and a scrubbing of her back that made her close her eyes in bliss.

She sank into the water, a smile on her face, and only opened her eyes to watch an altercation outside the bathing room. Apparently, other servants were trying to tow the redoubtable Sister Marie Clotilde into the bath and she was resisting with all the force of her ecclesiastical stewardship over the Sisters of Mercy in the Ottoman Empire. Lily let her bath attendant dribble jasmine oil across her shoulders. Apparently the Sisters of Mercy had never heard of the concept of "when in Rome," which seemed a bit ironic.

She had to smile when the bath attendants exclaimed over her red hair. One of the women combed it, while a bolder attendant draped the length of it over her own black hair, then giggled.

Lily could have groaned with dismay when she heard the distant sound of a gong, which was followed by her attendant taking her arm and coaxing her from the oversize tub. She knew it was pointless to insist that she was capable of drying herself, even though she did insist on toweling her own private parts, which made her attendants giggle again.

She knew the party was over when, wrapped in a towel, she returned to her room to find her ugly dress waiting for her, clean, starched and as glaringly out of place in a sultan's pleasure dome as she was. Lily had to smile as she eyed her clothes. Someone had decided her shift was too worn to resuscitate and had substituted a silk one, instead. She could only hope that it wasn't the sultan himself.

* * *

Not that she was inclined to ask, not even when she had left the harem and was turned over to a different eunuch on guard, who silently escorted her to the dining hall, inhabited by Abdul Wasiri and Major Wharton, looking too amused for his own good. Her hand went automatically to her hair, which yet another attendant had styled into charming ringlets, instead of her customary bun.

"Lovely as always," the major murmured, which made Lily's face turn even rosier than his.

"Major, you've been away from society far too long, if you think a gray dress has one iota of style," she whispered back.

"I meant you, not that burlap sack of a dress," he said surprisingly. Before she had time to be embarrassed at his unexpected plain speaking, the major performed an impressive salaam to their breakfast host. "Double dog dare you to do better than that," he said, out of the corner of his mouth.

"You lose, Major Wharton," Lily replied, as she sank into a deep and graceful curtsy. "Mama taught me this before I was introduced at court."

The American put his hand to his chest in surrender. "Lily Nicholls, you never cease to amaze me."

"You're easily amazed," she teased back, wondering where her polite upbringing had vanished to, and his, too, for that matter. Something about the major was different, but this was not the time to find out, especially since the sultan was watching her so intently.

Lily let the major take her arm and direct her to a low stool, where she sat as gracefully as possible. "Your Highness, it is the greatest pleasure to see you again and to thank you for your unparalleled hospitality," she said.

"My dear Mrs Nicholls, it will continue as long as you wish," he replied in his impeccable English. He tapped the little gong beside him. "And now, I will be pleased if you and the major will join me in a poor repast."

It was anything but poor, beginning with figs, grapes and rose-scented yogurt, served in crystal bowls on gold chargers. The major put his hand over hers when she reached for a grape. "Let the taster do his unenviable work first," he whispered in her ear.

She waited as the taster crawled toward his lord and master and dutifully sampled all the dishes first. When he didn't die, the sultan began breakfast with a handful of grapes.

"I've often thought a taster would be a good idea in the average officers' mess hall," Major Wharton said to their host. "Your Highness, you would be astounded at the lengths to which some junior officers will go to advance in rank."

The sultan laughed and gestured to the servant. "Then he is yours," he said.

The major shook his head, with every indication of real regret. "Alas, your Highness, I am not at liberty to accept your generous gift."

The sultan shrugged. "Perhaps you will win him in a card game." Then the sultan looked at Lily. "I hear that you passed a pleasant night, Mrs Nicholls," he said.

And how would you know? she thought, in suspicious alarm. "I did, your Highness. I thank you for your kindness to me and the Sisters of Mercy."

"You are welcome as long as you need shelter here," he replied, after a discreet belch.

"Your Highness, I am happy to report that work is already under way to repair the kitchen and the rooms beyond," Major Wharton said. "A day or two should see most of the work completed."

The sultan sighed. "Mrs Nicholls, I had hoped to keep you here much longer." To her surprise, he took her hand. "I can do one thing for you, my dear lady. Tonight, when you return, allow my tailor to borrow your dress so he can make two or three new dresses to replace what was destroyed in the fire."

Lily was touched, in spite of her skepticism. "That would be a great kindness."

She should have known the sultan had more on his mind. "Of course, nowhere in my realm is there a color that ugly. Sad, but true, my dear. I can substitute blue and green, possibly, and perhaps silk."

You're a sly one, she thought, impressed despite her misgivings. Still, it would be nice to wear something besides Miss Nightingale's version of sackcloth and ashes. She glanced at the major, who was trying not to smile. *And you are enjoying this, Major.*

"Nothing would please me more," she said to them both.

The sultan gave her a gracious nod; he was just warming up. "If there is anything else I can do for you, lovely lady, anything at—"

"A Christmas tree," she said, interrupting the sultan, which made the servants gasp.

I have erred, Lily thought in alarm. She looked at the sultan, who returned a suddenly frosty stare. "It's just a small thing, your...your Excellency, your Worship. I wanted to have a Christmas tree for the wounded men. It would mean so much…" Her voice dwindled away. "I shouldn't have interrupted you."

"You should not," he said severely.

When in doubt, cry, Lily thought, as her eyes welled with tears, almost—but not quite—of their own accord. She dabbed at her eyes delicately, not looking at the major, who was probably seeing right through her subterfuge. "Forgive me," she said, head down, voice meek. "I was just thinking of the wounded and their longing for a symbol of the season, something to raise their spirits. That's all."

Silence. Then, "What kind of tree?" the sultan asked, his voice tender now.

She looked up into his face. Her late husband had once complained that she was the only woman he knew who could cry and still look lovely, which meant he was putty in her hands. Perhaps sultans in the Ottoman Empire were equally susceptible. Lily glanced at Major Wharton, who was regarding her with some skepticism.

"A pine tree. Our Queen's consort is from Germany. He brought Christmas customs from his native land, when he married Victoria Regina," she explained. "Just a tree. We would decorate it for the men who have done so much to defend your empire, and who now languish in the hospital, far from home and family. That's all," she concluded. "I know there are pine trees in your lovely land."

"Hmm," the sultan said. "Hmm." He looked at her for a long moment and Lily watched a crafty look come into his eyes. "And what, my dear Mrs Nicholls, would you give me in exchange for such a favor?"

"My undying gratitude," she said promptly.

"Hmm." Again.

And then breakfast was over. With a bow and an off-hand wave in her direction, the sultan left the enormous dining hall. Lily looked at Major Wharton. "I shouldn't have said anything," she admitted.

The major nodded and helped her up from the low stool. "Lily, I used to be a trusting soul, convinced, in a childish way, that no one would ever wish to mistreat a Wharton." He laughed. "Especially not in Philadelphia!" He sobered immediately. "And then I came here to the Black Sea, with people's labyrinthine, devious ways." He leaned closer, his words for her ears only. She enjoyed the way his breath tickled her ear. "And met Captain McClellan."

Lily burst into laughter, delighted at this side of a shy man. She attempted a severe look. "Major, you jest. I know enough about men to suspect that my injudicious comments to the sultan—who already thinks I am lovely, lonely and reluctant to become a fourth wife—render me vulnerable to his advances."

"I agree," he told her, as they walked down the long hall, preceded by yet another eunuch.

She retrieved her wrap from a servant at the door. Outside, two carriages waited, each filled with disapproving French nuns. Major Wharton handed her into the less crowded one and swung himself up beside the native driver.

I should never have said anything to the sultan, Lily thought. *Is this going to come back to haunt me?*

Chapter Five

Her misgivings grew as the day passed, especially when a servant from the sultan's palace delivered a basket of fruit addressed to her, with a note reading: "Dear lady, I will find a tree. The price will be high. Wasiri."

Worried, she distributed the fruit among her wounded soldiers and took the note to Major Wharton, busy at his desk. He looked up with a smile when she knocked and entered.

"You've come to save me from report writing."

"Not precisely." She handed him the note. "Should I worry?"

He read the note and nodded, then read the note again. He blushed predictably. He took his time to speak, obviously weighing his words on some scale of delicate balance. "Mrs Nicholls, I don't pretend to understand the Oriental mind." He tapped the note on his wrist, then grinned, his shyness forgotten for a moment. "Or the mind of Excelsior Penrose, who has summoned me this afternoon to a scolding, I fear."

"For heaven's sake, why?"

"He's practically turning purple, just thinking about 'the flower of European womanhood'—good Lord, he is a proser!—'subjected to a godless harem.'"

"We were perfectly safe last night in the harem!" Lily exclaimed.

"I know." He looked out the window. "Still, I wish I understood the sultan's game. Surely he can't seriously think you'd be willing to become wife number four." He looked back at the report in front of him, shaking his head.

And here I am, adding to your worries, Lily thought. She quietly let herself out of his office.

Lily spent the rest of the day tending to her patients, part of her mind on them, part on her son, so far away from her…and another part on Major Wharton, who was going to get a dressing down for nothing. She directed the able-bodied patients to help the more feeble soldiers into the many-windowed, enclosed pavilion that she had renamed a solarium. When everyone was seated, she told them about the hopeful Christmas tree and was rewarded with a smattering of applause.

She set them to making paper chains and looked about for tin snips. "Any shape you want," she assured the men who were flattening tin cans. She supervised the work. One rogue of a soldier tried to pass off a tin phallus as a candlestick, but his fellow patients threw their pillows at him. The maneuver was successful, particularly the pillow in which someone had stuffed a thick book. His roar of outrage turned into a whimper of pain, which Lily wisely ignored.

As the afternoon passed, she glanced out of one of the windows to see Major Wharton walking on the lawn with Captain Excelsior Penrose. Their body language said everything. She felt her face grow hot as she watched the major's steady stride, hands behind his back, and Penrose's irate gesticulations. She couldn't help a sigh. Probably nothing Major Wharton could explain would ever head off a vitriolic letter destined for the British High Command, complaining about the American sending sheltered ladies to a harem.

As if any of them were sheltered now, not after a year and a half of washing filthy bodies, superintending basic needs or listening to soldiers and their longings for England and families. When all was quiet in the solarium, Lily sat on a window ledge in the hall, thinking of her own sacrifice and that of her young son. And there was the major walking beside the captain, who seemed to have a mountain of complaints to unload on a conscientious, caring man. It seemed unfair.

But maybe she was wrong. As she watched, just out of their view, something changed. The major was talking now, leaning toward the British surgeon, intent. She stared as Penrose reared back at some comment from the major and stalked into the hospital. She swore she heard the door slam, two floors below.

"My goodness, Major, what did you tell him?" she asked her own reflection in the window.

She didn't want to embarrass Major Wharton, but she had not overcome her curiosity as they met that evening in the small diet kitchen, piled high now with bowls and pans from the ruined kitchen. The nuns had returned to the seraglio, assuming she would arrive later.

Major Wharton joined her at the sink, drying the pans she handed him. She stopped, a sponge in her hand, which made him pause.

"I couldn't help noticing what you were attempting on the front lawn this afternoon," she said, dabbing at a bowl and not quite looking at him. "You were brave to try to explain the situation, but I fear Captain Pompous is even now writing a nasty note to the high command in Sebastopol."

The major gave her a winning smile, one without any shyness in it this time. "Then you would be dead wrong, Mrs Nicholls. True, I explained why I felt it best for you and the sisters to stay in the seraglio for another night. And as you can imagine, he reacted precisely as you must have seen, full of outrage, manly affront and Christian indignation."

"Yes! But won't you…aren't you…?"

"In a world of hurt, as we say in America?" he asked, taking the bowl from her. "Here's what you couldn't have heard from the window." He smiled at her, glee just barely jostling aside shyness this time. "I reminded him I was well aware of his continued dalliance with one Maeve O'Grady. You probably thought she was a respectable widow and a laundress, eh?"

Lily nodded, her eyes wide. "Isn't she? She's been so kind as to launder some of my…" It was her turn to blush this time. "Well, some of my dainties."

The major dried the bowl with a flourish. "I assured Excelsior that if he said one word about a perfectly reasonable solution to a difficult situation for you and the nuns, everyone in Sebastopol would know about

Mrs O'Grady, who—ahem—also rejoices in the name of Stephen O'Grady. Such a scandal that would be."

Lily stared at him, her mouth open. "How did…how did…?"

Humor triumphed over circumspection this time. "Close your mouth, Mrs Nicholls! I doubt the flies in the Crimea are healthy to ingest, especially after that long siege of Sebastopol."

"*Stephen* O'Grady? Heavens! Who…?"

"Told me?" He laughed then, and spread his dishcloth across a chair back. "Mrs Nicholls, I have told you this before: I am one of five members of the U.S. Army who has a paper stating he is an observer. It's signed by the president of the United States. I observe; it's official. I am a certified observer. Sometimes it's even useful. Imagine the scandal, should I reveal that little stinker. And so I told Excelsior Penrose."

There was no way Lily could stifle the mirth inside her, so she didn't even try. She sat down at the table, rested her head in her hands and laughed until she ached. The major calmly finished the dishes as her laughter eventually wound down into an occasional undignified snort, and then she dabbed at her eyes.

"I haven't laughed like that in years," Lily said, when she could finally speak.

"Does the body good," the major said. He took out his timepiece and observed it for a moment. "Mrs Nicholls, it is—"

"Major Wharton, my first name is Lillian, but I prefer Lily," she said.

He blushed predictably. "I do, too, Lily," he said. "You're right, of course. After all that candor, I suppose we should be on a first-name basis. Call me Trey. Silly name, but my parents were hoping that, after two sons, I'd be a girl and had nothing better to offer!"

When they had both finished laughing, he pocketed his watch. "Let me arrange for a dog cart to take you to the palace, before it gets any later." He laughed. "Unless you'd rather have Mrs O'Grady keep you company here for the night."

She shuddered in mock horror and was taking off her apron when she heard someone running. Lily glanced at the major. "I hope nothing else is on fire."

The major opened the door as the night orderly practically threw himself into the room. He gasped a few seconds until he could speak, and he looked directly at her. "Mum, the hemorrhage in Unit Four.... 'E's spouting again!"

"Then you'd best run for Captain Penrose," she said, retying her apron and starting for the door, every nerve alert.

The orderly shook his head. "I did, mum, but he's drunker than a lord. And Surgeon Guilford took the steamer to Yalta just this morning!" He grasped her arm, all propriety thrust aside. "Mrs Nicholls, can you help? Please say you can!"

She could and she did, running after the orderly to Unit Four, where the sergeant in question stared at his spouting stump in horror and his comrades looked on helplessly. She sat beside him, elevating his ruined arm and staunching the flow with pressure and styptic, all the while speaking calmly and telling the man that these things always looked worse than they were. She hoped it was true; she knew it was something her own father would tell a terrified patient.

With the orderly holding the lamp high and Trey

assisting her, Lily threw in a half-dozen more sutures. She had never done such a thing before, and admitted it in a low voice to the major when the job was done, and the invalid's eyes had closed in weariness and relief.

"I did the best I could," she murmured, looking at her bloody hands, which shook slightly now the emergency was past.

To her surprise, Trey knelt beside her as she still sat on the sleeping sergeant's cot. He covered her shaking hands with his own and just held them, until she felt the heart return to her body and her hands were still.

"You're an observer, too, watching Captain Penrose at work," he whispered.

"I suppose I am," she whispered back.

"I'm proud of you, Lily Nicholls," he said. He stood up and pulled her up, too. "It's too late for you to go to the sultan's palace. I don't trust anyone afoot at this hour. You're taking my bed tonight."

She opened her mouth to protest, but he put his finger against her lips.

"No argument, Lily. I'll see that you're comfortable, then come back here for an hour or so. If things look calm, I'll put the orderly in charge and stretch out on the sofa in my office. No argument," he said again.

Lily nodded, quite unable to feel shy about the matter, because she suddenly knew this man's heart. She had known for more than a year how decisive and organized he was; now she knew how kind.

After a few words with the orderly, the major escorted her to his quarters next to his office and left her there. Before he returned to Unit Four, Trey knocked on the door. When she opened it, he held out a nightshirt. "Granted, it is worlds too large for you, Lily, but

I suspect you're not choosy right now, considering that your entire wardrobe is singed beyond resuscitation."

She took it gratefully. "Perhaps I should have taken my chances in the seraglio. Didn't Sultan Wasiri promise me a new dress or two?"

Trey nodded. He looked around to make sure no one was listening, then leaned closer, like a conspirator. "Tell you what—when he sobers up, I can ask Captain Penrose if Stephen O'Grady could spare a frock."

She heard his laughter down the hall, and was still smiling when she closed her eyes.

Chapter Six

With all the soldiers that could be spared, and a sprinkling of servants from the sultan's palace, the kitchen and quarters were repaired within two days, to Lily's relief.

And her disappointment, too, she had to admit. Trey Wharton had proved to be an excellent man to share quarters with. Captain Penrose, still in no fit condition to see to his responsibilities, kept to his quarters. Major Wharton had written his own note to Miss Nightingale about the matter. "I'm telling her right here that you are staying in the hospital because the surgeon is incapacitated," he had said, showing her the letter. "I think there won't be any argument."

Before he had gone ward walking the next night, he had given her his voluminous report on hospital administration in the Crimea. "A little light reading, in case you are an insomniac," he'd said, as he took up his slatted lamp and closed the door.

Full of comments and questions, Lily had still been

awake when he returned an hour later. Almost before either of them seemed to realize it, they were in the office next to the sitting room—Lily wearing Trey's nightshirt and wrapped in his overcoat—and the major taking notes as she made suggestions to strengthen the document.

All joking aside, Major Wharton *was* an astute observer. "I don't know if you are aware of it—I barely am, anymore—but I used to have a childhood stammer."

Lily shook her head.

"The upshot was that I spent a lot of time watching people and how they did things. It was always easier to watch than to talk. I recorded my observations." He shrugged, a hint of red to his complexion, but not much. He seemed to be finding her easier to talk to. "I watched Miss Nightingale in Scutari Hospital. I did more than that—I studied her. Lily, she is a bona fide genius. She gave me a wealth of good ideas on how to manage people, wounds, time and money in fraught circumstances. You were in Scutari?"

"Yes." She put her hand to her mouth, unable to say anything for a moment, which earned her Trey's warm hand on her neck. "When…when she saw that I was sensible and not inclined to faint, Miss Nightingale sent me here, after that emergency had passed."

"Wise of her." He indicated the report, with her notations. "I intend to resign my commission when I return to the States. Let us see if this report leads to a hospital-administrator position for me in Philadelphia."

"And not with a bank?"

He shook his head. "Not interested. And I'm not interested in being a gentleman of leisure, either. What a boring life." He dipped his pen in the inkwell. "Lily,

I am thirty-five years old and know my own mind." He
put down the pen and looked at her, which made him
blush predictably. "That wasn't nice of me, to make fun
of gentlemen of leisure."

"Which my late husband was," she said and grew
bold enough to touch his hand, now that he had removed
it from her neck. "Don't task yourself over that. It *is*
boring to be a lady of leisure. I don't want to return to
that life, but what alternative have I?"

She had to give Major Wharton the credit due him.
Something about his candid nature had encouraged her
to voice a thought she had never been brave enough to
say before. At least she had been circumspect enough
not to say the next thing that wanted to come out of her
mouth: *Could you find me employment in your Phila-*
delphia hospital?

During the afternoon, Lily thought so long about
their comments that she almost—but not quite—wished
for the hectic days of only last autumn, when they had
all been too busy to think of anything except the wounded and the diseased. *What do I do now?* she asked herself, as she emptied bedpans and washed bodies. Since
the lifting of the siege of Sebastopol, her father-in-law
had written her several letters, urging her return to the
family fold in London, tempting her with a modiste
eager to make new frocks, boarding school—horrors!—
for Will, and leisure—oh, that word—to make calls
about town.

As Lily scrubbed the main hall, her eyes still on a
prime spot for the non-existent Christmas tree, she was
free to let her mind rove. *Nobody ever says anything*
about remarriage, she thought, remembering the times
her mother-in-law had let drop her own thoughts on

one love and no other, and how sad Lily's husband was dead so young. *A person could die of boredom,* Lily told herself and vigorously tackled the cold stones with the brush. *It won't be me.*

In mid-afternoon, the fruit basket from the sultan that she had come to dread arrived. She opened the note, and her heart leaped. *I have found you a tree. Do come and see it, Mrs Nicholls,* the note read. And there it was: *We have some business to discuss. Wasiri.*

She knew she would find the major in the warehouse next to the kitchen, where he had said he would be supervising an inventory. If she hadn't been so worried, she would have been more flattered to see the way his eyes lit up when she came into the room.

"Oh, my stars, tell me I shouldn't worry," she said as she handed him the little note.

He set down his clipboard and read it, smiling a little and shaking his head. "A persistent man, our sultan," he commented, tucking the note in his uniform pocket. "Would you like me to accompany you to his palace?"

She could have kissed him in her relief. He must have known, because he startled her—and maybe himself—by giving her a quick hug. "It's nice not to face this alone," she told him.

Trey didn't say anything as he released her; maybe it wasn't necessary.

As Lily sat beside him in the pony trap for the trip to the palace, she discovered that the short drive was long enough for a remarkable epiphany. She had done precisely what her mama's postscript to an earlier letter had mentioned: she had found love during wartime. She glanced at the major—a handsome man even in fraught circumstances, but more importantly, someone who never panicked, as far as she could tell, and who had a genuinely kind heart. She knew how many rules he had broken to get General Pasquier's dying son transferred to France, all in the hopes of allowing father and son to have even a few minutes together. And he hadn't done it for a dusty bottle of champagne. She was in the presence of a genuinely kind man, an intelligent man, a capable man, who also happened to be shyer than forest violets.

For all she knew, he had a sweetheart back in Philadelphia. If he didn't, there must be any number of female candidates vying for his heart in his Main Line society. It sounded depressingly similar to her own privileged life of emotions cushioned in cotton wadding, buttressed by the tomfoolery that a woman could only love once and that her chance had come and gone. It was idiocy, but not something a lady talked about.

But there were bigger fish to fry right now, she reminded herself, as they walked into the palace to be greeted by Sultan Abdul Ahmed's chief secretary. After a graceful salaam, he led them to the seraglio. Lily felt her heart sink into her sturdy boots. She hung back, not able to help herself.

"I have got myself into a mess over a dratted tree," she whispered to Trey. "*Why* was I so foolish?"

"When we—" and he emphasized *we* "—get ourselves out of this mess, you'll have to tell me why the tree is really so important."

She nodded, not even sure herself. But it was too late to worry over the matter, because there was the sultan, looking more benign than usual, perhaps because he was in his own harem, secure in the comfort of his ladies. *I doubt anyone asks the sultan if he only loves once,* she thought sourly.

The sultan and the major exchanged their usual lengthy pleasantries, which seemed to be part of doing business in the Ottoman world. She couldn't help but be impressed with how adroitly the major had come to an understanding of how to do business with Muslims. Maybe he *should* find his place in the crass world of commerce.

"And now, my dear Mrs Nicholls, I would like you to meet someone," the sultan was saying to her now and gesturing toward a set of beautifully carved doors.

She gritted her teeth with the impatience of it all, wanting to get over the business of the Christmas tree and what he was probably going to demand from her. Couldn't the man take no for an answer? Lily smiled as graciously as she could and allowed herself to be led along.

He showed them into what turned out to be a sumptuous bedchamber. Lily couldn't help a glance at the major. Good Lord, was the sultan going to seduce her right here, with witnesses? She moved closer to the major, who seemed somehow unconcerned and surprisingly serene. Of course, no one was threatening *his* virtue, obviously.

The room was pleasantly warm, the result of several charcoal braziers doing their work. The sultan led the way to a bed. *Heaven help me!* Lily thought to herself in panic, until she came closer and realized what a simpleton she had been.

Lying there was a small woman. Lily came closer, almost holding her breath at the frail life in front of her. Without asking permission, she perched herself on the bed and held out her hand, gently touching the woman's hand, then clasping it carefully in her own. If she had learned one thing in her painful time in the Crimea, it was how to conduct herself at someone's bedside.

She glanced at the sultan, curious to know who this woman was, wasted by age and apparent illness, but lovely still. One glance told her and it took her breath away.

I have been such a fool, she thought. She swallowed her stupid pride and looked at the sultan. "Your Highness, is she one of your wives?" she asked.

He nodded, kneeling on the floor beside the bed, putting his arm under his wife's head. "This is Habiba, the wife of my youth, my first wife, the mother of my sons," he whispered.

"Habiba," Trey said. "Lily, that means 'my dear one,' in Arabic."

She nodded, too touched to speak. Gently, she massaged the woman's arm. Habiba opened her eyes and Lily almost sighed with the loveliness of her brown, almond-shaped eyes. Forty years ago, maybe fifty even, Habiba must have been a vision out of an *Arabian Nights* tale.

The sultan's wife turned her head to look at her husband and Lily sighed again at the glance they gave one another. If Randolph Nicholls had ever looked at her like that, Lily knew she would still be in deep mourning at his untimely death.

She glanced at the major, seeking reassurance, and received another shock. He was looking at her in much the same way the sultan was regarding his wife. She blinked and the moment passed. It must have been a trick of the muted light in the room, she decided.

"I wanted you to meet my dear Habiba, Mrs Nicholls," the sultan was saying. "I know it will not be long before you leave this Soulali. Will you think of us now and then, when this war is long over?"

"More than you will know, your Highness," she whispered. "I have learned so much here." *And most of it today,* she added to herself.

She sat a few more moments, feeling the gentlest pressure on her hand, as Habiba pressed her fingers. Lily held her breath as the sultan's queen raised her hand.

"I have told her about your red hair and she wants to see it," the sultan said.

Without a word, Lily removed her bonnet, tossing it aside, and tugged at the pins that held her hair in place. She felt Trey's fingers in her hair, too, pulling at the strands to separate them. He ran his fingers through the tangle until her glorious hair was spread around her shoulders and down her back. She leaned closer then, so Habiba could touch it. The woman smiled and sighed, saying something to her husband. He nodded.

"She tells you thank you. She has always wanted to see red hair."

"I wish I could invite her to Scotland," Lily said. "She would see how commonplace it is."

The sultan laughed and translated her words. Habiba smiled, touched Lily's hair again and then closed her eyes in sleep, exhausted by so much effort.

"May your dreams be pleasant," Lily whispered.

They stood a moment more in the bedchamber, then the sultan ushered them out. Without a word, Lily reached for the major's hand and held it. She turned her face into his uniform sleeve until she had control of her emotions, then calmly followed their host.

He led them into the entrance hall again and there was the Christmas tree. It was scarcely a noble pine, but this was wartime, and all of the Ottoman Empire had suffered.

"I wish it were a larger tree, Mrs Nicholls," the sultan apologized. "Wagons are either still full of the wounded, or refugees, or supplies and food, moving here and there."

"I understand, your Highness," she said. "It will mean so much—so much!—to the men who are homesick for England." She took a deep breath. "You said the cost would be high for me."

"I did." The sultan seemed less confident then. "Perhaps I ask too much of a lady."

She knew then what he wanted, probably what he had wanted months ago, when she had foolishly thought he was asking her to be his fourth wife. She hadn't understood, but now she did.

"It's not too much, your Highness, considering your great kindnesses to us at the barracks hospital. And for the tree, of course." She fingered her loose hair. "You'd like to have a wig made from my hair for Habiba, wouldn't you? Certainly, you may."

Chapter Seven 6

"I like it, Lily, and I'm not just saying that."

Worried, Lily searched his face for the lie, but it wasn't there. There was nothing in Major Wharton's face but appreciation: no sympathy, no pity, nothing but the kind of delight she remembered from her son Will's face, when he saw something he enjoyed.

She held out her hand for the mirror, gritting her teeth. She had been brave enough through the process and Trey had sat right beside her through the whole ordeal. It was easy enough to pantomime that she wanted Habiba's chief servant to take everything. Her hair was curly and she knew it would look good enough, tight around her face. Still, she had felt a pang as she ran her hand down the whole lovely length of her red hair. Oh, well. She wore it under a matron's cap, so what difference could it possibly make?

Trey put the mirror in her hand. She raised it slowly to her face, horrified at first to see someone with big brown eyes—goodness, but they looked twice as large, without a wealth of hair to balance them—and let her breath out slowly. Tears welled; that was all. She turned her head to the side, reacquainting herself with her ears that had always been covered by her hair and cap. At least they were small ears, like Mama's. She sighed and looked at the major.

He hesitated a moment, then he touched her tight curls. His face turned beet red, but he didn't take away his hand, twining the stubby strands around his finger. "Fun, too," he told her. He peered closer at her face. "Not going to cry, are you?"

She shook her head as the tears fell. Without a word, he gathered her close and kissed the top of her head. "You did a brave and a good thing, Lily," he said and then released her, after dabbing at her eyes with a handkerchief held at the ready.

She wouldn't have minded if he had held her longer. He made no move to distance himself, so she had to be content with that. He turned to watch two palace servants carry the sultan's promised Christmas tree into the foyer. They had bound the limbs with twine to keep the tree from bouncing about over the deep ruts between the palace and the hospital.

"We'll set it in the main hall," she told him as they jounced over terrible roads, the tree held between them. "That way, the men from Units Two and Three—those who don't walk well—can see it from their beds."

He nodded. "I'll clip the twine, and set it in a bucket of sugar water outside the kitchen door. Our housekeeper used to do that." He scratched his head. "Not sure why. She claimed the cold air helped the tree hang on to its needles. No one ever argued with her."

* * *

Lily had done as he said, fluffing out the branches as he clipped the twine. He looked up at her and she tried not to shiver in the winter air, missing the extra warmth of her hair.

Trey grinned at her and opened the door to the kitchen. "Get inside! You can't imagine how I would dread composing a report to Miss Nightingale, describing your final hours deep in the grip of *la grippe,* because short hair had rendered you vulnerable."

She did as he said, warming herself in front of the oven. She wished he would stay in the kitchen, but after a nod in her direction, he returned to the hospital, muttering something about "that blasted report."

She waited a few minutes, thinking of the times he had left, only to return because he had something further to tell her, be it joke or serious business. Because he did not return, she decided to be philosophical, reminding herself that when the hospital finally closed, she would never see him again. There was no way their paths would ever cross again. She would never run into him in London, or glimpse him during a visit to the Lake Country. Fishing would never bring him to Scotland. He would be an ocean away, and there wasn't a thing she could do to change it.

The weight of her melancholy seemed to settle on her shoulders like mortar. She sobbed out loud as she changed from her one dress into the old nightshirt he had given her, because she had nothing else. She decided she would wear the garment until it turned to rags and disintegrated. With tears on her cheeks, Lily ordered herself to be calm and think about the pleasure of seeing Will again soon, and her parents. She had no idea what she would do with herself, once she left the Ottoman Empire, no idea at all.

Lily was sitting in bed thinking, her chin on her drawn-up knees, when Trey Wharton knocked on her door. She knew his knock.

"Y-yes?" she asked, wanting to get up and pull him into bed with her. Her face was hot with the mere idea.

He opened the door, but just stood in the doorway. He held a ribbon-tied document in his hand and her heart sank. He set it down on the small table by the door.

"It was on my desk. Looks like your marching orders, Lily. You've been given leave to steam from Constantinople right after Christmas, destination France and then England." He stood there a second, hesitating, then closed the door quietly. "G'night now."

She didn't hear his footsteps and her heart ached to think he was standing on the other side of the door, just waiting there for what, she wasn't sure. Every fiber in her body wanted her to leap out of bed and open the door, but something else—call it character, call it virtue, call it cowardice—prevented her. After a long moment, she heard slow, receding footsteps.

It wasn't the worst night of her life; that was probably the night after Balaclava, when every wounded man in the history of the world had seemed to pile up in the woefully unprepared barracks hospital in Scutari. It wasn't even the night her late husband Randolph had taken his last shallow breath and died. She had only felt relief that consumption no longer held him hostage in pain and suffering.

For hours she lay there, wishing to hear Trey Wharton's measured footsteps again. She had grown accustomed to his steps. For a year they had both ward walked, despite him not being a doctor. It hadn't mattered. Even though he was an American, and as he had so colorfully expressed to her, had no dog in the fight, he cared about the French and British soldiers in his hospital, the one Miss Nightingale had, in her wisdom, given to him.

He had walked even when she was too tired to walk, but had sat, hollow-eyed with exhaustion, on a bench in the main hall, too worn out to make it to her own bed off the kitchen. She lay in bed now, knowing she would miss his firm tread, and wondering if he would ever walk up and down with a child of his own, soothing away a nightmare, or teething woes. "I trust you won't be shy forever, Major Wharton," she had murmured late in the night. "Surely some day there will be a lady brave enough to chase you until you catch her."

At least she had two new dresses, one green, one blue and both silk, courtesy of the sultan. Lily washed and dressed in the morning, thinking about the Christmas tree she had bought with her hair: anything not to think about her departure papers on the table—she couldn't bring herself to touch them—or the fact that, in a few days, she would say goodbye forever to Major Trey Wharton, her American observer.

At least her hair was easy to tend. She smiled into her scrap of mirror, teasing the curls here and there, then covering it all with her matron's cap. Mama would mourn her lovely hair, but Papa would find it amusing. Ever practical, Will would probably hug her and remind her that it would grow. Now it was time to retrieve the tree and start decorating.

Lily opened the kitchen door and gasped. The tree

was gone! She put her hand to her mouth and sagged against the doorframe, her knees weak. When she could stand upright again, she looked around, her breath coming in little gasps until she felt light-headed. Nothing. She ran into the hospital. Maybe Major Wharton had risen earlier and set it in the main hall. That would be a kindness typical of him.

Nothing. Forcing herself to walk slowly—the men were still sleeping—she went into each ward, looking around. She went outside once more, not bothering with a shawl against the bitter cold. Still no tree. She pressed her lips tightly together to keep from sobbing. She took a deep breath, then another. She sniffed again. Pine.

Startled, she looked toward the stables, where the native coachmen generally gathered by their charcoal fire. All she saw this time was smoke. Her hands bunched into tight fists, she started to run, thinking of all the terrible things she would say.

The coachmen looked at her in surprise, as she stopped by their circle, suddenly uncertain. Her tears flowed when she saw the remains of her tree, smoldering and billowing smoke everywhere. The tree had been too green to burn for warmth, but they had tried. As she looked at the cold men—nobody dressed warmly because war had reduced them all to paupers—she remembered Trey's irritation only yesterday that the charcoal deliveries had been disrupted. He had made some comment about things going to pieces when wars were ending. These coachmen had never failed her in their delivery of the wounded.

They were cold and had tried to warm themselves with her Christmas tree, her foolish tree that probably meant more to her than to her patients, because she had been trying to hang on to some semblance of her normal family life, especially her son, in this time of abnormality. That was all the tree truly was, a graceful reminder of happier Christmases. She had tried to recapture better days with a silly tree and she had failed.

Lily turned away, shivering. She had given her hair for this futile gesture. She walked slowly back to the kitchen, her heart barely lifting when she noticed the major standing in the doorway, his face serious. She shook her head and tried to walk past him into the kitchen, but he gently took her by the shoulders and held her close when she began to weep.

She wasn't sure why she cried. Maybe it was for Randolph; maybe for Will, whom she missed with every fiber in her body; maybe because she knew in her heart she would never be as lucky in love as her own parents; maybe she cried for war and death and women in England and France who had lost their lovers; maybe she was just tired to the marrow of her bones. Whatever the reason, Major Wharton wrapped his arms around her and let her sob.

She wanted him never to let her go, but there was breakfast to prepare in the newly refurbished kitchen. The doctors would be coming soon for a cup of tea before they began morning rounds. The Sisters of Mercy were probably already through with morning prayers. The clock was ticking and many depended on her.

Lily pulled away finally, looking at the major, wishing one last time that he would say something that would stop her from leaving. She sniffed back unshed tears. Maybe the biggest reason for her sorrow was that the observer, for all his skill and experience, couldn't seem to see her love for him.

Chapter Eight

As foolish as she had felt over the Christmas tree, Lily knew herself well enough to understand that her training would take over, especially when so many people needed her. She had wanted to believe the major, when he looked her in the eye, his hands still gentle on her arms, and assured her there would be a tree.

She had nodded and smiled, because she knew he wanted to see that. It was pointless to mention that tomorrow was Christmas Eve. He could read a calendar as well as she could. After the noon meal, Trey had told her there would soon be a transport of the walking wounded by steamer for Constantinople. He had completed the paperwork for her to accompany them. She could leave on Christmas morning, or sooner, if the steamer was ready.

"At least it won't take me long to pack," she had joked, hoping to dissipate some of the bleakness she felt and could have sworn she'd seen reflected in his eyes also. *Say something to me,* she said to herself, wishing he could understand her heart. *That's how it is supposed to be done, you know, no matter that you are American and bound by your own orders. Do you think I find London irresistible? Think again.*

But Trey Wharton was not susceptible to thought waves and everyone seemed to need her. Her duties occupied her solidly from the noon meal to mid-afternoon, but she found a hundred ways to avoid the main hall, where the ambulatory men had collected all the ornaments they had prepared for the tree the coach-men had burned, the tree for which she had sacrificed her hair.

As the afternoon waned, one of the nuns delivered a note to her on the familiar, heavily embossed paper that came from Sultan Abdul Ahmed Wasiri. She managed her only genuine smile so far that day, pleased to see an invitation for her to visit that afternoon. There was a pony cart waiting for her.

She scribbled a note for Captain Penrose and left the barracks hospital.

As charming as ever, the sultan took her to the sera-glio, where a weaver sat cross-legged on a straw mat, attaching her shorn red hair to a mohair cap.

"A strand here, a strand there. Soon it will be complete, and my Habiba will have lovely red hair," he told her. He sighed. "Her own hair is so brittle. Now she will not cry when she looks in a mirror."

Lily felt a warm glow for the first time since her horror of early morning. "She will be lovely." She could see no point in telling the sultan what had happened to the tree. For all she knew of imperial wrath, heads would roll, and she didn't want that on her conscience.

After a brief visit with Habiba, Lily and the sultan sat in the antechamber off the entrance. He had sent for her pony cart again, and it was time to say goodbye.

It was also time to apologize. The sultan only nodded, his eyes bright, and tugged at his handsome goatee when she confessed that she thought he had proposed to her months ago.

"I think now that you were only trying to find a way to ask for my hair and I didn't understand," she confessed, feeling relief as she unburdened herself.

"It is true," he told her with a slight smile. "I do not think you would be happy in my harem." He looked at her, his eyes shrewd now. "Besides, I do not think Major Wharton would have ever allowed such a thing, not the way he feels."

"I beg your pardon?" she said, mystified. "What do you mean?"

The sultan made a grand gesture. "He told me one late night over cards how much he loves you, Mrs Nicholls."

Lily held her breath. The sultan watched her, then kindly suggested that she breathe. He tugged at his goatee again. "It was not your imagination that you feared I wanted you for my fourth and final wife." He shrugged, the gesture almost as grand. "Perhaps it is the devious mind of the east, my dear. I thought if I made enough overtures to you, he would find this a good excuse to advance his own cause." His eyes seemed to fill with sympathy then. "It is not so?"

You sly fox, Lily thought, amused in spite of her heartache. "I fear our major is simply too shy to find out how I really feel, your Highness. May…maybe he thinks I might not like his country."

"He should at least ask," the sultan suggested. "I think he is a brave man."

"He is, when he is fighting for his hospital," Lily said. "He is so used to helping others that I think he forgets about himself."

They were both silent for a long while. A servant crawled toward them to whisper that the pony cart was ready. The sultan dismissed him with a single finger and looked at Lily.

"Perhaps it is up to you to tip the balance," he said. "This is not something I would recommend for any female of my acquaintance, but you, Madame Nicholls, are a modern woman from a country with steamships, railways and matches that light with the flick of a fingernail."

Lily smiled at the image. "Proposing is not something that ladies do," she told him.

Another massive shrug. "Could you make an exception for an exceptional man?"

It had been a good question. She mulled it around that evening as she finished her own records and wrote her last detailed instructions in a journal. Steeling herself, she knocked on the hospital administrator's door, wanting to leave the documents with him. Perhaps also to say goodbye and take a long, last look.

He wasn't there, but it was late. He had probably decided to ward walk earlier, since it would be Christmas Eve tomorrow. She couldn't bring herself to go into the main hall, with its sad little box of tin ornaments and paper chains. She could say goodbye in the morning, provided Major Wharton was up. She knew the wounded were leaving early; Captain Penrose had prepared them for departure. Lily propped her report against the closed door and quietly went to bed.

It was still full dark when she woke. Lily washed in cold water and dressed quickly in her new green dress, determined to keep her mind on the business of the day. There were the wounded to shepherd to the steamer waiting in the harbor. In another day she would be in Constantinople, the storied gateway to Europe. She had not managed to make it home in time for Christmas, but then, neither had Mama and Papa, all those years ago. Christmas would keep. Next year, she and Will would have a tree, and the Crimea would be on its way to becoming a distant memory.

She couldn't say Major Wharton would ever be a distant memory, not when she planned to keep him fresh in her mind for as long as she lived.

She left her almost-empty valise by the front steps, then walked around to the administrator's office. She frowned to see her report still leaning against the door. *Where* are *you, Major Wharton?* she asked herself.

Lily debated a long moment, then told herself she was being foolish to avoid the main hall. After all, she was responsible for the dozen or so men she was to accompany to Constantinople; Captain Penrose, finally sober, would be hard pressed to get them ready all by himself. Besides, she couldn't let the mockery of an empty hall keep her from one last walk through the wards she had tended so well. If she was never useful again in her future life of leisure and ease, at least she could remember this time when people needed her.

She went into the main hall, gasped and stood there, stunned beyond words.

"What on earth…?" she managed to say at last, as her eyes took in the startling sight of Christmas ornaments suspended like magic in the air.

No, it couldn't be. Openmouthed, she stared at the space where the Christmas tree would have been, if the coachmen had not burned it. As her eyes became accustomed, she became aware that the ornaments were aligned in triangle shape, as though they hung on an invisible tree. She looked closer. The ornaments were hanging from the ceiling, each on its own string, every string aligned to foster the illusion of an invisible tree. There was even a pot of water for the invisible trunk.

She came closer and touched one of the strings. Up close they were visible, but just barely.

"It's surgical catgut, Lily. Amazing how it disappears from a distance."

She whirled around to see Major Wharton standing in the shadow by a ladder. She looked closer. His eyes were squinting and his shoulders slumped; she had not seen him so exhausted since the earlier days when the siege guns had boomed and the wounded had poured in. He must have been working all night on the tree. Or the non-tree—she had no idea what to call this little miracle of illusion in the main hall.

"I have decided to call it The One, The Only, The Famous Air Tree," he told her. "I must admit it was pleasant to put my West Point training to good use! I am an engineer. Here is your tree, my dear Lily Nicholls."

He leaned toward her, but did not touch her; he was still too shy. She knew if she did not make a move, she would regret it bitterly all her life. Without a word, she came close to the major, put a tentative hand on his cheek, then wrapped her arms around him. His arms went around her, but she kissed him first, her lips soft on his, and then firmer as he kissed her back with enough fervor and skill to suggest that she might be on to a good thing. Her hands were in his hair, which she couldn't help noticing was now longer than her own. He felt so good pressed against her body that she felt warm in places that hadn't been stimulated in years. Good riddance to barren widowhood.

"I don't want to leave you," she whispered into his lips. "I won't. Send the assistant surgeon with the men. I—what is that you said once?—double dog dare you to keep me out of your bed."

He nodded, his hands firm on her back, then straying lower. She had no objection.

To her surprise, he held her off and reached into his uniform pocket. He pulled out a few dusty leaves and berries.

"Mistletoe," he said, then started to laugh. "The sultan gave it to me yesterday afternoon. He summoned me to the palace after dinner and told me to take the mistletoe and make it work." He shrugged and tossed the dusty bundle over his shoulder. "Guess we don't need it."

They kissed again more decorously this time, considering that the men were starting to move about in the closest unit. He put his arm around her shoulders and walked her to the front of the Famous Air Tree. "You know, my dearest, it appears that our sultan does not miss a trick. Nearly a year ago, I spent one evening beating him at poker and unburdening myself to him. He was actually listening! I fear we have misjudged the mystical men of the Middle East. Maybe I should put in my report that we would be wise not to do so in future."

Lily cleared her throat, pleased to watch the Famous Air Tree shimmer in the breeze caused by Captain Penrose opening the main door. "I kissed you first, but I am relying on you to propose," she reminded her major.

He tightened his grip on her shoulders. "Then I had better be about it. Lily Nicholls, I love you."

He paused and, in the growing light of Christmas Eve morning, she saw him turn predictably red.

"I should continue the momentum, of course—another lesson from engineering school—but first, I have a confession."

She waited, amused.

"I have had your departure papers since that first requisition for a tree was turned down."

"You are a dirty dog!" Lily declared, softening her words with another kiss.

"Not at all, my love," he continued, more short of breath now. "I...I just couldn't let you go. Not then, and not ever."

He said it so simply. Lily kissed him again. "Still waters run deep," she murmured into his uniform front. "I do wish you would propose, Trey."

He laughed. "Marry me, Lily. I'll take extraordinarily good care of you and Will. Do you think he will like me?"

"He will love you," she assured him. "And my answer is aye."

"Then I suggest we find a minister—I know there is one in that hospital closer to Scutari—have him splice us, then wait back here for my marching papers. I'll give my report to Major Mordecai when we get to Constantinople and you and I will go to Scotland."

Captain Penrose was coming toward them now. He barely glanced at the magnificent, splendid, one-of-a-kind, Famous Air Tree. He looked even more tightly wound than usual.

"I think he has a bone to pick with one of us," Lily said. She stood on tiptoe and whispered in her major's ear. "What do you intend to observe in Scotland?"

"Lots of you," the major replied without a blush.

* * * * *

NO CRIB FOR A BED

282
201
81

Prologue

Away in a Manger

Away in a manger, no crib for a bed
The little Lord Jesus lay down his sweet head
The stars in the heavens looked down where he lay
The little Lord Jesus, asleep on the hay

Philadelphia, Pennsylvania—December 1, 1877

Dear Will,
To say that we are eager to see this Christmas would
be an understatement. We had thought to see you last
year at this time, but apparently man proposes and Sitting Bull disposes. Well, now he and his people are in
Canada and others of his confederate tribes are sur-
rendering there near you.

As much as you shake your head when I do this, I
was happy to pull a string or two on your behalf, to get
your furlough restored. Your fiancée was even more

delighted, as I am certain she has communicated to
you. The plan for last December's wedding—certain
to have been the social event of the Main Line—will
now become *this* year's wedding, complete with an
Indian Wars hero, for so the *Inquirer* has crowned you.
Tedious, eh? (I was never a hero in the Crimea—what
administrator is?—but that's the *Inquirer* for you.) Barring national emergency or Indian uprising, you and
Maddy will do us proud.

But we already are proud of you. May I be candid? It
has always been a sorrow of your dear mother and mine
that we were never to have children together. This, and
your own kind nature, have made you especially dear
to me. Indeed, I have never really thought of you as my
adopted son. You were always more, happy to let me
be your father and guide you as best I could. I recall
those early, disorganized days in 1861, days when you
dropped everything—friends, studies, your youth—
and served as the best scribe I could have had, as we
organized hospitals around the District of Columbia.
Many was the midnight hour when I would look over
at you sitting at the next desk, taking my dictation, and
have to remind myself that you were only sixteen. You
have long been an unsung blessing to this nation, even
longer a blessing to me. I understand your willingness
to serve now in the U.S. Army Medical Corps.

I know I am becoming maudlin. I suppose that happens, when one contemplates retirement. This gives you
an idea of my eagerness to have you home for Christmas, and then for your wedding.

Your mother sends her love, too. If any couple should
understand what it is to wait and work and worry during

war, it would be Lily and Trey Wharton. Come home soon, dear son.

Lovingly,
Papa

Chapter One

Captain Wilkie Wharton, Third Cavalry regimental surgeon, wasn't surprised when Mary Frances Coughlin refused his best efforts to carry her carpetbag. She did it in her usual good-humored way, though, which left him smiling.

"Captain, you know how my father feels about baggage," Frannie reminded him as she sat beside him on the Union Pacific platform in Cheyenne. "You've been six years, off and on, at Fort Laramie, so you *should* know."

Will grinned at her. "I know too well— 'Never pack more than you can carry yourself.' But that doesn't mean I cannot be a gentleman and offer."

"You have offered and that will do," Frannie assured him with that easy nature he had come to appreciate. During the past year, she had taught the enlisted men's children at the fort. Now she was returning home to Brooklyn, New York. Because her father was probably the fort's best hospital steward ever, Will had no qualms about leaving his green-as-grass assistant surgeon to doctor alone for six weeks, since he knew Paddy Coughlin was there to ward off ruin.

Mary Frances Coughlin was as sensible as she was pretty. He had long relied on her to read to patients in the hospital, or write letters for the illiterate. She never flinched from illness. He had commented on that once to Paddy, during one of their late-night efforts, when diphtheria was taking its toll on the fort's young ones. Paddy had merely raised his tired eyes to Will's tired eyes and commented, "She hasn't a flinching bone in her body, sir."

Although Will never mentioned the fact to anyone, Frannie's best skill in his hospital on the hill was probably her fine looks. Amazing what a sweet-faced woman could do to brighten a glum group of invalids. He couldn't call her a true beauty—his own fiancée, Madeline Radnor, took the palm there—but there was something so unfettered about Frannie's curly red hair that never seemed to remain subdued into a bun. Or maybe it was her snapping green eyes that could appear so interested in whatever sad story a soldier might choose to unravel. He couldn't have called her figure trim—again, Maddy won that contest. Will had decided Frannie's shape was what should appropriately be called generous.

Frannie Coughlin had always been so willing to listen to his patients that, in a weak moment, he had almost—but not quite—confided in her about Maddy and something that troubled him. Reason had triumphed at the eleventh hour and Will had kept his doubts to himself. Still, he had *considered* talking to Frannie.

Will checked his timepiece. The Union Pacific train

from the west was late, but he wasn't too surprised,
considering recent snowfalls. He had allowed himself
plenty of time to get home to Philadelphia for Christmas, and then his wedding midway between Christmas
and New Year's Day. He had brought along plenty of
reading matter—medical journals and even a novel—
and he intended to do nothing more than read and
eat and watch the boredom of the Nebraska plains go
clickety-clack past the window.

That had been the original plan, but he hadn't
objected when Paddy Coughlin had asked him to keep
half an eye on Frannie, who was sensible and good
company, and would give him no grief. There would
still be time to read and maybe reflect on his upcoming wedding, which was still troubling him in certain
respects.

Will had begun feeling a bit ill-used when he'd
received a letter from Lieutenant Ed Hunsaker, acting
post surgeon at nearby Camp Robinson, with the news
that he would be traveling east, too, with Nora Powell,
a captive white woman being returned to relatives in
Iowa. Ed's letter had seemed a bit testy to Will, as he
complained about having to travel in the company of
Nora Powell. *Well, who do you* think *would get that
duty, the adjutant?* Will had asked himself, at the time.

Still, Ed would be in charge of Nora Powell, poor
woman. Will remembered how talkative the man was
and predicted this would cut into Will's reading and
leisure time on the journey. Knowing Frannie as he did,
Will thought she might just distract Ed and keep him
company, to spare "her Captain Wharton," as her father
had once called Will in her presence. He had made her

blush; Will thought the camaraderie between father and daughter was charming.

He glanced over at Frannie, smiling to himself because she always looked so fresh: eyes lively and a smile on her face. Will blushed a little, remembering a dislocated shoulder—also known as Private Jewkes, the Third Cav's worst malingerer—who had once made the cheeky observation that if Captain Wharton, with his downturned mouth, had ever married Miss Coughlin, with her perpetually upturned mouth, their children could be happy and sad at the same time. He had laughed about it later, but not in Jewkes's presence. The private was incorrigible, but observant, Will had to admit.

"Do you think he's coming, Captain?" Frannie asked.

"I don't know. If they come, it'll have to be on the double-quick."

Man of medicine, he never would have admitted to Frannie that he almost hoped Ed Hunsaker *didn't* arrive with his patient. Not that Nora Powell was a patient, not really. She was more a prisoner, but even that wasn't accurate. Victim? Possibly, except that a true victim wouldn't have fought like a mother tiger to remain precisely where she was, in an Indian camp, with her little half-Indian children, assumed to be the product of rape.

So Ed Hunsaker had written to him from Camp Robinson, where his infantry regiment remained to keep the peace at the Red Cloud and Spotted Tail Agencies. Will had sighed over the high moral tone of Ed's letter. He had experience enough in watching Sioux and their families forced onto reservations. No one was ever happy.

Will had served nearly eight years on the frontier

now, but he had never seen a white woman returning from captivity, as Nora Powell was. Thirteen years a captive of the Ogalala Sioux, she had been found at the Spotted Tail Agency on a tip from the local Indian agent, who thought he had noticed a blue-eyed woman among the Indian women waiting for rations.

When she'd been finally separated from her children—"everyone screaming and crying at once," Ed had written—she had admitted to being Nora Powell, captured near Julesburg, Colorado, on an Indian raid in 1864. Beyond that, she wouldn't talk, but sat in silence, rocking back and forth and grieving for her children, who had been whisked away from her.

Even now, waiting for Captain Hunsaker and his 'prisoner' to arrive, Will owned to some uneasiness. Ed's letter, so righteously indignant, had offended him in some strange way he couldn't understand. Obviously there were saddened families who longed to know what had happened to women captured on the trail, and no one would argue with the belief that Nora Powell belonged with her own kind.

He couldn't help his uneasiness, remembering Ed Hunsaker's description of the shrieking and mourning when Nora's children had been pulled from her arms. Hunsaker had almost sounded smug about the whole situation, as though he knew best. Did he? Will had his doubts.

They must have showed on his face. "It bothers you, too?" Frannie asked.

Will glanced at her in surprise. How on earth did Frannie know what he was thinking? "You mean Nora Powell and her children?" he asked, keeping his voice low.

She nodded. Her face reddened. She moved a little

closer. "Captain, if it were me, I don't know if I could bear to part with my children, no matter how they had been conceived."

He nodded, somehow not surprised that Frannie would feel that way. Paddy Coughlin had told him how attached Frannie became to her little pupils in the enlisted men's school. Maybe women were just naturally that way. He smiled to himself. *And stupidly sensitive post surgeons, too,* he thought. *I think I agree with her.*

"I don't think anyone offered her a choice," he said. "I doubt it ever occurred to them." *That's a radical statement,* he told himself. *What must Frannie think of me?*

He glanced at her and saw nothing but sympathy on her expressive face. She sighed and looked away. He thought she said, "I'm glad it wasn't my decision," but she spoke softly and he could have been wrong.

Still no train. Will thought of all the complications the Union Pacific was prone to: buffalo on the tracks, hot boxes when the axle overheated, road agents or marauding Indians came to mind first, but seemed the most unlikely. Thanks to bone hunters, the buffalo herds were already shrinking. Pinkerton's had been particularly effective lately against road agents, so that seemed unlikely. And every soldier at Fort Laramie had commented on a definite slowdown to Indian troubles, since Sitting Bull's people were in Canada, and Chief Joseph's Nez Perce had been escorted to Indian Territory.

It's going to be long trip to Philly, Will thought, as he looked down the track again. *All I want to do is read.*

Chapter Two 3

Four hours later, the eastbound train arrived at precisely the same time as Captain Hunsaker with Nora Powell, her face bleak and her wrists bound. Shocked, Will glanced at Frannie, whose expression mirrored his.

It wasn't lost on Captain Hunsaker, who yanked off his winter cap and slapped his thigh. "Damn it, Captain Wharton, let's see *you* keep her in a wagon against her will!" he shouted, then looked around. Luckily, all the waiting passengers were inside and missed his little scene.

Trust Hunsaker to have no tact at all, Will decided. As senior medical officer at Fort Laramie with some clout over medical events at Camp Robinson, Will had heard plenty from others about Captain Hunsaker's poor bedside manner.

Hunsaker looked to be at the end of his noticeably short tether. "She tried to kill me on the way here! Nora Powell!" He spit the name out like a curse. "She's as savage as those wild Indians at the Spotted Tail Agency!"

Will gave his subordinate the patented frosty stare he had learned from a former commanding officer and which he had further cultivated to great effect in his years on the frontier. "Captain, remember yourself!" he snapped. "You have only a few minutes to get your luggage on the train with Miss Powell."

"Not I," Hunsaker protested.

"Oh, wait a minute," Will started. "I know you have orders to accompany her to...to..."

"To Utley-damn-Iowa! But I won't. It's going to be your job, Wharton." Hunsaker reached inside his over-coat. "Here. From my commanding officer." He stepped back with a triumphant look on his beet-red face.

Will read the official document with a sinking heart. "There is a measles outbreak at Camp Robinson?"

Ed Hunsaker nodded. He knew he had won and began to calm down. "I have to return immediately. She's all yours, Captain." He glanced at Frannie. "And your wife's."

"This is Miss Coughlin. I'm escorting her part way home as a favor to her father, Fort Laramie's hospital steward." Will knew he didn't need to blush over that; it was a common mistake. The post adjutant at nearby Fort Russell had made the same mistake earlier. Did they *look* like a married couple? Will wondered.

Captain Hunsaker glowered at Nora Powell, who glared back. "Just keep her hands tied and turn her over to her relatives," he said. "Good riddance to her and good luck to you!" Without another glance at his bound patient, he climbed back in the wagon, tossed out a bedroll and told the amused private at the reins to spring 'em.

Through it all, Nora Powell had stood quietly beside Frannie Coughlin, probably sensing some protection there, even though Frannie had done nothing more than stand between the captive woman and Captain Hunsaker, who possessed all the social skills of a radish.

Will turned to regard his new burden. "We will make the best of this, Nora," he said. He looked at her bound hands. The rope was tight and her hands bare in the cold. He came a little closer, but not too close, remembering that Indians never liked to feel crowded. She was a white woman, but from the file he had read earlier at Fort Laramie, back when Hunsaker had forwarded the details of her recapture from the Sioux, he knew she had been a captive since 1864. One issue could make this trip better or worse.

"Nora, do you remember English?" he asked. Unlike Hunsaker, he kept his voice low and quiet, because he knew how Indians talked to each other. "Do you?"

After a long moment, which he did not rush, the woman raised her blue eyes to his. She nodded, but was silent.

"Good."

She had small hands. Will took off his fur-lined gloves and gently placed one of them over her bound hands. "I'm going to leave the bonds on you for now," he told her. "Let's get you on the train."

He glanced at Frannie, who smiled at him. It was a peaceful, relieved smile, one he was used to getting from patients—the kind of smile that always made him gulp inside and wonder if they had any idea how little he really knew about anything. His professors at Harvard had never discussed feelings of inadequacy; maybe Harvard yard birds never felt inadequate. Truth to tell, most of his training in compassion had come much earlier from his dear Grandpa Wilkie, a former Royal Navy surgeon and the best man in his young world until Mama had remarried. Of many medical lessons, compassion remained the one he seemed to have learned the best.

He touched Frannie's arm. "See if you can get her seated. Put her by the window. I'll retrieve the bedroll our thoughtful friend from Camp Robinson tossed out."

Frannie nodded and put her hand lightly on Nora Powell's back. Will watched them, reminded all over again how Frannie seemed to have learned the same lessons his grandfather had taught him in Scotland. Something told him that the capable Miss Coughlin hadn't really needed an escort home to New York. Something else told him he was glad to have her along, even if people did think she was his wife.

He watched Frannie help Nora onto the train. Maybe she was susceptible to thought waves, because Frannie looked back at him. She winked at him, which made him smile at her, all the while thinking that his fiancée would walk down a street naked before she would wink at a man.

"Frannie, you're all right," he murmured, before picking up Nora Powell's pitiful bedroll from the slush. He stared down at the little bundle—all of Nora's possessions, except for two children. For one small moment, he thought his heart would break.

Chapter Three

Will handed his government travel documents to a highly dubious conductor. The man frowned at Nora Powell, who was making herself small against the window. Frannie sat next to her, a frown on her own face as she glared back at the conductor.

"She's not an exhibit in a zoo," Frannie whispered to Will as the conductor moved on.

Will seated himself across from the women. Without a word, he removed his glove from Nora's bound hands, then gently rubbed her cold hands with his warmer ones. He remembered when his mother used to put hot potatoes in his pockets and wished he could do something similar for this poor woman.

She started when he touched her, her eyes opening wide and then narrowing into slits. *She's going to bite me,* Will thought, but he kept rubbing her hands. "I'm not here to hurt you, Nora," he told her. "This nice lady is Mary Frances Coughlin, but we call her Frannie."

Frannie nudged her shoulder. "May we call you Nora?" she asked.

Nora nodded and relaxed noticeably, which meant Will could relax, too, and not fear for his fingers. When her hands were warmer, he sat back.

"Nora, I'm a surgeon. I'm on my way home to Philadelphia to get married. Frannie's going to New York. We're…we're going to take you home first."

He watched Nora's eyes as they filled with tears that spilled on to her cheeks. With her bound hands, she grabbed for him. "I want to go home now!" she said.

"That's what we're doing," Will repeated, relieved that she understood.

She had hold of his hand with both of hers. She shook her head. "Home!" she said again, louder. "Home! Not Iowa!"

Will felt the breath go out of him as he understood what she was trying to tell him. "Nora, I have my orders," he said, and it sounded lame and stupid to him. "You're to be returned to your Iowa relatives." He almost added, *It's the best thing,* but another look at her ravaged face told him the folly of that.

As the train left the depot, Nora Powell's soft weeping was drowned out by the hiss of the engine gathering steam and the clatter of the rails. Tears running down her face, she stared out of the window at the snow, the rabbit brush and sage scoured by the wind and the tracks that were taking her farther and farther from the family left behind at the Spotted Tail Agency.

Will was a competent surgeon, well trained and scientific in the best way he knew. As he listened to Nora's tears and watched the concern in Frannie Coughlin's eyes, he knew he was being measured and found woefully scant by some cosmic tribunal that he hoped wasn't the mind of God.

I have worries of my own, he told himself, thinking about Maddy and her boring letters, each more shallow than the last, as she went over every tiny detail of their upcoming nuptials. Did she honestly think he was interested in how many rosettes there would be on each bridesmaid's bodice? It was easy enough to read her silly letters and laugh them off, as he remembered her lovely face and breathy way of talking. Sitting across from real pain, he wondered at his own shallow character.

"I wish it were different," he murmured to Frannie.

"So do I," she whispered back.

He stared at Nora's bound hands, knowing what his mother would do, she who had worked for years to smooth the way for immigrants and the poor. She often spoke to him about her work, but he knew this had never involved Indians, and most assuredly not Indian captives who wanted to stay with their half-Indian children. He still knew what she would do.

"Nora, look at me," he said, in what he called his surgeon's voice, the one he relied on to get attention when he needed it.

She raised her eyes to his and he steeled himself against so much pain on one face. "Nora, I want to cut the bonds on your hands, but you have to promise me you won't try to escape."

She just stared at him, her face as impassive now as though she truly were Sioux.

"I mean it, Nora. If I cut the bonds and you escape, you won't get far."

A stubborn light came into her eyes, one he had seen

before, mostly on the face of mothers, who surely were the most tenacious creatures on earth. He swallowed, remembering a mother who had leaped through fire to snatch her child from a burning wagon when the regiment was set upon by Apaches in Arizona Territory. Neither had survived, but Will had never thought survival was on her mind when she plunged into the flames.

Maybe he could do better this time. "You might escape me, but look out of the window. It's snowing again and it's cold and you won't make it alive to Spotted Tail Agency. You're too far away."

He let her digest that fact, gazing out of the window, too, as dusk settled in. "Promise me, Nora," he said, a few minutes later. "I don't want to leave you bound because you're not a criminal. You're a mother who wants to go home. Let's find a better way."

Why he said that, he had no idea. "Maybe your relatives can help," he suggested, wishing it didn't sound so feeble. He continued his idiocy. "There are lawyers in Nebraska and Iowa."

Heavens! You're an imbecile, to talk about lawyers! he thought, disgusted with himself. He stopped, remembering other cases he had heard, where captive women had been returned to their families. He had heard tales and none of them had happy endings. And here he was, babbling about lawyers. He didn't even know if Nora Powell's relatives would show up to reclaim a tainted woman, much less advance one penny toward reclaiming her children.

"Or maybe they won't help you," he heard himself saying next. "I won't lie to you, Nora."

More silence.

"I just don't want you to run away, because you won't get where you want to be," he said simply. "That's what it comes down to. I don't want you to freeze to death. I'm trained to help people, but I can't if you escape."

After a long moment, Nora edged closer to the front of the seat and held out her bound wrists. "I won't escape," she said. "At least not now."

A glance at her face told him that was the best promise he was going to get today. "Very well." He took out his pocketknife and cut the cords.

Before he drew another breath, Nora had yanked the pocketknife from his hand. He watched, mouth open, as she looked at the knife, at him, then folded the knife and handed it back. "You should be more careful," she said simply. She sat back, leaned against the window and closed her eyes.

Will stared at her and then at Frannie, whose eyes were wide. Without a word, she moved away from Nora and sat next to him. Equally silent, Will put his arm around her, drawing her close for no discernible reason that filtered through his brain, except that he suddenly felt cold and she looked warm.

"I'm a fool," he said finally. "She could have killed me."

Frannie moved a little in his embrace and he let go of her, his face red. In another moment, Frannie had resumed her seat next to Nora. "You're no fool, Captain Wharton," she said, her voice quiet. "I think she trusts you to help her."

How am I going to do that? he thought, more miserable than before. "Frannie, all I'm trying to do is get home for Christmas and get married." Disgusted with himself again, he wondered if he had ever uttered a more imbecilic sentence in his life. He shook his head. "What a whiner I am," he admitted.

Frannie merely smiled. "Your secret is safe with me. Hopefully, your fiancée will marry you anyway."

282
222

60

60

Chapter Four

As the car grew darker, Will thought about Frannie's words, meant in jest, he was certain, but striking closer to the bone than Paddy Coughlin's daughter knew. He closed his eyes, thinking, not for the first time, that he was having trouble remembering what Madeline Radnor looked like. *I'm a beast,* he thought, but he knew he wasn't. True, he had a bad habit of leaving his dirty laundry on convenient doorknobs and apple cores here and there, but he never got so drunk that he couldn't remember where he was, or who was president of the United States.

He opened his eyes and looked at Frannie Coughlin, who was watching Nora Powell. He observed her carefully, seeing the concern in those lovely green eyes. He observed her reaching into her large and shabby carpetbag and pulling out a lap blanket. She draped it over Nora's slight frame. When the woman started, Frannie touched her shoulder and soothed her back to sleep.

Will asked himself if this scene would be different if Maddy were on the train and was suddenly pitchforked into caring for an Indian captive with two half-Indian children left behind somewhere on a reservation. He might wish his future wife would show compassion for a poor soul so decidedly beneath her, but he couldn't help doubting that Maddy Wharton would be any different from Maddy Radnor, Main Line debutante.

He probably wasn't being fair to his fiancée, considering that he hadn't seen her in two years, and there was every possibility that she had matured into someone who would embrace his decidedly unaristocratic life in the U.S. Army. In reality, though, her recent letters had more than hinted how nice it would be if he would resign his commission and set up a practice in a better part of Philadelphia, or in one of the affluent towns along the Main Line.

She wants me to specialize in diseases of the rich, Will had even written to his father in the last letter. Maybe he and Papa would have a moment to talk about the matter before the wedding and laugh it off as the stuff of cold feet.

He was already dreading his future wife's first look at his army quarters. As a post surgeon, he had more room than most officers his own age—four rooms, in fact—but he knew the size of the Radnor manor, situated across the street from his own Philadelphia home. Their future bedchamber at Fort Laramie was half the size of his parents' linen closet.

And there was the matter of servants. Before he had left Fort Laramie, he had cajoled a corporal's wife into promising to give his quarters a cleaning every week or so. Maddy had said she was bringing along a cook

and her personal maid. He hadn't the heart to tell her
that even if they were more than usually homely looking, the two would probably be married in a month or
less, sergeants and corporals being what they are in a
female-starved society.

"Captain?"

Startled, he looked up at Frannie, who was giving
him the same compassionate appraisal she had lavished
on Nora Powell.

"Yes, Frannie?" he asked, hoping he hadn't been
looking like a total no-hoper, rather than the capable,
unflappable, maybe even charming officer and gentleman he tried to be.

"You just looked a little dismal," she said.

"I feel dismal."

Frannie sighed and glanced at Nora. "She's in a tough
situation."

Will blushed, grateful for the gathering dusk and
hoping that Frannie Coughlin would never know that
he had been thinking of himself and not the Indian
captive. "And I had to go and promise her lawyers," he
whispered.

He was saved by the bell, the three-toned tinkle that
announced dinner was soon to be served in the dining
car. "When I get dismal, I eat," he announced to Frannie
and Nora, who had opened her eyes at the sound of the
bells. "Let's go."

Frannie shook her head. "I usually just wait until the
candy butcher walks through the car, so I can inspect
his sandwiches. I'm on a bit of a budget and I have to
get all the way to Brooklyn."

He appreciated her honesty and reminded himself

that the teachers of soldiers' children probably weren't in the top salary rung at any army post.

"I never eat alone, ladies," Will announced. "Let this be my treat."

"That's a lot of money, Captain," Frannie said, doubt high in her voice.

How to explain to this frugal miss, daughter of a hospital steward, that he was thrifty by choice, despite being buttressed by the Wharton fortune? For a fleeting moment, he wondered how his stepfather had ever explained the same thing to his mother, before they were married in 1856. It always struck him as ironic that his stepfather's branch of the Whartons was stuffed to the gullet with banking money, but they never talked about it.

"Frannie, I have enough. You know there is nothing to spend money on at Fort Laramie," he told her. "We're going to eat right on this train."

He knew he didn't have a stern face. He knew he could fake one when he had to. He gave Frannie The Glance. She saw right through him, but agreed to accompany him to the dining car. "We'll spend his money, won't we, Nora?" she said to the other woman and took her hand, so that she had no choice.

Dinner was mostly an unalloyed pleasure. Will watched Frannie studying the menu, a frown on her face, as she looked for the least expensive items. He watched her trying to gather her courage to tell him it was all too dear.

"Miss Coughlin," he began, which made her laugh, considering he hadn't called her that in an entire year. "Miss Coughlin, I'd be honored if you and Miss

Powell—" to his delight, he even coaxed a twitch of the lip from Nora "—will let me order for you. I'm a real connoisseur of Union Pacific grub."

It was "grub" that did it. Frannie laughed out loud, let go of the menu and said, "I surrender, Captain!"

She folded her hands in her lap. Will grinned at her with real affection, thinking of all the times she had helped him in the hospital simply by being there to read to his patients. He had never been able to show her any true gratitude before now.

He picked up the menu and caught the waiter's eye "We'll start with the purée of chicken soup, and follow it with rib ends of beef and browned potatoes." He looked over the elaborate menu to the two women seated across from him. "Unless either of you is partial to mutton and then I would give you my sympathies. No?"

He felt only relief when Nora smiled. "Well, then, no sheep for us. We can chase the rib ends down with lamb pie, *à la anglaise,* then clear our palates with olives and celery, before we charge ahead."

Both of the women were smiling now. Satisfied, he cleared his throat elaborately and returned to the menu. "Aha!" He stabbed the paper. "Here I see squash, green corn—heavens—green peas or beets. No beets, ladies—I forbid it. People who eat beets would probably drink their own bathwater."

Frannie laughed, which pleased him to no end. She had a hearty belly laugh, the kind that would send Maddy fleeing to another room. Nora laughed, too, then looked around, as if she wondered who had done that.

Will grinned at them both. "Green peas? Wise choice. Now let's take this dinner home with pumpkin pie and ice cream. Tea or coffee?" They agreed on tea and Will handed back the menu with a flourish that even made the waiter smile.

The Union Pacific did its usual best with the dinner he had chosen, but Will could have been eating ash cakes, for all he tasted it. His pleasure lay in watching Nora Powell work her way through every course with a single-minded intensity that told him worlds about her usual bill of fare. The ice cream on the pie made her eyes widen. "It's been years," she whispered. She savored a tiny bite, then a larger one, before she set down her spoon. "I wish I could share this with my children," she said, looking at the bounty in front of her, her face suddenly serious.

Please, don't let her cry, Will thought. Without hesitation, he launched into a vivid description of his first Christmas in Philadelphia after they had moved from Scotland, with strange food and customs, and his own fears of newly found cousins laughing at his thick Scottish brogue. "My stepfather swore he could only understand one word in ten," he told his little audience, then launched into his best Dumfries dialect.

To his relief, Nora smiled at his antics; so did the children at the table across the aisle. He glanced at Frannie, who watched him with an expression he could not interpret, and held his breath until Nora picked up her spoon again.

The waiter brought the bill when they had finished. "Captain, is she the Indian captive?" the waiter whispered as Will paid the bill.

"How did you know?"

"Not many secrets on a train, sir," was all the waiter

would say. He watched Nora leave the car with Frannie, then shook his head. "I'd rightly hate to be in her shoes."

"You're right," Will told him. "I'd hate to be in her shoes, too."

He let the women go ahead, standing a long moment in the space between the two cars, balancing easily as the train clacked its steady course across Nebraska. Hands in his pockets, he watched through the glass as Frannie settled Nora down again and put her arm around the woman, who seemed to be crying. Frannie drew her close, both arms around her then.

"Frannie, you're a woman in a million," he said out loud, and watched them until the cold penetrated his uniform and he was forced to enter the warm carriage.

Chapter Five

Will thought about Frannie as he stared at the medical journal in his hands. For several months, he had looked forward to this opportunity to read his back issues and think about nothing more strenuous than necrotic tissue and third-stage syphilis. When Paddy Coughlin had asked him to keep an eye on Frannie, he'd known she would be no trouble. He'd known he would still have time to read his journals.

Then Nora Powell had been thrown into the mix. Now he felt the full weight of her distress descending on him; he knew he had to do better. He closed the journal, not even bothering to mark his place. Duty called, but it was more than that.

He cleared his throat, wondering if he was about to blunder, but driven to ask by something his mother had told him once about the need for people in grief to talk, something her first husband's family had never allowed. "Nora, tell me about your children and your husband."

He thought he had made the mistake of the century

when Nora's eyes filled with tears. He held his breath as she dabbed at her eyes with her fingers, then looked at him. "You are the first Blue Coat to call him my husband," she said.

"He is, isn't he?" Will asked, startled. "Did he seek you out and throw the robe over you at a dance?" He had seen courting dances before, when he visited a Cheyenne tribe troubled with influenza. He thought them charming and certainly more fun than filling out a dance card. Plains Indians were worlds more practical than gentlemen making stupid small talk at a cotillion and hoping for a waltz.

He must have unleashed a flood. Nora leaned forward, her tears forgotten. She nodded and he suddenly saw the pretty woman under all the cares, hunger and devastation. "I had been watching him, too," she said, her voice shy.

"A handsome man is always worth a look," Frannie put in. "Is he handsome?"

Nora was silent a long moment. "He was."

"Oh," Will said, feeling stupid. He saw his mother's face in his mind, then, and remembered how gently she could counsel. "Where did he die, Nora? How did it happen?"

"We call it the Greasy Grass. I think you Blue Coats called it the Little Big Horn. Crazy Horse told me later that my husband was counting coup on a soldier when it happened." She raised her head proudly. "Thank you for mentioning him. He was a warrior."

"Then it is good to remember him," Will said, on sure ground now, because his mother was right. "Tell us about your children."

"Little Frog is eight summers. He is tall for his age.

My daughter does not have a name. She was born after the Greasy Grass and I was too sad to name her."

"Will...will someone else name her?" he asked, touched to see tears in Frannie's eyes. He swallowed a boulder in his throat.

"I do not know," Nora replied, after another long silence. "I do not even know who is watching after them. My husband is dead. His parents are dead. There was only me."

She said no more, turning her face to look out at the darkness. Will put away his medical journal, no longer interested in science when a greater tragedy loomed in front of him. *Heavens, what have we done?* he asked himself, unable to sit any longer. Not looking back at the women, he walked through two cars to reach the last platform. The first was a car like the one he had left, the other an immigrant car, with wall-to-wall people, babies crying, children milling about and food cooking. He breathed in the odors of cabbage, strange spices and unwashed bodies.

It was too cold for company on the platform. His mood lifted and he smiled to see a small clothesline, diapers flapping in the frigid air, turning into boards. As the train curved slightly north, he looked west, wondering where in that vast distance Nora's children were. He thought about Maddy, who had never known a hard thing in her life, and then Frannie, with her frugal plans to avoid the dining car. And here was Nora, wrenched from her children and heading toward who knew what.

And here I am, rich, educated and coming up short, he thought, not so much disgusted as sorry that the world wasn't fairer. Frannie should have a kind husband and a comfortable life, and Nora should have her children.

Cold, he leaned on the railing, driven by some idiocy to punish himself because he was blessed and they were not. He had no answers, so he went inside again, walking slowly through the immigrant car, observing out of habit.

He smiled at the children who gazed back, solemn. *New beginnings,* he thought, remembering Mama's immigrants at the community house, which his step-father's money had created in Philadelphia for people in need. As he walked, Will noticed a solitary female, barely more than a child herself, who appeared far gone in pregnancy. He never did understand people's instincts, because she gave him that patient look he had seen many times, when people thought he was a doctor and capable, in their minds, of making the lame walk and the dead rise. *I wish,* he thought. *I wish. Sometimes I can barely help myself.*

He nodded to her and continued through the car. He was nearly to the next car when he stopped, listening to labored breathing from a small boy leaning against his mother. All business then, Will crouched beside them, putting two fingers on the child's throat to find a thready pulse.

The woman eyed him with suspicion. He smiled at her and said, "I'm a physician." She only gathered her child closer.

Will looked around. "Does anyone speak English?" he asked, resisting the urge to raise his voice and speak more slowly, on the off chance that it would make a difference. He tried the same statement in poor French, passable Spanish, then slightly better German. Nothing. He stood up and left the car in a hurry.

Back in his own car, he rummaged under the seat for his medical bag.

"What's wrong?" Frannie asked.

"There's a child with lung congestion in the immigrant car," he told her, looking inside the bag, even though he knew everything was in its place. "Maybe I can help."

"Do you need me?"

The oddest thing happened then, as though the earth's axis had suddenly tilted. Maybe it was the way she asked—sincere and earnest and ready to help. Or maybe he had been taking her for granted all year, coming to rely on her because she was utterly sensible, perfectly kind and so lovely.

Do I need you? he asked himself. *Goodness, I believe I do.*

Will took a deep breath; the impulse simply had to pass. Maybe the bad air in the immigrant car had affected his brain. He was on his way to Philadelphia to marry a beautiful woman he had known since he was twelve. All the plans had been made. He shook his head to clear it.

"Are...are you all right, Captain?" she asked.

"I'm fine," he lied. "This shouldn't take more than a few minutes. You keep Nora company." He snapped his bag shut and hurried from the car.

His unsuspecting patient was still leaning against his mother. The wary look on her face vanished when Will took out his stethoscope. She offered no objection when he raised her son's shirt and listened to his chest.

Will concentrated on the sounds within, grateful not

to hear the crackling noise of pneumonia, but still not happy about the congestion. "I wish you could understand me," he said to the mother, who was looking at him intently now, as if trying to understand English.

"I can help."

Will looked around to see another worn traveler, dressed no better than the others and certainly smelling no better. "You speak English," he said with relief.

"Not much."

Will touched the sick boy, who had closed his eyes. "What language do they speak?"

"Russian." The man gestured more grandly. "Russians. Serbs. Some Greeks. A Pole or two. Latvians. Italians." He turned a kind eye on Will. "What can I do?"

Will looked at the pot-board stove, where a woman in a scarf and quilted jacket was boiling cabbage. The steam rose off the odoriferous pot, fogging the window. "Can you tell her to take her son close to the steam? He needs to breathe moist air." Will pantomimed breathing deep and motioned toward the boiling cabbage. "She needs to keep him warmer."

The man nodded, then spoke to the woman, who stood up immediately and took her son closer to the stove. Will moved her even closer, while his translator spoke to the others. In another moment, there was a second blanket around the child.

"Just keep him there. I will come back later to check on him," Will said.

When the Russian finished translating, Will stood there a moment longer, wishing he had a croup tent and the ingredients for a poultice. He walked through the car again, looking more closely at the immigrants. It suddenly seemed strange to him that they would be traveling east. Surely they had not come from the Pacific Ocean.

Curious, he found the conductor in the next car, talking to a salesman. When the conductor had finished his conversation, he looked at Will. "Everything all right in there, sir?" he asked.

"Well enough. There's a sick child, but I will check him again later. I was wondering, why are they heading east? I thought all immigrants went the other way."

"They overshot their destination," the conductor said. "It happens now and then with immigrant cars." He sighed the great sigh of the put-upon. "A few immigrants will miss their stops, or find no one waiting for them. We take them to Omaha, where hopefully they are straightened out." He shrugged. "Foreigners."

Will returned to his own car to see the porters at work converting the seats into upper and lower sleeping berths, with discreet privacy curtains. Frannie and Nora stood in the aisle, waiting for the porter to finish. Will handed him some coins when the porter had plumped up the final pillow.

"Nora and I will take the top berth," Frannie said. "You should be more accessible, in case the little boy needs you." She smiled at him. "It never ends, does it? My father mentioned to me that you had been planning to do lots of reading on this trip. Are we a great deal of trouble?"

"You have never been trouble," he assured her. "Did I ever thank you for all those hours you spent in the hospital, reading to my motley collection of malingerers, malcontents and misfits, better known as the U.S. Army?"

She laughed, reminding him all over again how much he enjoyed a hearty laugh from a woman. "Captain, if you had wanted an easier life, you would have stayed in Philadelphia."

"That's what my fiancée wants me to do," he said impulsively. He regretted his words the moment they left his mouth, because they sounded disloyal to Maddy and branded him as a complainer.

Frannie looked him in the eye; she was a tall woman and it wasn't hard. "Your malingerers will miss you, if you resign your commission. So will my father." She hesitated. "I will, too."

She blushed then and turned her attention to Nora Powell, who seemed to wilt before their eyes. "Nora, let us go to bed." She put her arm around the smaller woman. "Tell me you won't mind if I put my cold feet on your legs?"

I'd rather you put them on mine, Will thought, as he turned away, so the women could climb the ladder to the upper berth without his observation. A quick glance—he told himself it was a professional one—reassured him when Nora managed a smile at Frannie's gentle teasing. Such a glance also allowed him a glimpse of Frannie's trim ankles, his real object, he admitted to himself.

He took off his shoes and lay down in the lower berth, yawning, but keeping the curtains open so he could at least try to read another few pages in the medical journal. For the first time in his long medical life, the subject matter defeated him. He closed the journal again and lay on his back, his heart touched as he heard Frannie humming to Nora. He listened closer; it was "Silent

Night," which reminded him belatedly that Christmas was almost upon them.

His eyes closed. He wondered if he should visit the immigrant car one more time, but decided it could wait. Besides, all he wanted to do was think about Frannie.

282
238
44

Chapter Six

Will must have slept then, because someone shook him awake. As his eyes became accustomed to the night-time gloom of the rail car, he saw the conductor.

"The boy?" Will asked, already reaching for his shoes.

"No. It's worse. Hurry."

Will tied his shoes and tucked in his shirt. He pulled on his uniform jacket, but didn't bother to button it. As he stood up in the aisle and ran his hand through his hair, the curtains in the upper berth parted and Frannie leaned out.

"Do you need me?"

"I'm not sure," he whispered back. "If I do, I'll send the conductor for you. Is Nora asleep?"

"Yes."

She reached out and touched his shoulder, which made him smile in the gloom.

Stepping quietly through the next car, he followed the conductor into the immigrant car and stopped, his eyes wide at the sight of the pregnant woman struggling in labor as everyone watched and did nothing.

I should have checked her earlier, he thought, kneeling beside her. He pulled out his stethoscope and listened for her heartbeat. It was faint and he knew exactly what the outcome would be, even before he touched her distended abdomen.

He looked around for the conductor, who stared at the woman. "Help me get her to the floor."

The man did as he asked, then motioned everyone to move back and turn around, for privacy's sake. "I'll see if I can find out who she is," he said.

Will nodded, his eyes on his patient. Moving his hand over the woman's tight abdomen, he felt how far down the baby was, and rested his hand until he felt returning movement. The woman tried to raise her hand to his, but she hadn't the strength. Gently, he touched her face, then opened one barely shuttered eye, which was already starting to settle in her head.

"No one knows who she is," the conductor whispered when he returned and knelt beside Will. "Damned foreigners! They think she's Greek, but no one knows when she got on the car. She was alone."

"Doesn't matter now," Will said. "She's unresponsive and hasn't long." He took hold of the conductor's sleeve. "Get me some blankets, sheets and towels, and whatever you can find that's absorbent."

The conductor started to rise. Will tugged him down again. "Wake up Miss Coughlin in the berth over mine and tell her I need her immediately. Go now."

Railcar, battlefield or hospital, Will did what he always did, as the conductor hurried into the next car. He folded his hands in front of him, closed his eyes and

prayed. It was the quick, all-purpose prayer he reserved
for extreme emergency, and amounted to no more than
"Help me, Almighty God." He figured that, in some
form or other, healers from Hippocrates down to this
captain kneeling on the floor in an immigrant car had
asked as much and more throughout history, whether
from one god, three or ten.

When he opened his eyes, his brain was clear.
Quickly, he took out his small capital-knife kit and
spread it beside him on the floor, while the woman
grunted and moaned, trying to expel a baby that
couldn't be dislodged without assistance.

He felt a rush of cold air as the door opened. Frannie
knelt beside him, still in her nightgown. Unbidden, she
put her hands on the woman's face, stroking it, then
wiping the sweat with the sleeve of her nightgown. She
looked at Will, her eyes wide.

Will put his lips next to her ear. "Her heart is about
to give out. Frannie, she's dying."

"What do you want me to do?" she whispered back,
no hesitation in her voice and no fear. Will was so
relieved he could have kissed her.

"It's going to be ugly," he whispered back. "When
she breathes her last, I'm going for the baby. I'll have
to work fast. It'll look like butchery, because it is."

Frannie gulped and nodded. Even in the dim light,
Will saw how pale her face was and how every wonderful freckle stood out. "Just explain what you want. I'll
do...do my best."

"I knew you would," he told her, looking around at
another gust of cold air. His arms full of blankets, sheets
and towels, the conductor came back into the immigrant
car. Will directed him to tear a sheet in half and tie one

half around Frannie's neck. "Tie the other one around my neck." He looked at the conductor. "What's your name?"

"Joseph Pyle," the man said.

"Pleased to meet you," Will said. "Just keep everyone back. Hold up a blanket and face out. You don't want to see this."

Pyle gave him no argument. He turned around and held out the blanket, while Will explained to Frannie what would happen. "There's no time to apply retractors. I need your hands."

Frannie drew a deep breath, then made a small sign of the cross on the dying woman's forehead. She raised up and kissed his cheek. "Not quite the Christmas journey you envisioned, eh?" she asked.

He couldn't answer, because the laboring woman breathed her last. For the next minute he saw nothing but the task on the floor in front of him. Frannie did exactly as he ordered, not faltering when everything turned red. Above the sound of the train, he could hear her reciting the Rosary, something he was familiar with. He mouthed the words along with her as he cut, searched and pulled out a living child.

He was aware of another gust of cold air and saw Nora Powell out of the corner of his eye. She held out her hands for the baby. Gratefully, he deposited the child in her arms and quickly suctioned out the unresponsive infant's mouth. One second. Two seconds, then three, and the newborn cried.

Will sighed and breathed in and out until he was calm again. He removed Frannie's hands from her grip on the woman's ruined abdomen, placed them in her lap and wiped them. It was his turn to kiss her cheek and whisper, "Magnificent," in her ear.

With Nora's silent help, he cut the connection between the dead woman and her daughter, who was crying lustily now, a small and welcome sound in the quiet railcar. He didn't need to tell Nora what to do then, as she wiped off the baby and wrapped her expertly, papoose-style, in a strip of clean sheet. She wrapped the baby next in a towel and sat back, holding the infant close.

Frannie remained calm, arranging the dead mother's hair as he stitched her together, then wound her tight in a shroud of sheet. Together they rolled her onto a blanket. He had begun wrapping it around her, too, when Frannie stopped him with a hand on his arm.

"One moment," she said. "Let us look at her."

Will did as she asked, putting his arm around Frannie's shoulder as Paddy Coughlin's capable daughter prayed again. He knew the prayer and prayed with her. None of Trey Wharton's Episcopal leanings had made much of an impact on him, on Scottish boy Wilkie Nicholls, who had gone to Mass with dear Grandma Laura Ortiz Wilkie in Dumfries's tiny Catholic church.

"I didn't know you were Catholic," Frannie said, when she finished and he continued his work of wrapping the blanket around the Greek woman.

"It was a condition of my grandmother's priest in Alta California, when she married my grandfather," he explained, happy and relieved to have a normal conversation after the horror of his surgery. "Sometimes I need reminding."

"Maybe not so much after tonight?"

"Maybe not so much."

* * *

Under Will's instructions, the conductor and the helpful Russian translator carried the body to the ice-cold baggage car. "We'll be in Omaha in mid-morning," Pyle said, looking at his watch. "The Union Pacific will assume responsibility for the body and she'll be buried somewhere." He shook his head. "We'll try to find her relatives, but no one seems to know her name, or even when she came aboard."

Will watched Frannie, who was holding the baby now, crooning to it, breathing deep of that peculiar newborn fragrance. The conductor touched the baby's head, with its still-damp, dark curls, and Frannie stepped back, as though to ward him off.

"We'll take the baby, too, and find an orphanage," the conductor said. "Don't you get too attached, or anything!" he told Frannie.

Will could tell he was trying to make light of a devastating situation, but all Frannie did was frown at him and turn away. She started toward the sleeping compartment again, Nora walking beside her. Will watched them, gratified when Nora's arm went around Frannie's waist, sisters in a ritual that man had no part of. He wasn't unhappy with either of them.

"We'll see," he told the conductor.

"Your missus is taking a shine to that little one," the man said. "Better watch out."

My missus. Will thought about that later, as he sat in the dining car. The conductor had found a convenient bottle of single malt scotch. "No one will miss this," Pyle said as he poured them both a stiff one. He also set down a can of condensed milk and a bottle of warm sterilized water. "We're missing a key ingredient," he said, as he downed his scotch and filled the glass again. "A nipple."

"I have an eyedropper in my bag that will do until we find something better in Omaha," Will said. He sipped his scotch slowly, trying to get the iron taste and smell of blood from his system. This was no different from many another surgery, some under even less sanitary conditions, but there was something so wrenching about that poor woman dying anonymously, never to know her beautiful daughter.

Another swallow and he was done; better to stop while he was still rational. He thanked the conductor and took the canned milk and water back to his own berth, where, to his surprise but not his disappoint-ment, Frannie had curled up around the baby. They were asleep and he admired them both. Despite her rough arrival on a cold December, yanked from her dead mother, the infant seemed none the worse for wear.

"I'm going to name you Olympia," he said softly, touching her black hair. "Surely the gods were smiling on you tonight."

He stood up and opened the curtain to the upper berth. Nora Powell slept soundly, her hand opened and relaxed, which relieved him, somehow. He sat on his berth again and gave Frannie a nudge. She opened her eyes, but offered no objection when he pulled his blan-ket over her and the baby.

With a sigh, Will took off his shoes. He debated a long moment, then shook his head and removed his trousers and uniform jacket, draping them across the end of the bed. Frannie could call him a cad if she wanted, but he was too tired to care. *My missus.* He lay down, hoping the scotch had mellowed his brain enough to allow sleep.

He was almost asleep when Frannie touched his face. He kissed her fingers impulsively, waited for a slap that never came, then slept.

Chapter Seven

Olympia woke up a few hours later, making little mewing sounds practically in his ear, until he realized that, at some point in their slumber, he had wrapped his arm around Frannie and she was close to his chest, the baby nestled against his neck and hers.

Will lay there with Frannie and Olympia in his arms, enjoying her newborn fragrance. Medicine could often be a smelly proposition the deeper one delved, but newborns always compensated, with that unique fragrance.

"Frannie, Olympia is hungry," he whispered finally.

Frannie stretched and snuggled closer, her eyes still closed. She opened them wide a second later, when she realized where she was. "I should apologize," she began, then stopped. "No. This seemed like a good idea a few hours ago and it still does. Call me common."

"You're not," he replied. "I could have gone back to the dining room and finished that bottle of Scotch—oh, believe me, I could have. But I didn't want to."

Frannie sat up in the berth with Olympia in her arms,

which had the effect of pulling the blankets off his body. Will grabbed for them, shrugged and reached for his trousers instead. "Don't mind me," he murmured, as he buttoned up.

"You called her Olympia," Frannie said. "Goodness, when did you name her?"

"A few hours ago, when the two of you were sleeping," he said as he pulled on his uniform jacket. "The gods were smiling."

Frannie grinned at him. "And you were a little tiddly." She kissed the baby. "It's a good name for a Greek goddess, which she is. I like it." And then she was all business. "What are we going to do about the menu?"

He had done this before. In a minute he had mixed some of the condensed milk with the boiled water. While Frannie changed Olympia's diaper—a napkin from the dining car—he found the kitchen, corralled a yawning cook and soon had the milk lukewarm in a pan of water.

The two of them sat cross-legged and knee to knee in his berth—Olympia squalling now—and he used the eye dropper. "Put your little finger in her mouth while I drip in the milk," Will said. "I want her to learn about her sucking reflex. This will work until we find a baby bottle." *Maybe we'll find an orphanage, too,* he thought, then dismissed the idea at once. He didn't find it appealing. He could think about it later.

Frannie's doubts about the procedure amused Will, who knew by experience not to underestimate a hungry baby, even one as new as the little morsel in her arms. She relaxed as Olympia quickly adapted to the situation, then nudged Will with her bare foot.

"I think you're pretty good, Captain," she whispered.

He noticed Olympia's squirms and picked her up from Frannie's arms, putting her face near his shoulder as he patted her back. The reward was a substantial burp, which startled Olympia and made Frannie chuckle.

"You know, Frannie, under the circumstances, perhaps you could call me Will," he suggested.

The car was getting lighter. He could see her face plainly as she gave him a measuring appraisal. "Under the circumstances? Will, it is," she told him. "And do you know something? I prefer Francie. My brothers call me that."

"Francie, it is," he told her as he handed back Olympia and filled the eye dropper again. They continued feeding the baby, Francie's head close to his. When Olympia began to squirm this time, she put the baby to her shoulder and rubbed her back until the burp came.

Worn out with her efforts and by her full stomach, the infant slept, nestling her dark head into the hollow of Francie's shoulder. Francie kissed the baby and heaved a small sigh that sounded to Will like perfect satisfaction.

"Too much of that and you'll find yourself unable to let her go," Will said.

"And you think I haven't already succumbed?" Francie asked, her voice suddenly as serious as his own. "Will, you're not as bright as I thought."

"That probably isn't hard to imagine," he replied. "I could sit here and think about all the ways I could have changed the outcome of that hambone surgery. I could have taken a closer look at her when I went through the immigrant car earlier. I could have…"

He stopped, because Francie had put her finger to

his lips and then leaned forward and kissed them. He couldn't think of a single objection and kissed her back. Since Olympia was balanced between them, he steadied himself with a hand on Francie's knee. When they finished kissing, he left his hand where it was.

"My da says you have a bad habit of doing that," she murmured, her lips still close to his.

"Francie, I've never kissed your father."

She laughed softly and flicked his cheek with her fingernail. "You *know* what I mean! Da says you berate yourself every time someone dies, and pace around your office and mutter to yourself and second-guess." She lightly touched her forehead to his.

"All surgeons do that," he said in his defense. His hand was still on her knee. He felt his whole body growing warmer, which was welcoming, because he felt as though he had been cold for years.

"I doubt Captain Hunsaker second-guesses himself," she retorted.

"Maybe not all."

He didn't try to stop himself. He moved his hand under her nightgown, until he touched the soft hair between her legs.

"Just a minute."

Embarrassed, Will started to leave the berth, but she stopped him. "Just a minute, I said," she repeated, as she handed him the sleeping baby. She opened her valise on the floor and folded in a tablecloth he had borrowed from the dining car, making it a sheet. She took Olympia from him and set the sleeping infant in the open valise, tucking it partly under the lower berth, where it was firmly anchored.

After closing the curtains around them, she sat on

the lower berth and pulled her nightgown over her head. Without a word, Will pulled back the blanket again and removed his trousers. The uniform jacket was already off and getting wrinkled—where, he didn't much care.

"Are you sure about this, Francie?" he whispered.

She nodded. "Remember last night when Nora told you about her husband covering her with a blanket at the dance? You've now done that twice to me."

"Francie, that was…"

"Different? Tell me how some time, but not now, Will. I need you."

"Ditto here." He pulled the blanket over them without another word.

Chapter Eight

Will had occasionally fantasized about making love on a train. There was something pleasantly stimulating about the rhythmic clatter of the wheels that had appealed to the sybarite in his nature.

As he began to explore Francie's abundant curves, he tried to tell whatever part of his brain might still be rational that this was a supremely bad idea. This embarrassment of riches was his hospital steward's daughter, for goodness' sake. He explored Francie's breasts with his hand and then his lips, as he reminded himself that it was getting light; that the conductor knew where his berth was and could fling open the curtains with another medical emergency; that he was about one week away from marrying a beautiful lady who loved him.

None of his puny admonitions had the smallest effect on his body. If Francie had any similar objections, they weren't registering with her, either, from the eager way she touched him and kissed him more thoroughly than he had ever been kissed in his life. He knew he should have been gentlemanly enough to assure her that he would be gentle—on the chance—and what did he know?—that she was a virgin—but he didn't. Just as well, because he wasn't gentle.

With a sigh, Francie happily accommodated his rather assertive entrance into her body—good grief, where were his manners? She pressed against his back with her hands and heels as they both discovered that train rhythm was amazingly erotic: a satisfactory conclusion to his scientific experiment. He gathered her close, relishing every thrust and parry and holding himself off until she climaxed once and then again only delirious seconds later. She pressed her lips against his neck to keep herself from letting the entire train car hear her approval of what the two of them had just so energetically wrought, courtesy of biology and the Union Pacific Railroad.

If she could be so restrained, so could he. Will groaned into her ear when his own turn came, which only made Francie tighten her grip on him and unleash herself again. Man of science that he was, Captain Will Wharton, post surgeon, had no inkling that the average woman in 1877 was so talented.

But enough was surely enough, especially when the porter came through the car, sounding his summons to breakfast and announcing an arrival in Omaha in one hour. He knew he should be a kind fellow and unlimber himself from Francie's charms, but for the life of him, he had no urge to find the exit. Besides, she was still twining her legs around his—who knew that a gentle hand running up and down his back would be so soothing? Every single care he had boarded the train with in Cheyenne had flown away; he was jelly.

Francie shifted first, so he reluctantly did the polite thing and moved. She was all business for a moment, finding a cloth for him and her, probably the handful of napkins that he knew he would never, ever return to the dining car. And then she curled close to him, so they lay together as one. It was his turn to sigh and pull her closer, as she flung one leg over his loins as though she owned him. Maybe she did. He rested his hand on her head, massaging her scalp.

Someone had to say something, and again Francie was way ahead. "I'm not a virgin," she whispered. "It's been a while, though."

He had no trouble saying the right thing. "I'm not, either," he whispered back, "and ditto on the chronology."

She kissed his chest. "At the end of the war, I became engaged to Jemmy Doyle, sergeant in the Irish Brigade. Everyone knew the war was over. It was only a matter of time, and then we'd be married, so why wait?"

Francie was silent then, and he gently pulled her even closer. "It happens, Francie."

"I know." He sensed her great sorrow, mellow now, but evident. "Jemmy died at the battle of Sayler's Creek, right before Appomattox. That was twelve years ago."

"I'm sorry," he said and kissed her forehead.

"So was I." Another sigh. "Will you think me strange if I was sorry there was no child? I loved Jemmy Doyle."

And I love you now, he thought, beguiled with the knowledge that skidded to a halt across the stage of his mushy brain. *I wonder how long I have loved this woman?*

"I'm sorry, too, Francie," he told her. "You'd have made a fine sergeant's wife. Damn war, anyway." He kissed her again, then ran his finger gently along her jawline. "A moment of plain speaking here, Francie: I confess to having wanted to do this practically since the first time you set foot in the hospital to read to my miscreants."

"You're not serious," she said and it sounded like a statement of fact.

"I am, actually." He took a deep breath. "I'm not sure when it happened last night, but I'm being honest for the first time in a year of observing you. What are we going to do?"

Francie pushed herself on one elbow, the better to see into his eyes, now that their curtained berth was light. She opened her mouth to speak, when someone coughed politely outside the curtain.

"Yes?" Will asked. Better he should speak, since this was his berth.

He wasn't sure what Francie was going to say, but when she kissed his fingers, then made herself small under the covers, he suddenly prayed there wouldn't be any Philadelphia wedding. When Francie was safely behind him, Will opened the curtain a crack. "Yes?"

It was the conductor, with just the faintest whiff of scotch on his breath. *Someone had to finish the bottle,* Will thought, amused.

"Captain, you need to fill out the death certificate. We'll be in Omaha in forty-five minutes."

Will closed the curtain and hurried into his wrinkled uniform, helped along by Francie. He had to stop every few minutes to kiss her, and nearly called a halt to the whole proceedings when she made it her business to button up his trousers in such a lingering fashion. What a talented female. Barefoot, he padded down the aisle to the washroom and dragged a razor across his face in some approximation of military spit and polish. He took a moment to appraise himself in the mirror: brown eyes still as earnest, hair just as red, moustache still giving his somewhat baby face enough gravitas to suggest he could perform surgery on grown-ups, lips a bit bruised from hard usage by Mary Frances Coughlin.

Maddy will never know, he thought for one traitorous moment, and then he knew he could never marry her now, no matter how scandalous his ordinary life was quickly going to become. Good Heavens, the wedding of the season was going to turn into the debacle of the decade. Whartons and Radnors would rise up and smite him, and rip his club memberships to shreds. He'd be a lucky cur if Maddy didn't sue him for breach of promise.

"So be it," he told the man in the mirror, who managed to look both satisfied to the hilt and green about the gills at the same time. "If you're going to be a cad, might as well do a good job of it."

He put on his shoes in the corridor, narrowly avoiding stumbling into a full-breasted matron heading to the women's washroom and looking like one of Wagner's Valkyries. He parted the curtains to his berth to see Francie struggling into her shirtwaist. He obliged her by buttoning her up the back, seasoning the act with a kiss or two. The valise was lying open on their berth now, but it was empty.

"I woke up Nora at about the same time Olympia started making little noises," Francie whispered. She kissed his ear. "Hopefully, we were quieter."

He blushed and nodded. "I am never going to ask," he whispered back and Francie smiled.

"You and Nora take Olympia to the dining car." He handed her a greenback. "I recommend the French toast." Heavens, what a prosaic sentence. It nearly made him wince, considering that he wanted to crawl back into his berth for Round Two.

He cleared his throat, conductor-fashion, and parted the curtains on the upper berth to see Nora holding Olympia now. "Good morning, Nora," he said, hoping she had slept through all the early-morning activity in the berth below. Since she looked far more rested than he did, he thought that was the case.

"Good morning, Captain," she replied.

Maybe it was a trick of the light, but he could have sworn Nora gave him a slow wink. He closed the curtains, sweating in the cold air. He smiled at nothing and no one, until he thought of Maddy. *I am the world's biggest fool,* he told himself. *I can treat the common cold, but not the common cad.*

Chapter Nine

Will filled out the unknown mother's death certificate, attached it to the blanket shroud in the baggage car and arrived in the dining car in time to eat French toast doused with maple syrup. He felt almost too shy to look at either woman, then reminded himself not to be a fool in the presence of two capable ladies. They passed Olympia back and forth between them as they ate.

No one made better French toast than the Overland Limited. Or maybe he was famished from all that lovemaking. He decided, for once in his life, not to overthink the matter and just enjoy the pleasure of good food and whatever stimulus had come his way before breakfast.

Still, he worried. Will put down his fork. "Ladies, are we all agreed that Olympia is not going to any orphanage in Omaha?"

They nodded; even Olympia looked interested. Safe in Francie's generous grasp, she regarded him solemnly across the condiment bottles and then burped.

"*Really,* Olympia," he commented. "How will we pull this off?"

As it turned out, the conductor made it easy. Clipboard at the ready, he met them in the passenger car, once breakfast was over and the upper and lower berths had become seats again. Francie held Olympia close, crooning to her. It touched Will to observe that Francie and the infant both had the same long eyelashes. Given time, no one would know they weren't mother and daughter.

"Your wife has taken quite a fancy to the baby," the conductor commented, as Will signed one more paper.

My wife. "Yes, she has," he said without hesitation. "Mrs Wharton loves children."

"Captain, may I depend on you and Mrs Wharton to see that the child gets to the proper official, once we detrain? I have to catch the next train heading west, and must leave it to you, if you're willing, to find an orphanage."

"No fears," Will replied. He wondered—as he had not wondered since his youth in Dumfries—if the Christmas Star was also a lucky star. After all, it had brought his mother a new husband, and him a father, so many years ago. He smiled to himself, also thinking of his grandparents and their amazing courtship in California. "We'll do what's right." *We will, indeed,* he thought, his heart full, as he looked into Francie Coughlin's eyes and saw answers to all his questions about life and love and more practical things. Funny that it had taken him a year to realize he was in love.

It was a simple matter to watch as a security man accepted the shrouded body. Will initialed another document, then they walked away from the unknown woman, the baby safe in Francie's arms. Francie had lingered a moment beside the shrouded body on its stretcher. She touched her fingers to Olympia's lips and then to the blanket shrouding the baby's mother. He swallowed and turned away.

He turned away in time to see Nora Powell hesitating on the platform, her eyes on the westbound train that the conductor was boarding. Will took her arm, relieved that she did not shake him off and run. His arm went around her then as she turned her face into his military greatcoat and sobbed.

"Nora, just let us take you to Utley," he said, holding her close, not so much from fear that she would bolt, but that she needed something solid, which he knew he was now. "We're so close to Iowa."

"Suppose there is no one from my family to meet me?" she asked, after he wiped her eyes with his handkerchief.

A day ago, he wouldn't have had an answer for her, but that was a day ago. "Then you'll come with us to Philadelphia," he told her, without any hesitation. "You'll help my mother in her work with immigrants and I'll guarantee you one or two Whartons who are also attorneys." *Provided anyone is still speaking to me, after I jilt Madeline Radnor,* he thought. "There are ways to get your children back."

None of them seemed to take a breath as they saw their luggage transferred to an Iowa short line and then took their seats for the trip to Utley. Not until the train was under way did they all take a deep breath, then look at each other and laugh, conspirators in baby snatching.

That seemed to be the last smile Nora possessed. As

the day wore on, she withdrew into herself, staring out of the window, probably seeing nothing of the landscape and everything of the children she had left behind. Only Francie's hand in his kept Will's own doubts at bay. When she transferred her hand to his thigh—so proprietary—he felt only bliss, followed by an urge to find another lower berth, or, failing that, an accommodating linen closet; he was agile.

"Do you think someone will meet her?" Francie whispered.

He didn't know what to say. Nora had no place in either world; she wasn't quite Indian and she wasn't quite white now, either.

"Hard to say. There's such a stigma against white women returning from Indian camps." He tightened his grip on Francie in sudden, irrational fear at the idea of Francie in such a situation. What would a woman do? He knew that some officers' wives had been told by their husbands to save a final bullet for themselves, if they were ever caught between garrisons by a war party. He glanced at beautiful Francie, trying to see the matter through a woman's eyes, even though he knew he could not.

"In the same situation, what would *you* do?" he asked.

Francie knew immediately what he meant. "What Nora did," she said finally. "I want to live." She squeezed his hand. "Would…would you want me back?"

His eyes filled with tears. "Do you even have to ask?" The smile she gave him said the world.

It seemed a strange time to propose, but he did, and found himself with two fiancées, one he was supposed to marry in a week, and the other one holding a baby that everyone on the train assumed belonged to them. *How on earth did this happen to someone as prosaic as I am?* he asked himself. He had never given his mother or stepfather a lick of trouble; now he was about to become Maddy Radnor's worst nightmare and an embarrassment to his relatives, possibly as Nora Powell was surely an embarrassment to hers.

What did bother him was the deepening frown between Nora's brows and the way she kept twisting her hands until her knuckles were white. He accepted the sleeping Olympia when Francie moved across the space between the row and sat beside Nora. In another moment she cradled Nora in her arms, much as she had protected Olympia. *Bless your heart,* he thought.

Shadows lengthened across the land as the train rumbled on the Iowa short line. Snow fell in fits and starts, and he worried. He began to dread the moment when the conductor would call "Utley," and everything would come down to the kindness or cruelty of Nora Powell's relatives, the ones who had stayed behind when she, her parents and brothers had decided to cross a continent and seek a better life.

They were reluctant to move when the train stopped. Nora had no luggage beyond a bedroll, but Will had asked the baggage handler to remove his and Francie's, too. If they had to stay a few days in Utley to see the outcome, he wanted to have his razor with him.

The other travelers were greeted by loved ones and led away. By some instinct, he and Francie knew to stand on either side of Nora. Maybe they wanted to shield her from the reality that no one wanted her. Maybe they wanted to make sure she did not bolt from the platform, going where, he had no idea, because she had nowhere to run.

Soon it was just the three of them, plus Olympia, on the platform. The wind had picked up and was swirling snow around. Everyone had hurried away, eager to get indoors and out of the deepening cold. "Well, never mind," Will said at last, touching Nora's elbow. "We'll find a hotel and keep going in the morning. There's a place for you, Nora. Please believe me."

"I do," she said finally, her voice faint. "It's hard, though."

"I imagine it is," Will replied, putting his arm around her. "Please…"

"Unhand my niece, young man!"

Startled, Will turned around to see a tall, angular woman bearing down on him, shaking an umbrella. He held his hands up. "Ma'am, are you….are you…?"

"Cat got your tongue?" she snapped, wielding the umbrella like a sword until he stepped back. She turned to Nora and her glare softened into something remarkably like love, as far as Will could tell.

"Nora Powell, you dear one," she said softly. "I'm your Aunt Nellie Follensbee. I didn't mean to be late, but your uncle and his nitwit wife tried to argue me out of coming to get you. Passel of fools." She gently tucked her arm through Nora's, shouldering Will aside. "Let's go home."

Chapter Ten

Nellie Follensbee took them all home, cooing over Olympia, who slept in Francie's arms, then leading them to a waiting conveyance, where a big man in a snow-covered overcoat sat in the box and shivered.

Nora introduced them to her aunt as Captain and Mrs Wharton, and Will couldn't think of a reason to contradict her. Maybe he was too tired to launch into a lengthy explanation that he didn't care to make anyway. Francie did nothing, either, beyond giving him a side-ways glance that spoke volumes.

It wouldn't have mattered if Nora had introduced them as Attila and Mrs Hun; Nellie only had eyes for her niece. "You're named after me, you know," she told Nora as they sat close together in the hack. "We're both Elinores."

"I barely remember you," Nora confessed, as the hack came to a stop in front of a modest house with a wide porch on the edge of town.

"Doesn't matter. I remember *you,*" was Nellie's

comment as she helped her niece from the conveyance. "Your mother was my little sister." She dabbed at her eyes. "I have worried about you for thirteen years, and now you're home."

The words were so honest and so kind that Will felt tears in his own eyes. *It's not that simple,* he thought, as he willingly let himself be dragged into the orbit of Nellie Follensbee's generous hospitality.

Generous, it was. Nellie took Francie to a back bedroom with Olympia, where the redoubtable aunt made a bed for the baby in a bureau drawer. Will followed, just to lean against the doorjamb and watch with Nora. "She's going to wonder why our baby is wearing a Union Pacific sheet and fragment of a blanket," he whispered. "Maybe I'd better intervene before she thinks—ahem—Mrs Wharton and I are wretched, unprepared parents."

He kept his explanation short, mainly because Olympia was starting to make those sounds peculiarly her own that he already identified with hunger. As Aunt Nellie listened, her eyes wide, he told of the desperate surgery in the immigrant car and their unwillingness to consign so sweet a newborn to some orphanage in Omaha, even if there was one.

"Perfectly understandable," Nellie said in her crisp voice. "I would have done the same thing." She gestured to her niece. "Nora, you are probably more agile than I am. Upstairs in the attic is a whole trunkful of your own baby clothes. Let's pay a visit."

Veterans now of the care and feeding of Olympia, Will traded a soiled Union Pacific napkin for a clean one while Francie prepared the proper bottle they had acquired in Omaha. In a moment she was sitting in the armchair, stockinged feet propped on the bed, while Olympia dined.

Will sat on the bed, leaning back against the bedstead. Francie lifted her feet into his lap and he massaged them. "Do we dare hope Nora will be all right?" he asked, keeping his voice low.

He might as well have asked if the moon was made of cheese, for all the attention Francie paid him. She had that look of supreme contentment on her face, one he had seen after most of his deliveries. Olympia had captured Francie's little finger in her tiny grip and Francie stared at her in awe.

"During full moons I turn into a werewolf named Cecil," he said softly. Francie nodded.

She paid him no attention as he watched Olympia's proprietary grip and then Francie's lovely face. A year ago, when Francie had first come to Fort Laramie, he had been mildly amused by her abundance of little freckles. Now all he wanted was the leisure to count each one and maybe kiss it. He knew that under her glorious red hair, much brighter than his, was a brain both shrewd and equal to his own. He might have known Madeline Radnor for years, but as Will watched the woman he loved, he knew Mary Francis Coughlin was worth the upcoming scandal.

"I won't hold you to that proposal, you know."

He gazed at her. "I won't retract it."

She gave him a wistful smile. "You know better than I do that a gentleman doesn't jilt a lady for the granddaughter of a bog Irishman."

"This one does," he replied.

"At least think about it," she said, moving her feet

from his lap because she heard Nora and her aunt returning.

Thoughtful, Will joined them in the kitchen, leaving Francie to get Olympia to sleep. He sat at the table as Nora sorted baby clothes and told her aunt about life with the Ogalala Sioux. He had to hand it to Aunt Nellie; there were no clucks of dismay or looks of disgust at the life her niece had been forced to lead for thirteen years. He saw only genuine interest and then real dismay that she had a young niece and nephew motherless and fatherless at the Spotted Tail Agency near Camp Robinson.

"Captain Wharton thinks I need to get a lawyer," Nora said as she folded and refolded a small mound of nightgowns and receiving blankets.

"We have those in Utley," Nellie said, taking her niece's hand and holding it to stop her restless agitation. "What we need is political influence, but no one's ever heard of Utley."

"I can furnish that," Will told them. "My family knows a few people in Washington." He knew he had said enough. No need to tell them now that his stepfather was related to the vice-president's wife, and that he used to spend part of each school vacation in the home of the Secretary of the Treasury. "When Francie and I return to Fort Laramie, I'll go to Camp Robinson and see what I can do. I'll warn you that we might not get anywhere, but we can try."

Nora was silent a long moment. She smiled faintly when Francie joined them at the table, then shyly pushed the little pile of clothing toward her. Francie took them and kissed Nora's forehead.

Nellie took her niece's hand again. "Since we are

indulging in plain speaking, don't worry about your reception here in Utley, my dearest. This is a kind town. There will be some looks, and maybe some whispers, but time will pass."

"My other aunt and uncle…"

"…are nincompoops," Nellie said. "We just have to be brave a little bit longer."

Will thought about her words as he shivered through a quick wash in the lavatory and returned to bed in a nightshirt. A soft bed in a peaceful town was a far cry from last night's anguish in the immigrant car and he realized how weary he was. He knew he could have offered to sleep on the rump-sprung sofa in the room, but not when Francie had been so kind as to turn down the coverlet on what must be his side of the bed.

"No one's going to need you tonight. There's no emergency," was all Francie said as she gathered him close. He was asleep almost before she finished the sentence.

He had been dimly aware when she got up once to feed Olympia around two, and again as dawn began to gradually lighten the room. He lay on his back, hands behind his head, staring at the ceiling, comfortably warm. When Francie took off her nightgown and returned to bed, he wasn't the man to turn down such an invitation. They made love as quietly as they could, considering that he could hear Nellie snoring in the next room.

"Francie, I love you," he whispered, his arms around her. "It's funny. All I wanted to do on this Christmas trip home was read my stupid medical journals. Maybe I owe Captain Hunsaker something. Do you love me?"

She nodded. "It's probably not the smartest thing either of us ever did." She moved a little and made herself more comfortable at his side. "Do you know why I was going home to Brooklyn?"

"Call me self-centered. I never thought to ask."

"My brothers had arranged for me to meet a nice Irishman, a butcher from Killarney. They knew I would like him. 'You're thirty years old, Mary Frances,' they told me. 'Time you found a man.'" She raised up on one elbow. "Am I older than you?"

"Nope. I still have two years on you and I think I can take you in a fair fight."

Francie made a face and kissed his chest.

He chuckled. "Maybe we should introduce your butcher to my fiancée." He kissed the freckle beside her mouth. "One down. Thousands to go."

"This really isn't funny," Francie told him, massaging his stomach to soften the blow.

"I know. Do that lower."

"No! We have to catch a train."

He sighed. "Killjoy. What we really have to do is follow Nellie's advice and be brave a little longer. My family has good luck at Christmas."

What about Maddy's family? he thought, as Francie searched for her nightgown. *Do they have good luck at Christmas, too, or am I the worst cad in all thirty-eight states?*

Chapter Eleven

They changed trains in Chicago. He held Olympia to his shoulder while Francie dozed at his side. He smiled as the snowy Illinois countryside rumbled by, thinking of Nora's last words to him as they paced the platform in Utley. She had asked him how long he had loved Francie Coughlin, which surprised him.

"I don't think I even knew I did, until the train trip," he said, as they walked to the end of the platform and started back—two people with abundant nervous energy, unlike Francie, who sat so peacefully with Olympia and Aunt Nellie. "What made you think that?"

"It was the way you looked at her," Nora said, as the train whistle sounded in the distance. "It was the way my husband used to look at me, when I was down at the river, or gathering berries." She smiled. "He was shy, too. But you put your blanket over her, didn't you?"

"I did."

"I was hoping you would."

"Nora Powell, you're an observant lady." Impulsively, he kissed her cheek; she smiled.

"I'm a ruined woman that everyone in Utley will probably think should have killed herself."

"No. Your aunt's right, my dear. Give it time and make allowances for nincompoopery."

Will and Francie changed trains again in Indianapolis. Will had enough time to send his parents a telegram, advising them that the train would be late and he would take a hack to the house. The last thing he wanted was to see Maddy waiting for him on the platform, or the shocked looks his parents would exchange when he stepped off with a baby and a strange woman.

Francie tried to change his mind one last time, but he knew her heart wasn't in it. He knew his parents would love her and he doubted either of them could resist Olympia's solemn, dark-eyed stare, the same look she was giving him right now as he held her, studying his face, memorizing it in some baby way that meant he was hers forever.

"Francie, I've delivered a lot of babies. Why on earth did I succumb to this one?"

His dear one had no answer. All she could do was fix him with her own solemn look and tuck herself closer. With a lift in his heart, he knew he was hers forever, too. Women!

Will wasn't a total liar, because the train *was* late out of Indiana and late out of Pittsburgh, where they changed again, for the final time. After two days from Chicago of stop and start travel, overcrowding—it seemed like everyone in the midwest wanted to get to Philadelphia for Christmas—bad food and worse sleeping accommodations, they arrived late at night in the City of Brotherly Love, frazzled.

During that long layover in Indianapolis, Will had tried to coax his love into visiting the nearest justice of the peace and legalizing the until-death-did-them-part aspect of their already flourishing relationship. Francie wouldn't have it. "I want your folks to meet me first," she said.

"They're going to love you, whether you arrive as Mrs Wharton or Miss Coughlin," he assured her.

He was prepared to argue the matter until she succumbed, but her next reason stopped him, because it was so kind and so right. "It's more than that, Will. You're going to have to disappoint Maddy Radnor. Don't arrive married. Imagine how that would humiliate her." Francie kissed his cheek to ease his pain; he knew he had no comeback to so much consideration. Better to let Maddy down easy, without springing a wife and a child on her, too.

Still, he was greatly relieved when the conductor, sounding as weary as Will felt, called "Philadelphia."

Will was in no hurry to rise from his seat, which had nearly adhered to his backside by now. Besides, Olympia was slumbering in his lap, still curled up in her prenatal position, which he had pointed out to Francie in Ohio or Indiana. Maybe it was even in Iowa. "She'll stay that way a few more weeks," he had told her, always the physician. "Then one day she'll stretch out for good and leave the womb behind."

At least until those moments she'll want to crawl back inside, because it feels safer than the world around her, he should have added. The idea of facing Maddy was starting to make him wish for such a handy retreat.

Since Pittsburgh at least, while Francie had slept against his shoulder, Will had let Maddy's many letters about wedding details slowly unspool through his mind: her dress, brought all the way from Worth's in Paris; the numerous bridesmaids and their Worth frocks; the food, the invitations, the flowers, the ever-lengthening guest list. There was even a photographer.

His stepfather had discreetly written in a letter of his own that the Radnors weren't as high in the instep as they used to be and this wedding was costing them dear. Obviously, they expected some return from marrying into the well-heeled Wharton clan. Wilkie Wharton was an army surgeon, but Maddy was certainly trying her best to get him to resign his commission and earn better money—if he felt he had to work—by curing sniffles and piles from amongst the wealthy of their combined guest list.

The whole nightmare was going to make his ears bleed, if he kept thinking about it. *I am a cad, a cad, a cad,* he thought, the cadence matching the rhythm of the railroad. At the very least, he knew he would have to dip into family money to repay Maddy for his caddery.

It only took a glance at Francie to remind him that money was only money, after all. He had enough of it and he would still marry Francie and keep Olympia, too. No one would understand except, hopefully, his family, and they would return as man and wife to the frontier where they belonged. Some other rich physician could write prescriptions for hemorrhoid medication and throat lozenges. He'd stick to gunshot and arrow wounds, delivering babies under fraught conditions and tending to gangrene.

Somewhere in Chicago or maybe Indianapolis, he

had left behind his medical journals, because he had needed room in his valise for diapers. This trip was not ending the way it had begun, but then, neither had his grandfather's shipwreck off San Diego, or his mother's difficult sojourn in Anatolia. Some day when she was old enough to understand, he would tell Olympia and their other children that it was best to be flexible in love and things that mattered.

His home had never looked so welcome, blazing with lights and sporting an enormous wreath on the front door. He was amused to see Francie's wide-eyed stare at the size of what he knew was only a modest mansion in Philadelphia's best district. His family had never been show ponies—just rich.

"I don't know about this," she said, sounding uneasy.

He kissed her hand, then handed her Olympia, whose dark, solemn eyes were wide open, too. "If you want to meet my folks, this—to quote that rascal Brigham Young—is the place."

He glanced across the street to the Radnor house, also decorated, and flinched to see what he thought was Maddy's silhouette in the front parlor window. *This is going to have to be the fastest explanation in modern American history,* he thought, as he lifted the iron latch on the front gate and ushered his lovely lady up the carefully swept walkway.

Will felt a care or two leave his shoulders as he handed his overcoat and valise to the butler, whose eyes were lively with interest at the sight of Francie and the baby. His mother was next on the scene, hugging him, then stepping back in surprise when Olympia started to cry.

"What...?"

Will turned to see his stepfather, pool stick in hand, staring at Francie and Olympia. In another moment, Trey Wharton was grinning from ear to ear. "Wilkie Wharton, you are a dirty dog," he said. "I feel a tidal wave of explanation coming on, so let us adjourn to the sitting room and close the door." He laughed out loud and shook the pool stick at his stepson. "And if the first words out of your mouth are 'This isn't what you think,' I'm going to thrash you."

Will knew that tone. More of his care slid away, as he put his arm around Francie's waist and ushered her into the sitting room. "This isn't what you think," he said, and grinned when both of his parents started to laugh. Francie stared at them in frank amazement.

"It's an old family joke. Tell you later," he explained, deftly plucking Olympia from Francie's arms so his stepfather could help Francie with her coat. "Have a seat, my dear, unless you are as tired of sitting as I am."

She was, so they stood close together—somehow, Olympia was now in his mother's arms—and explained the last four days, taking turns. Will knew it had to be a rapid discourse, because he knew the next knock on the door would either be Maddy alone, or Maddy and her father with a brace of dueling pistols.

"That's the whole story. I…we…couldn't put Olympia in an orphanage. And a very kind and brave lady we dropped off in Iowa was smart enough to notice before I did that I have been in love with Mary Francis Coughlin for the better part of a year. Mama, I can't marry Maddy."

"No, you cannot," his mother said. She was on her feet, too, handing him back Olympia and embracing Francie, who burst into tears. "Welcome to this ramshackle family, my dear," she said. "What we lack in good sense, we make up for in dumb luck. When are you getting married?"

"The sooner the better," Will said, feeling his face go red.

"That's how it is?" his stepfather asked. "Francie, you and Olympia come along with Lily and me and we'll install you in Will's bedroom right now." He shook his finger at Will. "And tomorrow we're going to escort you lovebirds to the local registry."

"What about…?"

"Your fiancée?" Trey Wharton chuckled. "I doubt she has any better aim with dueling pistols than your not-so-future father-in-law has with trap guns! He's never hit a clay pigeon, to my knowledge. You'll probably have no more than a flesh wound."

Arm in arm, his parents left the room, holding the door open for Francie and Olympia. He was all by himself when he heard The Knock, and the butler showed Madeline Radnor into the sitting room.

Chapter Twelve

Maddy was as lovely as he remembered: dark hair, cobalt-blue eyes, lips full and lush, her figure slim and curved in all the right places. Every curl was firmly in place and her dress stylish and as neat as a pin.

Feeling like the worst hypocrite who had ever attached captain's bars, Will went forward to kiss her. To his surprise, she stepped back and folded her hands primly in front of her breast.

"Willie, it's good to see you, but we have to talk. Now."

Willie. She always called him that, even though he had pointed out more than a few times that there was a K in his name. Thank goodness Francie preferred 'Will.' Maddy must have seen him escorting Francie up the front walk, his hand on her back. He took a deep breath and opened his mouth.

Before he could speak, Maddy held up her hand. "I should go first, Willie."

"Ordinarily I would agree with you, my dear, but I…"

Am a real cad and need to spill the beans, he thought, as she held up both hands this time, as though she were orchestrating him. Maybe she was.

"No. I know it's late, but Mama saw your arrival. I must speak first, because I have a terrible confession."

Can't be worse than mine, he told himself, curious now. "Very well, Maddy, speak," he told her and had to almost forcibly suppress an image of his old springer spaniel.

"I have been untrue to you."

He was surprised, but still aware of his caddery. *I doubt you've climbed into bed with such a willing partner as I have,* he thought. "Oh?"

She drew herself up to the extent of her modest height. "I. Love. Another." It came out punctuated and in capital letters.

He could have melted with gratitude. "Well, my dear, perhaps you'd better explain."

She did, pacing in front of the fireplace with all the drama she usually reserved for hangnails and ripped hems and wrinkled collars. "It is Dale Turnbull."

Will had to turn away and cough, to suppress a fountain of mirth. Dale, he of the not-too-bright demeanor, jug ears and thinning hair? Never mind. The Turnbulls were even wealthier than the Whartons and Dale knew how to dress. He would always smell good, too, never like a regimental surgeon after a six-week detail in the hot sun.

"Dale." She had reduced him to monosyllables, which was just as well. That way he wouldn't laugh.

"It came on us so suddenly, Willie. I agreed to marry him, but not before I had confessed all to you."

She said it so sweetly and obviously meant every

word. Will hoped she had not been tormenting herself for long. Madeline Radnor had given him the perfect out. He could assume a wounded appearance and sulk, then marry Francie in peace and quiet, after the newly married Turnbulls were on their way to some watering hole or other to celebrate their nuptials. Maddy would find out eventually, but not from him. Or he could be honest.

It was his turn to hold up both hands. He took Maddy's cold fingers in his, noticing for the first time that she was not wearing his engagement ring. "Hold on, my dear. You really should have let me speak first. I, too, have fallen in love with someone else. Her name is Mary Frances Coughlin and she is the daughter of my hospital steward at Fort Laramie. It wasn't until this train trip that I realized how much I loved her." Introducing Olympia could wait, he decided.

After a long pause, Maddy did a strange thing, one that endeared her to him forever. She kissed his cheek, rubbing her own against his for a brief, perfumed moment.

"Willie, you always were a little slow to realize when women were in love with you. So we're both jilting each other?"

"It appears that way. I'd like to marry Francie tomorrow. She's upstairs now. When, uh, are you and—" goodness, he almost called him Jugs, an old childhood name "—and Dale getting married?"

She rosied up. "On the day I was to marry you! Why waste a good caterer and flowers? We'll leave for St Augustine right after." She touched his hand. "You're certainly welcome to bring your wife to the wedding."

"I think Francie and I will have to hurry back to

Fort Laramie, instead," he told her, walking her to the parlor door. "I have some work that won't wait at Camp Robinson."

She let him help her into her wrap. "You are such a brave soldier!" she exclaimed. "The *Inquirer* even called you a hero."

Poor, dear Maddy. She was destined to be beautiful, but slow of wit. Francie would never have believed one word of the *Inquirer*'s yellow journalism. Good thing Maddy was marrying Jugs Turnbull. His name would never appear in any newspaper except on the financial page, which no lady ever read.

He walked her across the snowy street, shook her hand at her own front door and wished her a Merry Christmas. When he turned around to look at the Wharton mansion, he saw that the front door was open. Francie stood there: red-haired, Catholic as he was, generous, smart and destined to be his best Christmas gift ever.

As he crossed the street to her, he stepped aside for a group of Christmas carolers intent on reaching his parents' front door before he did. Will stood back to watch them. He listened as one little boy in an overcoat much too large jingled a bell to announce their arrival and the others spoke to each other in a variety of languages.

He grinned, thinking this must be a choir assembled at the immigrants' center where his mother held forth. He gestured over their heads to Francie, who joined him on the walk beside the choir. He cuddled her close.

"Is everything all right with your former fiancée?" she asked.

"Quite all right. I'll tell you later. I'd rather kiss you now."

And he did, as the choir sang "Away in a Manger."
The little boy with the bell giggled to see them, but Captain Wilkie Wharton paid him no mind. When he was
just holding Francie, Will allowed himself a momentary
worry: there was an Irish butcher certain to be disappointed when Mary Francis Coughlin didn't show up
in Brooklyn. As he stood there with his arms around
his true love, Will decided that a man can only worry
about so much on the eve of his wedding.

Epilogue

~~~~~~~~~~

Dear Mama and Father,
I'd have written much sooner, but a lot has happened since we returned to the garrison. First, Olympia Wharton is thriving. Second, Father, you have my deepest gratitude for your prompt intervention in the matter of Nora Powell and her two children. In the past I have sometimes resented your ability to arrange matters to grease my youthful path, but as Mama would probably remind me, you are skilled in administering, be it hospitals or politicians.

Thank you from the bottom of my heart. I would almost give a year's salary—it's not much—to have seen the expression on the face of the Indian agent at Camp Robinson when he received those letters from *both* of Pennsylvania's senators, demanding that Nora Powell's two Indian children be taken immediately to me at Fort Laramie. The additional note from Vice-

President William Wheeler was a nice touch. Captain Hunsaker delivered the children into my darling Francie's care and there they remained for all of February while the wheels of government ground on.

The result, as those senators may have told you by now, was the arrival last week of Aunt Nellie Follensbee and Nora Powell in Cheyenne, where Francie, Olympia and I returned two lonesome children to their mother. Such a reunion! Under the stipulated terms, more properly they are in the custody of the redoubtable Miss Follensbee, who was accompanied to Cheyenne by an equally formidable attorney from Utley, Iowa. I've never been so happy to see the right thing done. Believe me, that doesn't always happen out here.

Mother, this will amuse you: Francie is in the family way. She hasn't worked up her nerve to tell me yet, but I studied medicine at Harvard, know how to read a calendar as well as the next physician, and have considerable experience in identifying the cause of a slightly green look, early in the morning. Should I just let her surprise me?

With love from your son,
Wilkie

* * * * *

HISTORICAL

Where Love is Timeless™

HARLEQUIN® HISTORICAL

COMING NEXT MONTH
AVAILABLE DECEMBER 27, 2011

SCANDAL AT THE CAHILL SALOON
Cahill Cowboys
Carol Arens
(Western)

THE LADY CONFESSES
The Copeland Sisters
Carole Mortimer
(Regency)

CAPTURED FOR THE CAPTAIN'S PLEASURE
Ann Lethbridge
(Regency)

A DARK AND BROODING GENTLEMAN
Gentlemen of Disrepute
Margaret McPhee
(Regency)

REQUEST YOUR FREE BOOKS!

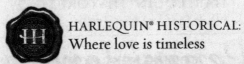

HARLEQUIN® HISTORICAL:
Where love is timeless

2 FREE NOVELS PLUS 2 FREE GIFTS!

YES! Please send me 2 FREE Harlequin® Historical novels and my 2 FREE gifts (gifts are worth about $10). After receiving them, if I don't wish to receive any more books, I can return the shipping statement marked "cancel." If I don't cancel, I will receive 6 brand-new novels every month and be billed just $5.19 per book in the U.S. or $5.74 per book in Canada. That's a savings of at least 17% off the cover price! It's quite a bargain! Shipping and handling is just 50¢ per book in the U.S. and 75¢ per book in Canada.* I understand that accepting the 2 free books and gifts places me under no obligation to buy anything. I can always return a shipment and cancel at any time. Even if I never buy another book, the two free books and gifts are mine to keep forever.

246/349 HDN FEQQ

Name	(PLEASE PRINT)

Address	Apt. #

City	State/Prov.	Zip/Postal Code

Signature (if under 18, a parent or guardian must sign)

Mail to the **Reader Service:**
IN U.S.A.: P.O. Box 1867, Buffalo, NY 14240-1867
IN CANADA: P.O. Box 609, Fort Erie, Ontario L2A 5X3

Not valid for current subscribers to Harlequin Historical books.

Want to try two free books from another line?
Call 1-800-873-8635 or visit www.ReaderService.com.

* Terms and prices subject to change without notice. Prices do not include applicable taxes. Sales tax applicable in N.Y. Canadian residents will be charged applicable taxes. Offer not valid in Quebec. This offer is limited to one order per household. All orders subject to credit approval. Credit or debit balances in a customer's account(s) may be offset by any other outstanding balance owed by or to the customer. Please allow 4 to 6 weeks for delivery. Offer available while quantities last.

Your Privacy—The Reader Service is committed to protecting your privacy. Our Privacy Policy is available online at www.ReaderService.com or upon request from the Reader Service.

We make a portion of our mailing list available to reputable third parties that offer products we believe may interest you. If you prefer that we not exchange your name with third parties, or if you wish to clarify or modify your communication preferences, please visit us at www.ReaderService.com/consumerchoice or write to us at Reader Service Preference Service, P.O. Box 9062, Buffalo, NY 14269. Include your complete name and address.

HH11B

USA TODAY bestselling author

Penny Jordan

brings you her newest romance

PASSION
AND THE PRINCE

Prince Marco di Lucchesi can't hide his proud
disdain for fiery English rose Lily Wrightington—
or his attraction to her! While touring the palazzos
of northern Italy, the atmosphere heats up…until
shadows from Lily's past come out….

*Can Marco keep his passion under wraps
enough to protect her, or will it unleash itself, too?*

Find out in January 2012!

*Brittany Grayson survived a horrible ordeal at the hands
of a serial killer known as The Professional…
who's after her now?*

*Harlequin® Romantic Suspense presents a new installment
in Carla Cassidy's reader-favorite miniseries,*
LAWMEN OF BLACK ROCK.

*Enjoy a sneak peek of
TOOL BELT DEFENDER.*

*Available January 2012
from Harlequin® Romantic Suspense.*

"**B**rittany?" His voice was deep and pleasant and made
her realize she'd been staring at him openmouthed through
the screen door.

"Yes, I'm Brittany and you must be…" Her mind suddenly went blank.

"Alex. Alex Crawford, Chad's friend. You called him
about a deck?"

As she unlocked the screen, she realized she wasn't
quite ready yet to allow a stranger inside, especially a male
stranger.

"Yes, I did. It's nice to meet you, Alex. Let's walk around
back and I'll show you what I have in mind," she said. She
frowned as she realized there was no car in her driveway.
"Did you walk here?" she asked.

His eyes were a warm blue that stood out against his
tanned face and was complemented by his slightly shaggy
dark hair. "I live three doors up." He pointed up the street to
the Walker home that had been on the market for a while.

"How long have you lived there?"

"I moved in about six weeks ago," he replied as they

walked around the side of the house.

That explained why she didn't know the Walkers had moved out and Mr. Hard Body had moved in. Six weeks ago she'd still been living at her brother Benjamin's house trying to heal from the trauma she'd lived through.

As they reached the backyard she motioned toward the broken brick patio just outside the back door. "What I'd like is a wooden deck big enough to hold a barbecue pit and an umbrella table and, of course, lots of people."

He nodded and pulled a tape measure from his tool belt. "An outdoor entertainment area," he said.

"Exactly," she replied and watched as he began to walk the site. The last thing Brittany had wanted to think about over the past eight months of her life was men. But looking at Alex Crawford definitely gave her a slight flutter of pure feminine pleasure.

Will Brittany be able to heal in the arms of Alex,
her hotter-than-sin handyman...or will a second
psychopath silence her forever? Find out in
TOOL BELT DEFENDER
Available January 2012
from Harlequin® Romantic Suspense
wherever books are sold.